PRAISE FOR THE *NEW YORK TIMES*
BESTSELLING CAT IN THE STACKS MYSTERIES

"Courtly librarian Charlie Harris and his Maine Coon cat, Diesel, are an endearing detective duo. Warm, charming, and Southern as the tastiest grits."
—Carolyn Hart, *New York Times* bestselling author of the Death on Demand Mysteries

"Combines a kindhearted librarian hero, family secrets in a sleepy Southern town, and a gentle giant of a cat that will steal your heart."
—Lorna Barrett, *New York Times* bestselling author of the Booktown Mysteries

"Ideal for Christie fans who enjoy a good puzzle."
—*Library Journal*

"[A] pleasing blend of crime and charm."
—*Richmond Times-Dispatch*

"Humor and plenty of Southern charm. . . . Cozy fans will hope James will keep Charlie and Diesel in action for years to come."
—*Publishers Weekly*

"James just keeps getting better and better. . . . It's an intelligent read, so well-written that I couldn't stop reading it. Every single time I turned out my light for the night, I found myself thinking about the story, flipping the light switch again, and reading just 'one more chapter.'"
—*MyShelf*

A Cat in the Stacks Mystery

SIX CATS A SLAYIN'

Miranda James

BERKLEY PRIME CRIME
New York

BERKLEY PRIME CRIME
Published by Berkley
An imprint of Penguin Random House LLC
penguinrandomhouse.com

Copyright © 2018 by Dean James
Excerpt from *Careless Whiskers* by Miranda James copyright © 2019 by Dean James
Penguin Random House supports copyright. Copyright fuels creativity, encourages
diverse voices, promotes free speech, and creates a vibrant culture. Thank you for buying
an authorized edition of this book and for complying with copyright laws by not
reproducing, scanning, or distributing any part of it in any form without permission.
You are supporting writers and allowing Penguin Random House to continue to
publish books for every reader.

BERKLEY and the BERKLEY & B colophon are registered trademarks and
BERKLEY PRIME CRIME is a trademark of Penguin Random House LLC.

ISBN: 9780451491114

Berkley Prime Crime hardcover edition / October 2018
Berkley Prime Crime mass-market edition / November 2019

Printed in the United States of America
1 3 5 7 9 10 8 6 4 2

Cover art by Dan Craig Inc. / Bernstein & Andriulli
Cover design by Katie Anderson

This book is dedicated with great love and thanks to Martha Farrington, my second mother. Her love and support have made a huge difference in my life, and I am grateful that I walked into Murder By The Book so many years ago and found a home.

ACKNOWLEDGMENTS

First, as always, thanks to my amazing editor, Michelle Vega, and the team at Berkley who do so much for me: Jennifer Monroe, Tara O'Connor, and Elisha Katz. Rock on, ladies!

Thanks also to my agent, the inimitable Nancy Yost, and her team: Sarah E. Younger, Natanya Wheeler, and Amy Rosenbaum. My career couldn't be in better hands. Y'all rock on, too!

Without the wonderful friends in my life who support me on a daily basis, I wouldn't get very far doing anything. So many of them to thank: Julie Herman, Patricia Orr, Terry Farmer, John Kwiatkowski, Carolyn Haines, Don Herrington, Sally Woods, McKenna Jordan, Brenda Jordan, Megan Bladen-Blinkoff, Sandy Wallesch, my fellow Femmes Fatales, and my sisters in the Cozy Mystery Share a Palooza on Facebook: you're all a privilege to know.

Finally, a special thanks, as always, to the readers who have taken Charlie and Diesel to their hearts so fervently. My appreciation for your enthusiasm and support is tremendous. Every book I write, I write for you.

ONE

I opened the envelope and read the enclosed invitation. After the import of it had sunk in, I balled up the stiff card and threw it across the kitchen. I muttered a curse to myself.

Diesel, my Maine Coon cat, saw this action as an invitation to play. He darted after the wadded-up card and started batting it around the floor. I watched, my mind busy trying to come up with polite ways to say *not on your life* to the issuer of the invitation.

"What's Mr. Cat playing with?"

The voice of Azalea Berry, my housekeeper, broke into my thoughts. I looked up to see her, hands on hips, staring at the large cat playing soccer across the room.

"An invitation," I said.

"Who's inviting the cat somewhere?"

Azalea's deadpan expression at first had me thinking she was serious. Then I saw the twinkle in her eyes.

"I wish it *was* for Diesel." I couldn't quite keep the sour note out of my voice. "It's addressed to me, unfortunately."

Spatula in hand, Azalea turned back to the stove. "Eggs'll be ready in a minute. Who's it from?"

"The new neighbor," I replied. "The one who bought old Mr. Hardy's house."

"Oh, *her*." Azalea's tone indicated that she didn't care for Geraldine Albritton any more than I did. "What kind of invite is it?"

"She's having a Christmas party. According to the invitation, it's a *Neighborhood Meet-and-Greet*. And it's next week."

"She's not giving people much notice. What if they all made other plans for that night?" Azalea set a plate of scrambled eggs, country ham, and biscuits in front of me. Diesel saw that I now had food, and he left off batting his new toy around. He came up to my chair, placed a large paw atop my thigh, and emitted a sad chirp. Starvation was imminent.

"More than likely she's thinking the curiosity value will bring them. I don't know how many neighbors have dropped by to welcome her to the neighborhood so far, but you can bet there will be more than a few people who haven't who'll be wanting to see the inside of that house."

Azalea snorted. "People are always wanting to find out about their neighbors."

"True." I put my attention to the food on my plate and let my mind contemplate the looming situation. Azalea refilled my coffee cup before she left the kitchen for the laundry room.

I believed I knew my neighbors well enough to predict that most of them would not react kindly to the overtures of a pushy newcomer. Based on my limited acquaintance with Geraldine—*call me Gerry*—Albritton, I felt pretty sure that, unless she toned herself down, many of my neighbors wouldn't want to have much to do with her. Southerners have always prided themselves on their hospitality, but by the same turn, they weren't always ready to welcome strangers to the inner circle. Gerry Albritton might not find people in this neighborhood as ready to embrace her as she probably expected.

Though I desperately wanted to forget every second of our first meeting, I couldn't suppress it. The memory of it hung around, refusing to be banished. I recalled it as I ate my breakfast.

Gerry Albritton had moved in a month earlier, and a week later, I decided to do the neighborly thing. Armed with a small basket of baked goods—some provided by Azalea and others from Helen Louise Brady's French bistro—I walked across the street that morning to introduce myself. I told Diesel we were going to meet the new neighbor, and he chirped happily in response. He was always ready for fresh conquests. He soaked up admiration like a hairy, chirping sponge.

I rang the doorbell. Perhaps twenty seconds later the door opened, and I beheld Ms. Albritton for the first time. Until then I'd caught only brief glimpses of her out the front windows as she went in and out of the house. Up close she was shorter than I had reckoned, probably only about five four and petite with it. I felt far too large as I loomed over her.

Dressed as if she was heading out to a formal dinner party—high heels, pearls, diamond rings, and the ever-fashionable little black dress—Ms. Albritton had an air of

3

sophistication about her. She smiled widely at the sight of me, and I smiled back a bit uncertainly. I wasn't sure whether she actually noticed Diesel, as she appeared to be so focused on me.

Before I could introduce myself, Ms. Albritton spoke. "You *have* to be Charlie Harris, the handsome widower of Oak Drive." She batted her eyelashes at me, tilted her head, and offered a coy smile. "Come right on in, I've been just about dying to meet you. You're even better-looking close up." She laughed, a light, tinkling sound. "I've only been able to peek at you from a distance before now. I just *know* we're going to be friends, so you just call me Gerry and I'll call you Charlie, okay?"

Rattled by her flirtatious manner and thoroughly taken aback, I stared at her and made no attempt to respond. She didn't appear to notice, though. Her gaze shifted down from my face, over my chest and farther south. I resisted the urge to squirm.

Then she seemed to realize that Diesel was with me.

"And *this* is the famous *Diesel*. Oh, you are such a handsome boy. Like father like kitty, and both of you so tall and strong-looking."

I glanced down at the cat. Diesel stared at Ms. Albritton as if mesmerized. Thus far he hadn't made a sound, unusual for him. He looked up at me and offered what sounded like an interrogatory trill. He hadn't met anyone quite like her before, not with that coquettish manner and tone, at least.

I found the dregs of my composure and responded to Ms. Albritton after Diesel's appeal. "I am Charlie Harris, Ms. Albritton, and yes, this is Diesel." I thrust the basket of pastries toward her. "We wanted to welcome you to the neighborhood."

She accepted the basket with another coy smile. Her hand brushed mine. "Aren't you two the *sweetest* things?" Her Mississippi drawl drew the words out a few extra beats. "Y'all come on in. I'm afraid the house is still a wreck, but I know you'll overlook it. A poor woman on her own moving into this *wonderful* neighborhood. I can't tell you how *thrilled* I am this house came up for sale. All the time I was growing up here I wanted to live in this neighborhood, and when I moved back recently I couldn't believe a house on this street was up for sale." She turned and walked away.

At that point in our brief acquaintance, the last thing I wanted to do was enter this house, but I couldn't be rude and simply walk away—or rather, *run* away, if I had my druthers. I didn't feel up to fending off a lonesome widow this morning. I intended to tell Ms. Albritton that Diesel and I couldn't stay, that we were expected somewhere even though it was my one day off during the week and I had nothing planned.

I followed her into the living room and discovered to my distaste that the furniture and decor consisted of what I privately called industrial horror. For a moment I thought I had wandered onto the set of a futuristic movie. Everything I saw was either stark white or deep black, except for dashes of color from photographs placed around the room and on the walls. There was not a book in sight—to me, always the sign of a person with whom I probably had little in common. Most of the rooms in my house had shelves full of books.

Gerry Albritton motioned me toward a leather sofa with tubular black legs. I took one corner, and Diesel huddled by my legs. I could tell that he found the atmosphere of the room as sterile and off-putting as I did. Our hostess set the gift basket on the coffee table, the top of which appeared to be made of some kind of white synthetic substance. Then, to my alarm, she seated herself so close to me that her knee brushed against mine.

My deeply ingrained manners precluded my being rude to her. But I decided to make an exception. I got to my feet quickly, before Gerry Albritton had a chance to speak.

"I *do* apologize," I said, trying hard to sound sincere, "but I just this second remembered that my daughter is coming by any minute to drop off my grandson. It's my day to babysit. I'm sure you'll excuse me."

"Now, that's just too bad." My hostess sounded put out with me and wasn't bothering to hide it. "I was really hoping for a chance to get to know you better." Then she smiled, and her tone became friendly again. "But of course children and grandchildren come first." She rose from the sofa. "It must be so nice to have family like that. I'm all on my own." Her expression had suddenly turned forlorn.

"That's too bad," I murmured. Diesel and I followed her to the front door.

"You'll have to come back when you can stay longer." Gerry Albritton laid a hand on my arm and squeezed it. "I know we're going to be good friends."

"How kind," I said. "We hope you'll be happy here." Diesel and I scooted out the door and headed home. I was never so glad to get away from someone in my life.

I suppressed another shudder as I tried to push the

memory of that encounter away yet again. Since that time I had done my best to avoid Gerry Albritton and had been mostly successful. Diesel and I ran into her twice on walks, but on both occasions I got us away from her as quickly as I could. The woman made me uneasy. It was more than her aggressive friendliness, simply something I couldn't define, that made me wary of her.

I still hadn't told Helen Louise about Gerry's blatant flirting with me. I wasn't sure why I hesitated to share it with Helen Louise. Perhaps it was because I suspected so strongly that Gerry had an underhanded purpose in behaving like that. The more I was exposed to it, the more I began to think the flirtatiousness had a forced quality to it. Until I could figure out what lay behind it, I planned to keep it to myself.

Compounding the situation was the mystery surrounding Gerry Albritton herself. Right after that first meeting, I questioned Melba Gilley, my friend since childhood and my coworker at the Athena College Library, to discover what I could about my new neighbor.

Gerry claimed to have lived in Athena when the subject arose during my first encounter with her—yet Melba didn't know Gerry Albritton, and Melba knew everyone who had lived in Athena over the decades.

"Only Albrittons I know don't have a single Geraldine in the family," Melba said, obviously puzzled. "I could be wrong, of course, but none of the Albritton boys our age married a Geraldine, either."

"That's the name she claims now," I said. "Maybe she used to go by a name besides Geraldine."

Melba frowned. "Maybe, but I don't think so. If I got a good look at her, I could probably figure out who she is."

"I asked her if she's related to the city councilman, Billy Albritton," I said. He did not represent my district, but I had seen him around town, and his picture turned up in the local weekly newspaper on a regular basis. He was around seventy, I thought.

"I know Billy and his sister, Betty," Melba said. "I'll ask him if he knows her. I don't get along well with Betty."

I didn't want to delve into Melba's potential feud with Betty Albritton, so I didn't inquire why the two didn't get along.

"Talk to Billy, if you like," I said. "Gerry professed not to know him, though. Said it must be a different set of Albrittons."

Melba snorted. "All the Albrittons around here are one big family. Some of them are pretentious as all get-out, but that's another story." She locked gazes with me. "What's all this interest in another woman, anyway?"

I hesitated. "I'm curious about this woman because something seems off about her." I didn't want to tell Melba about the flirting, or she might take it into her head to confront Gerry Albritton herself on Helen Louise's behalf. Melba was fiercely protective of her friends.

"Like what?" Melba asked.

I shrugged. "I can't really say. She seems fake somehow. But maybe I'm making way too much of the whole thing."

Melba shook her head. "No, you've got great first instincts about people. If you're feeling like something's off about this whoever-she-is, then something sure is off."

I had to smile. Melba never failed to support me, and her friendship all these years was a blessing I never took for granted and hoped I never failed to return.

When I came out of my reverie I discovered that my plate was empty. I noticed that Azalea stood by the stove, and she was staring at me.

"I don't reckon you heard me," Azalea said.

"Sorry, I didn't. What did you say?" I asked.

"Wanted to know if you wanted another biscuit and more ham."

"Gracious me, no, thank you. I've had plenty." The truth was, I would happily have eaten another biscuit or two, packed with ham, but I had to make some effort to keep my waistline under control.

"If you're sure." Azalea gazed at me a moment longer. When I didn't respond, she sighed and turned back to the stove.

Diesel had resumed batting the crumpled invitation around the kitchen, and I knew I had to take it away from him. I couldn't ignore the invitation, much as I would have liked to. No, I would probably have to give in and accept. But only if Helen Louise was available to go with me, I decided. The invitation had said *and guest*.

I heard the front doorbell ring, one sharp, quick note. I pushed back from the table and rose. "I'll get it," I said.

Diesel preceded me. He loved visitors and was invariably first to the door.

I opened the door, a smile of greeting ready, but no one waited on the other side. I was about to step forward onto the porch, but Diesel's growl alerted me.

As I halted and glanced down, I heard faint sounds of mewling from the area near my feet. I had been about to step into a box containing five kittens.

TWO

▨▨▨▨▨▨▨▨▨▨▨▨▨

Two days after The Great Kitten Rescue, as Stewart insisted on calling it, my new four-legged boarders came home from the veterinarian's office. Dr. Romano, Diesel's vet, had checked all five kittens thoroughly. She estimated they were about eight or nine weeks old, ready to be weaned. They were healthy and had obviously been cared for before they wound up on my doorstep.

Prior to my discovery of the note in the box with the kittens, I considered taking them to the local shelter. I didn't think I could cope with five additional felines in the house. The note changed my mind, though. In block print, it read, He *says he'll drown them.* Please *take care of them for me.* The emphasis on that first pronoun bothered me. I immediately imagined a heartless father or stepfather who didn't want to feed five cats. The poor author of the note was desperate to save them.

The paper with its ruled lines had been torn from a

school notebook, and that made me think the person who wrote it was young, perhaps an adolescent. The letters were well-formed enough that I figured they weren't written by a young child. I showed it to Dr. Romano, but since the paper contained no real clues to the identity of the writer, she shrugged and confessed to being as puzzled as I was.

The upshot was that I had five more mouths to feed. I had been worried that Azalea would have a fit with more cats in the house, but after she held one of the kittens, an orange tabby, I knew the battle was over. Azalea pretended to be gruff and tough much of the time, but at heart she was kindness itself. I suspected that at least one of the kittens might go home with her, if at all possible, once I resolved the mystery of their sudden appearance in my life.

In addition to the kitten Azalea favored, there were two other orange tabbies. The remaining two kittens were tabbies also, but dark gray with black markings. These two reminded me of a much-loved cat I'd had once, named Marlowe. She was named for the Elizabethan playwright, and I had adored her. I decided that I'd call one of these kittens by her name. Fortunately for me, Dr. Romano had determined the sex of each kitten. There were three males, the orange tabbies; and two females, the gray tabbies.

The two females were easier to tell apart. One was darker than the other, and that was Marlowe. I decided to call her sister Bastet, in honor of the cat in Elizabeth Peters's Amelia Peabody books. Two of the boys looked almost identical and were dark ginger. After some thought, I settled on Fred and George, the names of the ginger-headed Weasley twins from the Harry Potter books. The other was lighter, and I named him Ramses, again in honor of a character from the Peabody books.

Azalea was one major concern. Diesel was the other. He had been around other cats occasionally, like Endora, the Abyssinian belonging to the Ducote sisters and their ward, Benjy Stephens. Adult cats were one thing, however. Five kittens—five *active* kittens—were quite another matter. Diesel exhibited a lot of curiosity about the brood. He was tall enough to look over the side of the box they arrived in, and while I stood at the door staring down at them, he regarded them for perhaps thirty seconds before he turned his head to look up at me. He meowed, and I would have sworn he was asking me, *Well, what do we do now?*

"That's a good question," I responded, looking down at him. "First thing is to bring them into the house because it's chilly out here." Diesel moved back when I bent to pick up the box. The kittens squeaked and mewed in alarm, and I spoke in soothing tones to them. "It's all right, little ones, you're safe. We'll look after you." Diesel warbled as if to reinforce my promise.

From then on, Diesel stayed near the kittens whenever possible. I first considered keeping them in the utility room—until I remembered the tendency of kittens to find tight spaces to squeeze into. The utility room offered several such possibilities, none of them particularly salubrious for small fry. I discarded that idea because I didn't want to have to move appliances in order to rescue stuck felines.

Finally I settled on the living room for the daytime. I moved furniture around in order to clear a corner of the room. Using two small, wide bookshelves turned on their sides, I created an effective barrier to contain the quintet. At least for a week or so, I told myself ruefully, before they learned how to climb over the barricade. If we had already put up the Christmas tree in the room, I would have probably put them in the den. But our family tradition was to put it up on Christmas Eve. Perhaps by then I would be able to find out where the kittens belonged.

Inside the kitten corral, I placed two litter boxes and two cat beds, along with water and food bowls. The space was large enough for play, plus Diesel could sit atop one of the shelves and monitor the activity of the inmates. He appeared to enjoy this task. In fact, he didn't want to leave the kittens when I was ready to go to work on the second day we had them.

"I suppose it's just as well he's staying here today," I told Azalea as I gathered my briefcase and my coat. "He can help babysit so that you don't have to worry about them climbing out somehow and getting lost in the house."

Azalea chuckled. "Suits me fine, Mr. Charlie. You go on to work and don't worry about us."

I nodded. "Call me if you need anything. I can run by the grocery store when I come home for lunch if necessary." I headed out the back door into the garage.

As I backed down the driveway to the street, I kept my eyes on the rearview camera in my new car. My previous car hadn't had this device, and I was still getting used to it. Suddenly a flash of movement on the screen startled me, and I hit the brakes as I was about to back into the street.

My heart thudded from what might have been a near miss. I turned to look back and saw a smartly dressed young black woman standing on the sidewalk a few feet away. She was waving at me. I put the car in park and rolled down my window.

"Good morning, Mr. Harris." She stepped closer and stooped enough so that I could see her face without craning my neck out the window. "Sorry if I startled you, but I saw you backing out, and I wanted to catch you before you got away." She smiled.

I tried not to sound grumpy when I replied, but I might not have been completely successful. "What can I do for you, ma'am? If we've met, I regret to say I don't remember your name."

The young woman, who I judged to be in her late twenties, smiled again. "Oh, we haven't met, but I know all about you. My employer, Mrs. Albritton, told me about you. Actually, she sent me out to catch you."

I suspected a trap. I had avoided face-to-face contact with Gerry Albritton for the past couple of days because I had still not made up my mind about the blasted holiday party she was throwing. I had no doubt she had sent this young woman to get an answer out of me.

Gerry's assistant continued to speak. "My name is Jincy Bruce."

"Nice to meet you, Ms. Bruce." I repeated my question. "What can I do for you?"

"Gerry wanted me to ask you about her party," Jincy replied. "She knows how busy you are, but she's trying to nail down the guest list before she gives the caterer the final numbers. She needs to do that this afternoon."

I interpreted the smile that accompanied this message as apologetic. Was chasing down guests part of Jincy Bruce's regular duties? I wondered.

I was tempted to say that I had other plans, simply to

be contrary, but I realized that was a childish response. So I forced myself to smile before I answered.

"Please tell Gerry that I will be delighted to attend and that I will be bringing my partner. I believe the invitation was issued to me *and guest*."

"Your *partner*?" Jincy looked confused for a moment; then she grinned as if struck by something amusing. "Oh, *I* see. Thanks, Mr. Harris, I'll let Gerry know. Bye, now!" She waved as she turned to hurry across the street.

I sat there a moment, puzzled by Jincy Bruce's reaction to my statement. What had she found so amusing? Was it my use of the word *partner*? What was so funny about that?

Still puzzled, I put the car in reverse and continued backing into the street. Had the day not been on the chilly side with a hint of rain later on, I might have walked to the Athena College Library. The drive took less than ten minutes because the campus lay so close to my neighborhood, and it was an easy walk when the weather complied. Today, however, I might need the car, not only to run an errand later but also to stay dry if the rain came as predicted.

Going to work at the archive without Diesel felt odd. Over the years since I found him, wet and shivering in the bushes of the parking lot at the public library, he had rarely missed a day accompanying me. I knew Melba would be disappointed not to see her little buddy, but she would get a kick out of hearing about Diesel the kitten-sitter.

I stuck my head in Melba's office to wish her a good morning. She looked up from her desk with a grin—that slowly faded when she realized I was alone.

"Good morning, Charlie." She got up from the desk

and walked toward me, her expression anxious. "Where's Diesel? Is he sick?"

"No, he's fine." I grinned. "He decided he'd rather stay home with the kids today."

Melba laughed. "Has he decided to be their nanny?"

"Looks like it," I replied. "Frankly, I'm relieved that he has taken to the kittens so well. I was worried that he would be upset with five more cats in the house."

"He's such a sweet boy," Melba said. "Have you found out any more about who left those babies on the doorstep?"

"No, not yet. I haven't really had much time, other than to make a few calls around the neighborhood. So far nobody knows anything about them. Or at least, that's what they're saying."

"They're probably better off with you, anyway," Melba said. I had told her about the note I had found with the kittens. "Imagine someone wanting to drown those five darling little babies." She shook her head. "That's one mystery that maybe you shouldn't solve."

"Maybe not." I had considered that option but hadn't made a final decision yet.

"Speaking of mysteries, though," Melba said, "I've been doing some calling around of my own since you first told me about that new neighbor of yours, Ms. So-Called Geraldine Albritton."

From her tone, I figured Melba had not dug up anything yet.

"I managed to get a hold of Billy Albritton, and he says he doesn't know any Geraldine Albritton. He couldn't talk but a minute, though, so I didn't get to ask him anything else.

"Then I talked to a couple more Albrittons I know, and not a single one of them has ever heard of a Geraldine in the family. And you know what that means?" Melba fixed me with a stern gaze. "It means that woman is an impostor. You'd better find out who she really is and what she's up to before she causes any serious trouble."

THREE

||||||||||||||||||||||||||||||||

"I'd swear she told me she's lived in Athena all her life."
I frowned. "Why would she lie about that?"

Melba shrugged. "Maybe she's not lying about it.
Maybe she did grow up here. I bet you what she's lying
about is her real name."

"What can she be trying to hide? Jail time, for example?" I could come up with numerous lurid possibilities
based on the thousands of mysteries I had read since
childhood.

"Could be. What if she's hiding from an ex-husband or
a stalker?" Melba asked. "Maybe she's really from somewhere else, and she came here under a new name to get
away from an abusive man and just happened to pick Albritton." She shrugged. "If you want to get real crazy,
maybe she's in some kind of witness protection program."

"Hold on a minute," I said. "Let's not get *too* carried
away and get the FBI involved. She could very well be

hiding from someone, but if she is, then that's her business."

"Unless she's running from the law." Melba looked grim. "She could be wanted for the Lord knows what somewhere else, and here she is, trying to hide out in Athena to keep from going to prison. We don't need a dangerous criminal right under our noses."

I knew if I laughed I would hurt Melba's feelings, but she was getting more and more off-the-wall with her speculation. After a cough to cover an inadvertent snicker, I said, "There could be some offshoot of the Albritton clan that people have forgotten about. Didn't you tell me that it's a big family?"

"Yes, it is. Old Mr. Albritton, the one who died last year at ninety-nine, had thirteen brothers and sisters, and they all married and had children, and those children have children, and so on, so you might be right."

"You'll keep digging, I'm sure."

"Darn tootin', I'll keep digging." Melba shot me a look full of determination. "I want to know who that woman really is and what she's after."

"Let me know if you find out," I said in a light tone. "In the meantime I'm going to go upstairs and get to work."

Melba nodded, but I could see that her mind was still preoccupied with the mystery of Geraldine Albritton. I knew the problem would worry her until she found an answer.

I had more than enough to do that day without spending time thinking about my mysterious neighbor. Two graduate students from the history department had been working in the archive recently. One was a master's degree student, the other a doctoral one. Both specialized in

Southern history, and the archive held several collections of diaries and private papers of great interest for Mississippi and for Southern history in general. The students could only work with the documents under my supervision, however. No one was allowed to remove documents from the archive without special permission, and that was rarely given.

To my surprise, neither student was waiting, as at least one of them usually was. Moreover, neither made an appearance that morning. I finally remembered why. The semester was almost at an end, and their Christmas and New Year's break loomed closer. This was finals week, and they were far too busy elsewhere. They might even have headed home already for the holidays. I had the office completely to myself. No Diesel, no students.

With the quiet around me, I decided I would have a productive day with few distractions. That meant I could get on with cataloging a collection of nineteenth-century Southern novels from a recent donation. The donor had collected the work of writers like John Pendleton Kennedy, William Gilmore Simms, Kate Chopin, and George Tucker. I had to resist the temptation to read instead of catalog, though, because—with the exception of Chopin—I had not read these writers. Two of the books even featured inscriptions by the authors, and that made them even more interesting to me. I liked that personal touch.

I happily spent a couple of hours immersed in cataloging after I finished checking and responding as needed to my e-mail. A little after ten thirty, the ringing of my office phone pulled me from my absorption in creating detailed notes about the copy of Kennedy's *Swallow Barn* from the collection. I laid it aside to pick up the receiver.

"Charlie Harris. How can I help you?"

"Hey, Charlie, hope I'm not bothering you, but I wanted to talk to you a minute if you've got the time," a man's voice said.

After a moment's hesitation I recognized the caller as Milton Harville, the owner of one of the pharmacies in town. The business had originated with his grandfather and had remained in the family since. Milton's daughter Jenny had recently graduated from pharmacy school and had joined her father in the store. The Harvilles had also lived in my neighborhood for several generations, and Milton and I had been in the same class in school. We had been friends since elementary school.

"Hi, Milton, sure thing, what's up?" I replied.

"Well, I feel kinda funny even asking about this, but you and me, well, we've known each other forever, besides being neighbors, so I reckoned you might not mind talking about it."

Milton, whose house stood in the middle of the block on the street behind mine, had always taken forever to get to the point in a conversation, and today was no exception. He was a nice guy, so I responded in a friendly tone. "Talking about what?"

I heard an indrawn breath at the other end of the line. Then the expulsion of a sigh. "It's this new neighbor of ours, Gerry Albritton. You must have met her by now, surely."

"Yes, I've met her," I said. "She can be a little overwhelming." That seemed a safe enough comment.

"You're not kidding," Milton said. "Pushy ain't the word, I gotta tell you. She's been after me and Tammy about this party of hers. Tammy don't want to go, but you know I'm in business, and I can't afford to offend potential customers. Gerry looks like she wears a lot of makeup, and she could be a real good customer. We sell a lot of cosmetics here, you know. So, I feel like we kinda have to go to this shindig of hers, even if I have to go without Tammy, but I'll never hear the end of it if I do go without her, so I'm wondering what the heck I oughta do." He paused for a breath, then hurried on before I could respond.

"So, I got to thinking about our neighbors, and you're the one who's closest in age to me, so I decided I'd ask you what you're going to do about it. Are you going? And is Helen Louise going with you? Because if Helen Louise is going, I can probably talk Tammy into it because she loves Helen Louise's place and is always going in there and buying cakes and pastries to bring home. It's a wonder I can fit through the door, I eat so much of that stuff."

I seized my chance when he paused. "I am going, and I imagine Helen Louise will go with me, though I haven't asked her about it yet. I'm sure enough of the neighborhood will be there, for curiosity's sake, if nothing else, so no one person will have to spend much time talking to Gerry Albritton. That should make Tammy feel better." I didn't know Tammy well. Milton had met and married her when he went to pharmacy school in Jackson, and they didn't move back to Athena until Jackie and I had moved to Texas. In the years since I had come home to Athena, I saw her occasionally in the store, but she hadn't been particularly friendly. A cold fish, in my opinion, not exactly a woman that I would have pictured the gregarious Milton marrying. He seemed devoted to her, though.

"Well, maybe so." Milton didn't sound all that sure.

"You know what Tammy's like, she thinks every woman I talk to is trying to lure me away from her, and I keep telling her, I don't have time for that stuff, I have a business to run, and besides, I've never wanted any woman besides Tammy ever since we met, but you know how she is. And I sure ain't no movie star, never have been, so I can't figure out why Tammy thinks women are so hot for me all the time."

Milton was right—he didn't have movie-star looks, but he was still an attractive man. He worked out and had all his hair, and he had a friendly, engaging manner that served him well at the pharmacy. His wife went overboard with the jealous routine, but I figured there were probably more than a few of Milton's female customers who shopped more often than was strictly necessary at the pharmacy in order to chat with him.

I decided not to address Tammy's possessiveness; otherwise Milton might complain about it further, and I'd be on the phone several minutes more. Instead I reiterated my previous comments.

"I sure hope you're right," Milton said, "but the Lord only knows what Tammy might do." He paused for a moment, and I was hoping he was ready to end the conversation. Instead, he surprised me with his next words.

"I can't help thinking I know her, Charlie, but I don't know how I know her, you know what I mean? There's something about her that's familiar, and it's been nagging at me. But for the life of me, I can't put a finger on it. You ever had that feeling about someone? Because if you have, you know how annoying it can be, it's like a little worm in your brain wiggling around trying to find the way out."

I suppressed the sudden mental image I had of a worm

burrowing in my brain and addressed Milton's main point.

"I've had that feeling, certainly, but not about Gerry Albritton," I said. "Remember, I was gone from Athena for a long time, so there are a lot of people here now that I don't know. I'm pretty sure I've never met her before."

"Well, if you say so," Milton replied. "Look, guess I'd better get off the phone, you've probably got a lot to do, and I'd better get back to work before Jenny fires me." He chuckled.

"All right," I said. "Tell Jenny hello for me, and I guess we'll see you at the party, if not before." I ended the call before Milton could launch into another ramble. He was one of the nicest guys around, but have mercy, he could talk the trunk off an elephant and probably its ears and tail, too.

I stared blankly at the work on my desk awaiting my attention. I thought about what Milton had said. He had the feeling he knew Gerry Albritton, but he couldn't remember how or why. I wondered if I ought to share that with Melba. Maybe if the two of them got together they might figure it out between them without any further help from me.

I laughed at that idea. This was one rabbit hole I didn't need to fall into, trying to solve a mystery where there probably wasn't one. None of my business who Geraldine Albritton was, if she wasn't who she claimed to be. Besides, Tammy didn't need to come into the store and find Melba and Milton in a corner somewhere, talking ninety to nothing. She'd try to scratch Melba's eyes out.

For another hour I managed to keep focused on work. When I checked the clock next I discovered that the time was eleven forty-six. Might as well stop now and go home for lunch, I decided. My neck and shoulders needed a break. I tended to hunch over the desk while working.

On the way down the stairs I heard my cell phone ringing, and I dug it out as I reached the bottom of the flight. I glanced at the caller ID. Azalea. Probably wanted me to run by the grocery store.

"Hello, Azalea, what can I pick up on the way home?" I said.

"Mr. Charlie, are you about ready to come home for lunch?" Azalea sounded annoyed, and I figured the kittens had gotten loose and she needed help finding them.

"Yes, I'm on my way out of the building this minute," I said.

"Good. Somebody's been peeking in the windows," Azalea said.

FOUR

I cut Azalea off in my haste to get going. "Call the police. I'm on the way."

I stuck my phone back in my pocket and hurried out of the building to my car. Traffic thankfully stayed sparse. I made it home in under seven minutes. When I pulled in to the garage and stopped the car, I saw no sign of the police. I thought they might have arrived by now. Athena wasn't such a large town that the police were ever very far away.

Heart pounding, I stumbled once climbing out of the car but managed to get to the kitchen door without falling. I opened the door and stepped inside to find Azalea and Diesel waiting. Considering the situation, I found their calmness unnerving. Azalea was frowning at me.

"Did you call the police?" I asked.

Azalea shook her head. "No need to call them. I would've told you, Mr. Charlie, but you hung up on me.

Didn't try to call you back because I figured you'd be rushing to get here."

Diesel came to me and rubbed against my legs. He could tell I was worried and wanted to reassure me. I scratched his head to let him know I was okay. My heart rate began to drop back toward normal.

"What about the prowler?" I asked. "Weren't you afraid he might try to break in?"

Again my housekeeper shook her head. "No, I wasn't afraid of any such thing. Whoever was peeking in the windows wasn't a grown man or woman."

"Do you mean a child or a teenager was the peeping tom?"

Azalea nodded. "Child. Couldn't be more 'n about ten, I'd say."

"Did you get a good look at him or her?" I asked. "I wonder if it was the child who left the kittens on the doorstep."

"Reckon it likely was," Azalea said. "All I saw was dark hair on top of a head a couple times. Caught a glimpse out the corner of my eye when I turned around. Head ducking down out of sight of the window." She indicated the window over the sink. "By the time I got to where I could see better outside, whoever it was had run off. I didn't see no point in going chasing after them."

"No, no point by then," I said. "I'll bet it was the kittens' owner coming to check on them." A thought occurred to me. Why wasn't the child in school? The local schools weren't out for the holidays already, were they? I thought they had a couple of more days to go, at least.

Even if the schools weren't out, a child could have

sneaked away from the elementary school that was about five blocks from this house, I reasoned. The more I considered the idea, the more I was convinced it was probably the answer. Identifying that child, however, would be problematic. I could hardly go to the school and ask if anyone noticed a dark-haired child sneaking off or back on to the school grounds around lunchtime.

Chances were that the child would return at some point for another attempt to catch sight of the kittens. I suggested this to Azalea, and she agreed.

"I'll be on the lookout from now on," she said. "Now, how about lunch?"

"Sounds good," I said. "I'll just go wash my hands and have a look at our newest little boarders."

Diesel followed me to the first-floor washroom under the stairs and waited patiently outside while I completed my ablutions. Since I left the door open, he didn't try to crowd inside with me as he would have done if I had started to shut the door.

"Let's see about the kitties," I told him as I finished drying my hands. He chirped several times and trotted ahead of me as I walked to the living room. When I arrived he was sitting atop one of the bookshelves, surveying the scene.

The kittens were playing with one another, and I watched their roughhousing for a moment before I realized that there were only four of them. After a closer look, I determined that Ramses had somehow managed to get out of the corral. "Well, that was sooner than I expected," I told Diesel. "I didn't think they'd get out for another week or two. Can you find him, boy?" I hoped Ramses hadn't managed to get far.

Diesel trilled loudly and leapt off the bookshelf. He started hunting around the room while I watched. I figured he would find the stray more quickly than I could, by scent if nothing else. He could also see under and behind furniture more easily than I could.

Sure enough, after a moment Diesel located Ramses. Diesel scrunched the front half of his large body under the sofa, and I heard a combination of chirping and mewling before Diesel emerged with Ramses. He herded the errant kitten back toward me and the corral, scolding all the way.

Ramses ran to me, perhaps to get away from the fussing Maine Coon, and before I realized what he intended, he had scaled his way halfway up my pant leg. I winced as the sharp, small claws connected with flesh a few times. I scooped him away from my leg and held him close, cupped in my hands, his face only a couple of inches from mine.

"Okay, Ramses, I didn't intend for you to emulate your namesake and start having adventures at this age," I told him. In the series in which the character Ramses featured, he had been a terrifyingly precocious child, prone to wander on his own even as a toddler.

Feline Ramses stared at me, apparently fascinated by the close proximity of my face. Without warning, he leaned his little head forward and licked the tip of my nose.

"I'll take that for an apology," I said, and the kitten mewed. I stroked his head with one finger. "Now listen here, Ramses. Let's not go exploring anymore for a while yet, okay?" He mewed again, and I put him back in the corral.

Diesel had watched me the entire time I held the kitten, and once Ramses had been returned to the fold, Diesel resumed his vantage post atop the bookcase. He trilled to let me know he intended to keep watch for a while. At least, that was how I interpreted his communication with me.

Back in the kitchen I informed Azalea of the errant kitten, and she chuckled as she set a plate of roast beef, mashed potatoes with gravy, and green beans at my place at the table. "Little scamp. He'll be out again before you know it."

"Not as long as Diesel is there keeping an eye out for attempts at jailbreak," I said.

"Mr. Cat acts like he's their daddy." Azalea set a glass of iced tea on the table along with a small plate of buttered rolls.

I cut into the roast beef, so tender it nearly fell apart simply from the touch of the knife. I forked a bite into my mouth and savored while I chewed slowly. After I swallowed, I said, "Perfection as usual, Azalea. No one can do roast like you do."

"You say that every time I cook a roast." Azalea regarded me with a faint smile.

"And every time it's true." I grinned. After a mouthful of potatoes and gravy, I said, "We've got to come up with another solution for keeping the horde from getting loose all over the house."

"What about one of those cages they put dogs in?" Azalea asked.

"That's one possibility, if there's one big enough for all five of them," I replied. "I wouldn't want to separate them if I don't have to. I'll have to think about it."

I had never cared for the sight of dogs in crates, even though friends assured me that crate-trained dogs felt safe and comfortable with them. Stewart crated Dante occasionally, but given the poodle's tendencies to get into mischief when left on his own, I understood why Stewart did it. Dante had a penchant for gnawing on Stewart's most expensive shoes.

In the case of five growing and curious kittens, however, a large crate or cage might be the safest choice. I would check with the vet's office to find out where I might get a large one that would keep the kittens contained but allow them room to play. I hoped I could find one and get it installed in the next couple of days, because I had little doubt that where Ramses led, the other four would soon follow. Diesel and Azalea would do their best, but they couldn't watch the kittens every minute.

Besides, I realized, having the kittens safely contained meant that Diesel could come to the office with me or to the public library. I believed he would understand that the kittens would be out of harm's way in the cage and would then be happy to accompany me as usual. I had become so used to having Diesel with me almost everywhere I went, and when he wasn't with me, I definitely felt his absence.

That decided me. A cage it would be.

Once I finished my meal, I called the vet's office and spoke to the receptionist. I told her what I needed, and she reminded me that Athena had one of those chain pet stores. I had forgotten that, because I never had gone inside it. I thanked her for the information and ended the call. I could make a run by the pet store this afternoon after I finished at the archive.

Before I left to return to work I went to the living room to check on Diesel and the kittens. Diesel blinked sleepily at me as I approached the corral, and he yawned, his tail swishing. I rubbed his head while I took in the scene inside the bookshelves. All the kittens were asleep, snuggled together on one of the two makeshift pet beds I had made for them out of several old quilts.

How tiny and defenseless they looked. I couldn't imagine how anyone could be cruel enough to harm such innocent little creatures, but sadly I knew it happened every day. I would do what I could to ensure their safety while they were in my care, and I intended to solve the riddle of their appearance on my doorstep. I felt sad for the child who'd had to give them up to protect them. They would all go to good, loving homes, one way or another, if they couldn't return safely to their original home.

I turned and walked softly back across the hall to the kitchen. "All quiet on the kitten front," I told Azalea. "At the moment they're all napping."

Azalea nodded. "Maybe they'll sleep for a while now. I have plenty to do before Miss Alex comes by with the baby." Her face creased in a smile. "That little Rosie is the most precious thing."

My granddaughter, Charlotte Rose Harris, was now almost two months old, and every time I saw her I wanted to melt into the floor. She had Sean's dark hair and her mother's pert nose. She was not a placid child, unlike her cousin Charlie, who was hardly ever fussy. Miss Rosie reminded me greatly of her aunt Laura, who had also been a fractious baby.

"I know Alex and Laura both appreciate you helping look after the babies," I said. "I'm going to run by the pet store after work, but I should be home by four at the latest to help you."

Azalea looked at me. "The day I can't take care of a bitty baby is the day they put me in the old folks' home. Don't you rush home on my account. Miss Rosie and I will be fine. Besides, Miss Alex is only going to go get her hair done and do a little shopping."

I knew better than to argue. "All right. See you later." I headed to my car. I glanced in the rearview mirror and then into the camera to guide me back toward the street. As I kept close watch on my backward progress, I saw the small figure of a woman walking down the sidewalk across the street.

Something about that woman looked awfully familiar. I stopped the car and turned in the seat to look at her. She turned into the walk at Gerry Albritton's house and approached the front door.

I shook my head as I recognized the woman.

Melba Gilley, secret agent, was on the hunt for information.

FIVE

When I returned to work I thought about leaving a note on Melba's desk, asking her to come see me when she got back from her lunch hour. Knowing my friend, however, I figured she would make a beeline for my office the minute she set foot in the building to fill me in on her visit to Gerry Albritton.

I didn't have long to wait. Barely half an hour passed after I returned to my office before Melba hurried through my door.

"I bet you can't guess where I've just been." Melba almost skidded to a stop by the chair in front of my desk. She plopped down in the chair and looked at me, her expression smug.

"Gerry Albritton's house." I tried not to laugh at her obvious annoyance at my answer.

"How did you know?" She sounded cross.

"I saw you practically running down the sidewalk

while I was backing out of my driveway after lunch. Didn't you see me?" I said, and she shook her head. "I'm surprised you didn't trip and break a leg, you were going so fast." I couldn't help exaggerating because I loved to tease her when she was in one of her snoopy moods.

Melba glowered at me. "I've got a good mind not to tell you what I found out."

I grinned. "You'll bust a blood vessel if you don't, and you know it."

She snorted with laughter. "You're right about that."

"So spill, what did you find out?"

Melba hesitated, and I could see that she was choosing her words before she responded. "Nothing concrete," she said after a moment. "I tried asking her questions, but she deflected them. I even mentioned Billy Albritton, but she pretended not to hear me. I didn't learn anything much." She paused and shook her head. "I don't think I've ever seen her before, but there's something about her that's so familiar. It's driving me crazy, but I can't figure out what it is."

"Maybe she looks a little like somebody else you know," I said. "I get those feelings sometimes because of a superficial resemblance. Now, you, I've always thought, remind me a little bit of Paulette Goddard."

"Really?" Melba said, looking pleased. "I loved her in that Bob Hope movie, the one with the haunted castle."

"*The Ghost Breakers*," I said. "That's a fun movie, but we're getting off the track."

"It's no use right now getting back on track," Melba replied. "The harder I try to figure out who that woman reminds me of, the more confused I feel."

"Tell me this, do you think she's really an Albritton?" I asked.

Melba shrugged. "No. I think she just picked a name out of the Athena phone book, and that one must have sounded good to her. She sure didn't act like she knows anything about the family." She rose from the chair. "I'd better get back downstairs before Andrea starts looking for me. If I get busy with work, maybe it'll come to me about who she reminds me of."

"See you later," I called after her as she headed out the door.

I busied myself with my own work. I needed to focus on the tasks at hand, not spend time thinking about two mysteries, the origin of the five kittens and the truth about Gerry Albritton.

For about half an hour I managed to stick to my resolve while I cataloged more of the collection I'd been working on before lunch, but after that my mind began to wander. Then one question came to the forefront of my consciousness.

Should I make a concerted effort to find out who left the kittens on my doorstep?

If I did manage to track down the child who had done it, would I cause trouble for her or him? Perhaps I was being oversensitive, but the wording of the note left with the kittens—especially the emphasis on the word *he*— made me hesitate. I had thought about going door-to-door in the neighborhood to inquire whether anyone's cat had recently given birth to a litter. I knew most of the families within a couple of blocks on my street and part of the street behind my house, but not so many in the surrounding streets, other than to say hello when I encountered them somewhere in town.

One idea struck me. Gerry Albritton's holiday party was coming up next week. If most people in the neighborhood turned out for it, I could work my way through the crowd asking innocuous questions. Everyone always wanted to talk to me about Diesel anyway, and discussing my cat would serve as a natural opening to a more general chat on the subject of house pets.

That provided me with one excellent reason to attend a function that otherwise I wanted to avoid. I could enlist Helen Louise in the campaign to dig for information as well. Between us, we ought to be able to find out something, or at least eliminate families from the inquiry.

With that decided, I could get back to work and actually do the job I was supposed to be doing. Though I missed having Diesel in the office with me, I worked happily until three thirty. Then I gathered my things, turned out the lights, and locked the door behind me.

There was no sign of Melba downstairs. I would catch up with her later. I knew that when she figured out why Gerry Albritton seemed familiar, I would be the first to hear about it. I headed out to my car to drive home.

When I neared my driveway, I spotted my daughter-in-law's car parked on the street in front of the house. My granddaughter was barely two months old, and Alex hadn't been venturing out of the house much since Charlotte Rose had made her appearance. Sean hadn't said much, but I figured that Alex was struggling a bit with motherhood. I knew that Rosie, as we called her, was not the happy baby that her little cousin Charlie was. Rosie was more fretful and demanding, and I thought caring for the baby was wearing Alex down.

Sean was helping with Rosie as much as he could, but he had a law office to run—a job he usually shared with Alex. They couldn't afford to shut down the office while Alex was on maternity leave so Sean could be at home, too. Alex's father, Q. C. Pendergrast, had *un-retired*, as he called it, in order to help, but he had suffered a stroke a few months ago and was still recovering from its effects. He could only do so much.

I thought Sean and Alex needed to bring another lawyer into the firm, but they had been reluctant to do that. Now, however, it seemed more imperative to me than ever. I had expressed my opinion when it was solicited, so both my son and daughter-in-law knew how I felt. Now it was up to them to act on my suggestion.

As I was getting out of the car, I realized I had completely forgotten about the pet store. I hesitated a moment. I really ought to get this taken care of today. But I wavered. My granddaughter was here. I decided the pet store could wait.

When I walked through the door into the kitchen, I immediately spotted Alex at the table feeding Rosie. I stopped and watched for a moment. I didn't think Alex had heard me enter the room, her attention appeared so fixed upon her child. I glanced to my right and saw Azalea standing near the stove. She was also watching Alex and the baby, and her expression was unreadable.

"Hello, Alex," I said, my voice low. I greeted Azalea, and she nodded in response.

Alex offered me a wan smile as I bent to kiss her

cheek. "Hi, Dad, how are you?" Rosie continued her noisy suckling at her mother's breast.

"I'm fine," I said. "How are you? Did you get all your errands done?" She nodded. "That's good. Nice to have a break." Alex nodded again. She seemed as dispirited as I had ever seen her.

I tried again. "Rosie seems to be doing fine, too. You're taking such good care of her."

Alex sighed. "Seems to me that she's almost always hungry. The rate she's going, she'll be an Amazon by the time she's sixteen."

I squeezed her shoulder. I could see that she was tired, and I figured she wasn't sleeping well. Laura had been a fussy baby, too, and I remembered the many nights of fractured sleep that her mother and I endured before she finally grew out of that stage.

"She's like her aunt, Laura, that's for sure," I said as I took a chair opposite Alex and Rosie.

"How on earth did you manage with Laura?" Alex said, interest sparking briefly in her eyes.

"Jackie and I both went around dazed for months," I said. "Eventually Laura started sleeping through the night, and we were able to get back to sleeping ourselves."

"I hope Rosie starts sleeping more soon. All the trouble she has with colic, I guess." Alex sighed. "I am so exhausted now, I don't know what I'm doing half the time."

I hesitated before I responded because I knew Alex was sensitive on the issue I was about to broach. Looking at her drawn face, though, I felt I had to speak up.

"I think you and Sean really need to rethink your decision about a nanny," I said.

Azalea spoke before Alex could respond. "Now Miss Alex, you listen to Mr. Charlie. You're wearing yourself out, and my cousin Lurene's daughter Cherelle loves babies and would love to help you out. Don't mean you're not a good mama because you need help." She smiled. "I had to have help with Kanesha, because the good Lord knows that child was a handful from the moment she came into this world and hasn't stopped being one since. If I hadn't had my own mama to help, I swear I would have left Kanesha on somebody's doorstep just so I could sleep."

Alex had started shaking her head the moment I began to speak, but she stilled the movement as Azalea talked. I hoped Azalea's words would get through to my daughter-in-law. She obviously needed help with the baby, but she was a proud young woman who always wanted to show that she could do anything and do it well. But in this small bundle of fussiness I thought she finally had to realize that there were some challenges she might not be able to handle alone.

"You're right." Alex sighed. "Sean has been begging me to let him find help, but I wouldn't let him." Tears began to roll down her face. "I feel like such a failure."

Azalea moved quickly to put an arm around Alex's shoulders. She stroked Alex's head, now bent toward her nursing child. "Now see here, you are not any kind of failure, you just hush that kind of talk. Looking after a fretful baby is a trial to anyone, and you stop feeling like it's your fault."

"Azalea's right, sweetheart," I said. "The best thing you can do for yourself is to have the strength to admit you need help. No one is going to fault you for that."

"Thank you, Dad." Alex didn't appear to be wholly convinced by our assurances, but I hoped if we continued to encourage her, she would accept help.

Before I could say anything further, we all heard loud meows coming from another room. Only Diesel could produce that decibel level, and after a glance of apology to Alex and Azalea, I hurried from the room.

I took a couple of steps into the living room before I halted in amazement. Diesel sat on his hind legs in front of the drapes at the large picture window, batting futilely at kittens climbing the drapes. I counted quickly. Yes, all five of them clung to the drapes at various points about three feet high.

Diesel successfully batted one loose—George, I thought—and warbled in a threatening tone. He placed a large paw on top of the wriggling kitten and pinned him to the floor, even as he gazed up at the remaining four mountaineers.

"I'm here, boy." I hurried to join Diesel at the drapes and started extracting the other kittens from the drapes and placing them inside their obviously ineffective corral.

"What am I going to do with you little monsters?" I said to the kittens, all of whom were now tussling with one another. Beside me Diesel chirped and meowed, no doubt in agreement. These kittens were proving more challenging than I had expected, and I had to get the situation under control.

SIX

||||||||||||||

I posed my question about the kittens to Stewart and Haskell later in the day. "I was planning to go to the pet store this afternoon but didn't make it there. I simply forgot, I guess." I shook my head. "I don't know what my memory's coming to these days. Anyway, I called them about half an hour ago, and they don't have a big enough cage in stock at present. They said it would take a week or so to get one, and I told them I'd think about it. I'm not sure what to do, but I obviously need to do something sooner than that."

"Haskell and I were discussing that ourselves," Stewart said, sounding a bit smug. "I think we've found, well, *Haskell* has found the solution."

"Really? What's your idea?" I asked, turning to Haskell.

"I can build something for you that ought to do what you want," he replied. "You buy the materials, and I'll supply the design and the labor. With Stewart's assistance." He glanced at his partner, and Stewart nodded, smiling.

"Sounds great to me. I can't tell you how much I appreciate this," I said.

"Glad to help out," Haskell replied.

"How long do you think it will take?"

"A few hours, I reckon. I can do it tomorrow," Haskell said. "Long as I don't get called in for anything." His work schedule could be unpredictable, I knew. He sometimes got called to fill in for another deputy or in cases of emergency.

"Wonderful," I replied. "Write down what you need, and I'll get it this evening."

After that, we discussed the dimensions of the enclosure Haskell proposed to build, and once we had settled on those, Haskell started jotting down the items he needed. He made a few calculations as he went, and within half an hour he had completed his list.

I drove to the building supply store right away. I estimated that by the time I located everything and had it loaded and paid for, I'd be home again in time for dinner. Helen Louise was joining us tonight, and I was looking forward to talking to her about the upcoming holiday party at Gerry Albritton's house. I was able to spend a little more time with Helen Louise since she had made the decision a couple of months ago to start cutting back on her hours at the bistro. I didn't think she had cut back as much as she really needed, for the sake of her own general well-being, but she was slowly making progress.

At the store I simply handed over Haskell's list, and store personnel found everything for me. I went to high school with the owner of the place. His family had owned the business since the early part of the last century, and customer service was a priority for them. The whole errand took less than an hour, and they delivered everything about thirty minutes after I got home. Haskell and Stewart helped unload it all, and Haskell assured me they would have the enclosure assembled by the following afternoon.

Later, over the dinner table, Helen Louise and I, along with Stewart and Haskell, enjoyed the chicken salad Helen Louise had made. We talked about the party while we ate.

"I've already had a call from Milton Harville," I told the others. "He didn't sound all that keen on the party."

"Because of Tammy, I'm sure," Helen Louise said. "I don't think I've ever known anyone as possessive as she is. Poor Milton can hardly talk to women customers at the pharmacy without her going crazy."

Stewart laughed. "I know this will sound bitchy, but I can't imagine any woman besides Tammy ever looking twice at Milton. He is the kindest, most generous man I know, but he doesn't exactly have the most sparkling personality. Plus he talks and talks and talks, and you end up spending three times as much time at the pharmacy as you need."

"I know what she sees. A healthy paycheck." Haskell scowled. "I knew her in high school, and the only guys who interested her were the ones with money. Back then Milton was already working for his dad and his grandfather, and he always had a little cash to throw around. Unlike some of us."

"According to Milton, Gerry Albritton was mighty

friendly to him." I glanced at Helen Louise. "As she was with me."

Helen Louise grimaced. "I think she plays up to men as a matter of course. No telling what she's really after."

"I can see why you don't want to go to her party, Charlie." Stewart grinned at me. "Our Charlie doesn't like the man-eater type."

"No, *our* Charlie doesn't." I frowned at Stewart. "There will be plenty of men at the party, I have no doubt, and she's welcome to lavish her attention on them."

Helen Louise laughed. "Most of them will be with their wives, at least if the guests are all from the immediate neighborhood. I can't think of any single men, offhand."

"Will the grande dame of the neighborhood be there, do you think?" Stewart asked.

I looked at him, puzzled. "Who is the grande dame of the neighborhood?"

"Deirdre Thompson," Stewart and Helen Louise said in unison. They laughed.

"I'm sure she was invited," Helen Louise said. "Our hostess must know by now who Deirdre is."

"And surely Deirdre has condescended enough to call upon the new addition to the neighborhood," Stewart said. "She always has done in the past."

"She did when I moved in to the house after my aunt's death." I recalled the occasion with grim amusement. Deirdre and Diesel had taken one look at each other, and Diesel had left the room. Deirdre hadn't lingered, either. I shared this with the others.

Hearing his name, Diesel warbled loudly from the

doorway. I looked over to see him accompanied by Fred and George. I groaned and pointed to the trio. "This is why I desperately need a way to pen up these miscreants." Even before I finished speaking, the two kittens had galloped across the floor and made as if to climb up Haskell's legs, which, fortunately for him, were covered in denim.

Haskell grabbed the kittens before they had ascended to the table. He grinned at them. "Maybe I should start on their corral tonight instead of waiting for tomorrow."

"Thanks, but I suppose the house will survive one more night," I said. Diesel lay down beside my chair. The poor boy looked exhausted. I said as much to the others.

"Babysitting is a tough job," Helen Louise said. "Especially when there are five of them. Poor Diesel. He's such a sweet boy, looking after the kittens."

Diesel raised his head and chirped. I reached down and rubbed his head.

Haskell rose from the table, Fred and George cradled in his arms. "Back in a minute." He left the kitchen.

Diesel didn't stir. I thought he had gone to sleep.

"Do you think Haskell and I are included in the invitation?" Stewart asked. "I'd give a lot to see Deirdre in action with all the lesser mortals from the neighborhood."

"I don't see why not," I said. "The more the merrier."

"I haven't seen dear Deirdre around much lately," Stewart said. "Not since her third husband died. I suppose she's been busy shopping for number four."

Helen Louise laughed. "How many eligible men her age are there with enough money to interest her?"

Stewart grinned. "Oh, I imagine she has widened her field for this one. I heard somewhere that she's been spending a lot of time in Memphis lately."

Haskell returned, sans kittens. "Who're you talking about?" He resumed his seat.

"Deirdre," Stewart said. "On the prowl for a new husband."

"Not that Deirdre isn't an interesting subject," Helen Louise said, "but let's get back to Gerry Albritton. Have you noticed the two for-sale signs in the neighborhood?"

"The ones with Albritton Realty on them?" Haskell asked.

Helen Louise nodded.

"Where are they?" I asked. "I don't recall seeing them."

"There's one on my street, about three blocks from my house," Helen Louise said. "Where Mr. Murdoch lived."

"Our old high school principal?" I asked after a moment's reflection. "I saw that he died a few weeks ago."

"More like two months," Helen Louise said with a wry smile. "But you've had a lot on your mind since then, with a new granddaughter and baby Charlie."

I nodded. "Where's the other sign?"

"Three streets over, toward the railroad tracks," Haskell replied. "Family named Merriman owned it for years. Elderly lady was the last one living there, and she died about two months ago."

"And here's our neighbor Gerry selling two houses in the area," Stewart said. "I wonder how many other elderly neighbors there are around us."

"Why do you wonder that?" I asked.

"Maybe Gerry is bumping them off so she can sell their houses," Stewart said. "There are quite a few old folks in this area. We could start seeing those signs popping up all over the place."

Haskell regarded his partner's flippancy with a repressive frown. "Be careful where you say things like that."

Stewart rolled his eyes. "I wouldn't say that in front of anyone else." He paused for a grin. "Well, hardly anyone else."

Haskell shook his head, and Helen Louise and I exchanged wry smiles. Stewart's irreverent sense of humor occasionally went a little too far, but as long as he confined such remarks to the present company, there would be no harm done.

Stewart rose from the table. "On that note, dear ones, I think it's time I fetched Dante and took him out for a walk." He gazed at Haskell. "Will you join us?"

Haskell stood. "No, I'll clear the table. My turn, I think."

"I'll help you," I said, also rising. "No, you stay where you are." Helen Louise had started to get up, but she sank back in her chair at my words. "You were on your feet at the bistro today."

"I'm not going to argue," she said.

Haskell and I had the table cleared by the time Stewart returned with his poodle on a leash, ready for their walk. Both master and dog wore sweaters. Diesel roused long enough to chirp tiredly at his friend, while Dante wiggled and woofed ecstatically upon seeing his good buddy. Dante pulled at his leash to approach the cat, and Stewart allowed the leash to extend. Dante licked Diesel's face. The cat put a large paw on the dog's head and pushed him away.

Stewart and I chuckled, and he drew Dante along toward the front door. "We'll be back soon," he said.

I put away the leftovers while Haskell loaded the dishwasher. We chatted in desultory fashion as we worked.

By tacit agreement, it seemed, we avoided further discussion of Gerry Albritton. Frankly, I was tired of the subject.

My respite from my irritating neighbor didn't last long, however. Stewart and Dante returned after a few minutes. As he entered the kitchen, Stewart brandished a piece of paper.

"Wait till you see this flyer, Charlie. It was stuck to the front door," he said. "I spotted them at several houses up and down the street."

I took the flyer, which was the size of a regular piece of copier paper, and scanned the contents. I began to read aloud.

"Tired of mortgage payments? Fed up with costly repairs? Ready to downsize and move? We buy houses, no questions asked, no inspections required, at good prices. Give us a call, and let's do business."

I looked at Helen Louise. "The contact information is for Geraldine Albritton's real estate office."

"What on earth is she up to?" Helen Louise frowned. "Is she trying to buy up the whole neighborhood?"

SEVEN

||||||||||||||||||||||||||||||||

"She's certainly not going to buy *this* house." I crumpled the flyer with both hands before discarding it in the trash bin under the sink. Having done so, I shut the cabinet door a little more forcefully than necessary. I wasn't sure why the flyer made me angry, but that was how I felt.

Diesel, evidently alarmed by my tone, sat up and began to meow. I called him to me and began to stroke his back when he stopped and leaned against my legs. Dante was in Stewart's lap, whining because he wanted to play with the cat. Stewart kept him firmly in place.

"Everything's all right, boy." I had to take a few deep breaths to calm myself, and Diesel relaxed under my touch.

"No doubt it's standard business practice with her," Helen Louise said. "Although she seems to have come out of nowhere. I certainly hadn't heard of her or her real estate business before."

"I hadn't, either," Stewart said, and Haskell shrugged. "Not something I pay much attention to," he said.

"I wonder where the money is coming from." I resumed my seat at the table, and the cat settled down by my legs. "Surely it takes substantial capital to go around buying houses. What if several people all want to sell at the same time? That would run into hundreds of thousands of dollars."

"She either has amazingly good credit," Helen Louise said, "or she has big cash reserves."

"Or someone putting up the money for her," Stewart said. "It's strange that no one seems to know where she came from. She basically popped up like a mushroom after a good long rain."

"She's definitely an enigma." I shrugged.

Stewart laughed. "I'm looking forward to this Christmas bash of hers even more now. No telling what might happen."

As if they had heard Stewart's last few words and considered them an invitation, the five kittens came running and tumbling into the kitchen. Ramses was in the lead, and George brought up the rear. Diesel jumped up from beside my legs and darted toward the playful youngsters. Dante jumped out of his master's lap, the leash still attached to his collar, before Stewart realized what the dog was doing. The poodle joined the melee on the floor, barking excitedly while Diesel batted at kittens in an attempt to stop their antics. Two of the kittens seized sections of the leash in their mouths and began to chew.

Laughing, Stewart hastened to catch Dante and free the leash from sharp kitten teeth. Haskell and Helen

Louise were also laughing as they both got up to help. They grabbed a kitten in each hand, and that left Ramses rolling and scrambling as Diesel continued to bat at him. I scooped up Ramses and brought his face near mine. He purred, and I could have sworn he tried to smile. He certainly looked smug for having led the charge, as it were.

Diesel seemed to sag with relief now that the junior set had been caught, and he stretched out on the floor. The kittens had worn him out.

"What do we do with them now that we've caught them?" Helen Louise held up Fred and George and grinned.

"Take them home with you," I said promptly.

Helen Louise shot me a look that I had no difficulty interpreting. I chuckled. "I guess not."

Haskell held Marlowe and Bastet close to his chest. "Unless you want them roaming free all night, you're going to have to put them in a smaller room."

"You're right," I said. "If it weren't so chilly tonight, I'd put them on the porch, and they could ramble to their hearts' content." I thought for a moment. "The downstairs bathroom is too small for all five of them and their beds and litter boxes. I guess I'll put them in one of the bathrooms upstairs for tonight."

"Might as well do it now," Haskell said. "How about the one in Laura's old room?"

"That bathroom's fine," I said. Laura's former bedroom was closest to mine upstairs.

"Y'all keep the kittens entertained." Haskell turned over his two little monsters to his partner. "I'll get the bathroom ready for them."

Stewart offered to help, but Haskell waved him away. "Won't take me long." He left the kitchen.

"He certainly is handy to have around," Helen Louise said.

"He is," Stewart said. "He doesn't mind doing things to help out, though. He likes to keep busy."

In the brief silence that followed Stewart's remarks, I heard Haskell trotting up the stairs. He returned to the kitchen in less than ten minutes, I reckoned.

"Everything's ready," he said.

I rose from the table. "Thanks for doing that."

Helen Louise and I got the kittens settled upstairs in their temporary quarters. After I shut the door, we stood in front of it and watched. Two little paws appeared underneath the door.

"Didn't take them long to find that," Helen Louise said.

"They're all a little too smart for their own good, I think." I turned to lead the way out into the hall. I left the bedroom door open.

"I'm going to head home in a few minutes," Helen Louise said. "It's been a long day."

"Are you working tomorrow?" I asked. "I can't remember what you told me the other day about your schedule."

"No, thank goodness, I'm off. Henry is in charge, and he and the others can handle everything," she said as we reached the bottom of the stairs.

"Good," I said. "Any plans?"

"I'm going to sleep late." She followed me into the empty kitchen. "Then at some point I'm going shopping. I want a new dress for this party. I haven't bought anything new in ages."

"You'll be a knockout no matter what. The belle of the ball."

She grinned. "That's the plan."

I laughed. "Gerry Albritton may have a heart attack on the spot, especially since you're a good eight inches taller."

"That's her lookout, not mine," Helen Louise retorted.

"Absolutely." I drew her into my arms for a kiss. After a brief but satisfying interlude, we stepped apart. I glanced around the room. No sign of Diesel.

Helen Louise read my mind. "He's probably sound asleep on your bed."

"Probably." I watched while she gathered her purse and jacket. I held the jacket for her while she pulled it on. We went into the garage from the kitchen and out into the driveway, where she had parked earlier. The streetlights glowed in the early-evening darkness, and I felt the chill from the damp air.

Helen Louise unlocked her car before she turned to give me another quick kiss. "Get back inside. You don't want to catch a cold."

"I won't." I watched until she backed her car into the street and headed the few blocks to her house.

I started to head into the garage, but a flash of movement in my right peripheral vision stopped me. I turned and headed into the yard. I didn't see anyone or anything moving now. I halted and stared hard at the shrubbery in the beds on either side of the front door.

I waited. Nothing moved, but I was feeling the cold more every second I delayed going back inside.

Maybe I imagined it. I shrugged and walked to the garage. When I reached the entrance to the garage, I turned to glance one more time in the direction of the front door. Still nothing.

Shrugging, I hit the button to close the garage door as

I stepped into the kitchen. The house stood quiet around me. I paused for a moment before walking to the living room to survey the scene. The area the kittens had occupied needed to be cleaned, and I didn't want to leave it for Azalea in the morning.

After setting the bookshelves upright and out of the way, I swept up the scattered litter and stray kitten hair; then I found one of those lint roller devices to remove more hair from the drapes. While I worked, a thought struck me.

What if I really had seen something or someone moving in the front yard a few minutes ago? *Might have been the child who left the kittens on the doorstep.* Perhaps I should have investigated further in case the child was still lurking in the shrubbery. I really didn't think that was likely, however.

Surely the parents wouldn't let their child run around in the neighborhood after dark without supervision. But I knew there were negligent parents who didn't keep an eye on their children like they should. I would never have let Sean and Laura run around the neighborhood on their own at night.

I turned off the light in the living room and took the dustpan and broom to the utility room. Azalea would probably find dust or hair I had overlooked, but I had been as meticulous in my cleaning as I knew how. Then I realized that Haskell and Stewart would have the new corral built and in place by the time Azalea returned on Monday morning. The real inspection would take place once the kittens were either returned to their original home or placed in new forever homes.

Upstairs I got undressed and into my nighttime apparel

of shorts and a T-shirt. Diesel lay stretched out on his side of the bed, his head on the pillow. He opened his eyes, yawned and stretched, and then appeared to go back to sleep. I climbed in with him, turned out the light, and soon drifted off to sleep.

I woke the next morning to the sound of Diesel warbling loudly from the floor beside the bed. Evidently, I didn't respond quickly enough, because I felt a large paw on my arm. After a couple of yawns, I pushed aside the covers and sat up on the side of the bed.

"All right, boy, I'm awake." I looked in the cat's face. "What's so urgent?"

He turned and padded to the door.

"Give me a minute," I said. "Bathroom first, then I'll follow you."

Less than two minutes later I trod down the stairs behind him. He headed across the kitchen and into the utility room. He sat beside his litter box and meowed loudly.

"Sorry, I guess I forgot to clean it out yesterday."

Diesel meowed again.

"I'm on it." I quickly took care of the litter box, and after that I rinsed out and refilled his water bowl. Then came the dry food and half a can of wet food.

I left him happily munching his breakfast and wandered into the kitchen for coffee. I realized as I glanced at the window over the sink that it was still dark outside. A quick check of the clock on the wall informed me that it was about three minutes shy of five thirty.

After hitting the button to start the coffeemaker—it was set for six thirty every morning—I grabbed a jacket off the rack in the hall and opened the front door. I intended to retrieve the newspaper, and I had the door halfway open before I remembered that today was Saturday. There would be no paper.

About to close the door, I spied a folded piece of paper stuck to it with a tack. I removed the tack and unfolded the note. I immediately recognized the childish scrawl.

They're gone! I thought you'd take care of them! What did you do with them? Where are they?

EIGHT

||||||||||||||||||||||||||||||||||

I stared at the note for several seconds, until I became aware of the chill air against my bare legs. Hastily I moved back and shut the door. I put the jacket back on the rack and walked into the kitchen, head down, contemplating the note.

Poor kid was my first thought, but then I realized I felt a little irritated. Why would the child assume that I had already given up the kittens? Hadn't it occurred to the youngster that I had simply moved the kittens?

Perhaps the child was used to being let down by adults, I thought a moment later. After all, an adult had apparently threatened to drown the kittens.

I frowned. Hadn't I been making a groundless assumption that the person the child referred to in the original note was an adult? It might be simply an older brother, a teenager who enjoyed tormenting his younger sibling. Either way, the child had no reason to trust adults, other than the fact that I was known in the neighborhood to be an animal lover.

I laid the note on the table and went to the counter to pour my coffee. Cream and sugar added to the cup, I settled in my usual place and sipped my coffee. The hot liquid felt good going down, and the slight chill I'd felt earlier dissipated.

Contemplating the note again, I thought about the best way to allay the child's fears about the kittens. The easiest way would be to respond to the note, pin it to my front door, and leave it. And if I happened to keep an eye out for the child in hopes of finally catching sight of him or her, that was all to the good.

Diesel sauntered up to me, laid a paw on my thigh, and trilled. I rubbed his head for a bit. Finally content, he stretched out by my chair, most of him under the table. Taking care not to disturb the cat, I got up to find a pen. I rummaged in the catchall drawer and found one.

Back at the table, I thought briefly about my response to the note.

The kittens are fine. I moved them to a different room overnight. They will soon be back in the same spot. I promise you I will keep them safe.

Surely that ought to do it, I thought. I drank more coffee, thought about breakfast, and drained my cup. I decided to put the note back on the front door in case the child sneaked out early to come look again.

What had I done with the tack? I couldn't remember. I patted the pockets of my shorts. Ah, there it was.

Note safely tacked to the front door, I came back to the kitchen and tried to decide whether I was hungry enough yet to start preparing breakfast for myself. While I pondered

this weighty matter, I heard footsteps, both human and ca-
nine, on the stairs. Moments later, I heard the front door
open, and Stewart—he was usually the one—took Dante
out for his morning walk.

Stewart and Dante returned soon and, as I anticipated,
came into the kitchen instead of heading back upstairs.
Dante pranced around Diesel, tapping the floor with one
dainty paw to entice his friend to play. Diesel ignored
him, but Dante persisted despite the lack of response.

"Good morning." Stewart peered at the paper lying on
the table in front of me. "What's that all about? Another
message from the kid?"

"Yes, with a response from me. Poor child sounds upset, but hopefully this will reassure him or her." I started
to get up.

"No, I'll take it back." Stewart disappeared into the hall
but returned quickly. "All done. Are you going to lie in wait
for this kid?"

"Off and on," I said. "I don't intend to spend the entire
day watching the front door. The child might not come
back until tonight, and I would have wasted an entire day
sitting there."

"True." Stewart poured coffee into his favorite mug.
He took a chair to my left. "Haskell and I can keep an eye
out for someone lurking in the bushes while we work on
the cage."

I chuckled. "Speaking of lurking in the bushes—last
night after I said good-bye to Helen Louise, I was about
to walk back into the garage when I thought I saw something moving out of the corner of my eye."

"Near the front door?"

"I wasn't sure," I said. "I stopped and looked, but everything was still. I figured I had imagined it and came on inside. But now I'm thinking that what I saw was the child sneaking away after putting that note on the door."

"Possibly," Stewart said. "You didn't see anything on the door at the time?"

"Perhaps if I'd really been looking at the door, I might have," I said, "but I wasn't. Sooner or later I will find out who this child is."

"I'm sure you will." Stewart had a sip of coffee. "Haskell should be down soon, and we'll get started on the cage."

"I really appreciate this," I said. "I'll cook breakfast for you."

"That's kind of you, but I'm going to be having a cold breakfast." Stewart grimaced. "My cholesterol is up, and I need to lay off the bacon and sausage for a while. So it's a bowl of granola, yogurt, and fruit for me this morning."

"What about Haskell? Is he having a cold breakfast, too?"

"Yes, he's going to have the same, although I suspect he may want toast as well." He smiled fondly. "He does like his buttered toast and jelly."

"Don't we all," I replied. *Not to mention buttered biscuits, cheese grits, scrambled eggs, bacon* and *sausage. Maybe country ham, too.* I shook my head, thinking guiltily of my own cholesterol levels, always a little above the norm.

"What's wrong?" Stewart asked.

"Food cravings." I laughed. "The minute anyone starts talking about healthy food, I immediately think of all the things for breakfast that you shouldn't eat every day. Which I do."

"There's plenty of granola, yogurt, and fruit," Stewart said, his tone bland. "Feel free to help yourself."

"Thanks. I might just do that." I pushed back from the table. "Before I eat anything, I'm going back upstairs to feed the kittens and clean their litter boxes. Then I'll have a shower. Diesel, do you want to come with me?"

The cat, who had evidently ignored the poodle long enough that Dante had finally given up, meowed. I gathered the cans of food and the bag of dry crunchies and placed them on a tray I dug out from one of the cabinets.

"See you in a bit," I said to Stewart, who nodded.

Diesel raced up the stairs ahead of me. He seemed to know our destination. When I reached the second floor, I saw him disappear into Laura's old bedroom.

I made sure to shut the bedroom door to limit the possibilities if any of the kittens escaped from the bathroom. Diesel stood ready in front of the bathroom door, from under which I could see small paws protruding. Diesel growled and batted at the paws, and they were quickly withdrawn.

Balancing the tray on one hand, I opened the door enough for Diesel to slip in. After a few seconds I slipped into the bathroom, too. As I had guessed, the kittens had swarmed over Diesel. My boy had been smart enough to lure them about three feet away from the door.

I fed the kittens and gave them fresh water before I attended to the litter boxes. When I finished, I spent a few minutes playing with them, holding and stroking each one in turn. Ramses wiggled the entire time I held him, impatient to get down and join in the fray with his siblings. The others seemed to enjoy the attention I gave them.

I left Diesel in the bathroom with the kittens, promising to return after my shower. He appeared to be happy staying with the active quintet.

Twenty minutes later I returned—showered, shaved, and dressed in more appropriate daytime attire. I called to Diesel before I opened the door, and he warbled in response. I opened the door wide enough for him to ease out, and he did so. I managed to close the door before any of the inmates escaped.

The sun had begun to rise, I noticed as Diesel and I walked into the kitchen. I heard sounds of activity coming from the direction of the living room but decided that I wanted my breakfast before I went to see how the cage was coming along.

I contemplated yogurt, granola, and fruit, but not for long. I suppressed the little voice that was urging me to follow Stewart's example. I prepared cheese grits, a couple of slices of buttered wheat toast, and two sausage patties. Diesel sniffed appreciatively, but he would be disappointed. No sausage for him. They were too highly seasoned.

By the time I finished eating and drinking another cup of coffee, I could see sunlight streaming through the kitchen window. The weather forecast had promised a clear, chilly day. That was good, because if everything went as planned, Sean and Frank, my son-in-law, would arrive at nine to start installing Christmas lights on the front of the house. Frank, with his experience in stagecraft and set design, had drawn up a tasteful plan for illumination. Had it not been for his enthusiasm and Sean's willingness to assist, I probably wouldn't have bothered. Time enough for that when baby Charlie and Rosie were old enough to enjoy the holiday.

After clearing up the small mess I had made cooking and eating breakfast, I headed through the hall to the living room, accompanied by Diesel. We stopped in the doorway to survey the progress.

My volunteer carpenters had put down a drop cloth to protect the hardwood floor. From what I could see, Haskell and Stewart had completed one segment of the frame and were now working on the second one.

"You're making good progress," I said.

Haskell glanced up. "It's not a complicated design, but it should be sturdy enough to do what you want."

Diesel padded over to inspect the completed segment, for the moment propped against the wall. He sniffed it, then prodded it with a paw. He looked my way and chirped, as if to tell me he approved of the work. Haskell and Stewart continued to work, oblivious to the cat's actions.

"Is there anything I can get you?" I asked. "Water? Coffee? Juice?"

"No, thanks," Stewart said. "Soon as we finish this bit we're going to take a break and have breakfast."

"Okay. I'll be around, though, if you need me," I said. "Come on, Diesel. We'll be in the den for a while."

I retrieved my laptop, and the cat and I got comfortable on the couch. While I caught up on e-mail, Diesel snoozed beside me. I had nearly finished with e-mail when my cell phone rang. I set the laptop aside because the caller was Melba. I knew the conversation could last awhile.

"Good morning," I said.

"Morning, Charlie," Melba replied, sounding perky.

After an exchange of the usual pleasantries, Melba said, "I got to thinking about Billy Albritton."

"What about him?" I asked, puzzled.

"About why he kind of brushed me off," Melba said. "I got to thinking about it last night, and it seemed to me he didn't mind talking to me—he's always been flirty, you know—until I brought up Geraldine Albritton."

"Obviously you think that means he knows something about her and didn't want to let on that he did," I said. "Right?"

"Right. He's slick, all right, else I would have caught it then, but at the time I believed him when he said he was in a hurry." Melba laughed. "I'm not going to let him get away with it, though."

I tried not to chuckle. "What are you going to do? Show up at his house and bang on the door until he lets you in?"

"If I thought that was what it would take to get a real answer out of him, I'd do it." Melba's tone held a touch of frost. "You know I would."

"Yes, you sure would," I replied.

"I'm going by his appliance store first thing Monday morning," she said. "I don't think he's there on Saturday. I'll insist that I have to talk to him, and only him, about replacing my washer and dryer. If he thinks he's going to get some money out of me, he'll be more willing to talk."

"Fond of a dollar, is he?" I didn't know the councilman myself.

Melba's snort resounded in my ear. "You better bet he is. Like all the Albrittons. Most of them started out poor, and some of them still are. The ones like Billy who've managed to make a few bucks hang on to them as hard as they can."

"I have no doubt you'll wear him down," I said.

"I'll let you know," she replied. "In the meantime, you mind if I come over and see those babies you're fostering?"

"Sure, come on," I said. "Are you thinking about adopting one?"

"I might," Melba said. "There'll never be another Diesel, but it might be nice to have a cat of my own around the house."

"I think you'd love having a cat."

Diesel meowed loudly.

"Did you hear that?" I asked.

Melba chuckled. "I did. Tell that sweet boy I'll be seeing him in about twenty minutes. That okay?"

"Sure, see you soon." I ended the call. "Your friend Melba's coming over to see you and the kittens."

Diesel meowed again. He knew Melba's name.

"Come on, let's go to the kitchen and make some fresh coffee for Melba." I rose from the couch. Diesel oozed off onto the floor, rolled onto his back, and stretched. I laughed and headed out the door.

I took a detour to the living room to let Stewart and Haskell know that company was arriving soon. They acknowledged my announcement but didn't look up from their work. The second frame was complete, and they were now stapling the wire mesh into place.

Diesel met me in the kitchen. While I rinsed the coffeepot and prepared the maker for another round, he disappeared into the utility room. I heard crunching noises when I turned off the water.

By the time the doorbell rang to announce Melba's arrival, the coffee was ready. Diesel scampered ahead of me to the door to greet the visitor.

When I opened the door, Melba looked at me with a frown. "I just saw the weirdest thing. I thought I saw a child's head sticking up out of the shrubbery."

NINE

I stepped past Melba to get a clear view of the front of the house. "Which side?"

Melba pointed to my left. I stepped onto the lawn and began searching the shrubbery. I continued around the side of the house and into the backyard, but with no results. The child had disappeared.

Melba and Diesel waited for me at the door. "Did you see him?" she asked.

I shook my head, frustrated. "No, not a sign. Come on in." I stopped to look at the door, having remembered the note I had left there. I was not surprised to see that it was gone, tack and all.

I motioned for Melba to precede me. Once we were all inside I shut the door and led the way into the kitchen. "I made us fresh coffee. Let's have some, and you can tell me exactly what you saw."

"All right." Melba chose a chair while I poured coffee

for us. Diesel settled on the floor by her chair. I knew she liked cream and sugar in her coffee, and I set those on the table.

While she stirred her coffee, she said, "It was when I was pulling in to the driveway. I happened to glance over toward the front of the house, and I thought I saw something moving in the shrubs. I stopped the car a moment, and then this head popped up. I blinked, and then it was gone. The kid must have realized I was in the driveway and ducked down."

"Anything descriptive you can tell me about the head you saw?" I asked.

"Darkish hair on the short side," Melba said. "Looked like a girl's cut to me, but I can't be sure." She sipped at her coffee. "This is good. Are you going to check for footprints?"

I laughed. "I'm not Sherlock Holmes. What would I do with footprints?"

Melba shrugged. "That's what they used to do in old mystery movies. You could make a plaster cast."

"If I had plaster on hand, I could," I said. "But I'm not in the habit of keeping it in stock."

"It was just a suggestion. You don't have to sound so snarky." Melba scowled at me. "You're the one who goes around solving mysteries, not me."

"I'm sorry," I said, penitent. "I didn't mean to make fun of you. It simply struck me as funny. Can you really see me getting down in the dirt in the flower bed, pouring plaster and whatever else you do to get a cast?"

Melba laughed. "Well, no, I reckon not. I bet your knees aren't any happier than mine doing that kind of thing."

"No, they're not." I grimaced at the thought. "Okay, dark-haired child, probably a girl. Did you get any impression of height or age?"

Melba considered my question while she drank her coffee. She shook her head. "No, not strong enough to be helpful. I didn't see enough of her to judge. I couldn't tell whether she was crouching at the window or standing upright."

"How about the size of the head?" I was grasping for anything that could help identify the child.

"Wasn't real big, so I'd say a younger kid maybe."

"Thanks," I said. "I figure ten years old at the most." I told her about the note I had put on the door for the child. "She had obviously already taken it down, but if she was looking in the window of the living room, she might not have read the note yet."

"Does it matter?" Melba said.

"No, I don't suppose it does. She'll read it at some point."

"Have you thought of rigging up a camera there by the living room windows? You could probably get video of the kid and be able to identify her from that," Melba said.

"I hadn't really considered it," I replied, "though I suppose I should think about it. I wouldn't have a clue how to do it myself."

"I bet you Frank would know how. Sean might, too. They both know a lot about computers and wiring and things like that."

"True." I drained my coffee and set the cup aside. "They'll both be here at ten to put up Christmas lights on the front of the house."

Melba got up to refill her cup. "You haven't done that

before. Why'd you decide to do it this year?" She returned to her chair. "Surely not because most of your neighbors do it every year."

"Certainly not for that reason." I had never gone in for competitions with neighbors over holiday decorations. "The family suggested it because we used to do it in Houston when Laura and Sean were young. I guess now that they both have children of their own, they want to revive the tradition."

We finished our coffee, and Diesel and I took Melba up to see the kittens. After half an hour with them, Melba looked like she was ready to adopt all of them. She seemed particularly taken with Ramses. He easily claimed first place in the personality stakes among the five, but the adorability factor stood consistently high. By the time we left the kittens, I think Melba had already begun planning for adoption.

"Until we know where they came from," I reminded her, "I can't give them away. I don't imagine the child will be able to keep any of them, frankly, given the situation, but things could change."

"I know," Melba said, "but I'm an optimist." She gave me a quick hug, and Diesel a rub on the head, at the front door. We watched until she was in her car, and then I stepped back inside and shut the door.

I checked my watch. About three-quarters of an hour before Sean and Frank were due to arrive. Diesel and I spent a few minutes in the living room, watching Haskell and Stewart. They had the mesh on both segments now, and Haskell had begun work on the door. They were making such rapid progress, I knew it wouldn't be long before we could bring the kittens back downstairs.

Diesel stayed with them to supervise, and I went upstairs to retrieve my book. I had been in a historical-mystery mood lately, and I was revisiting an old friend, Ellis Peters's medieval monk, Brother Cadfael. I had already reread the first five in the series and was now midway through the sixth, and perhaps my favorite, *The Virgin in the Ice*.

Back in the den, I settled down with the book. When Sean and Frank arrived, I was deeply immersed in twelfth-century England. I would have preferred not to have been interrupted because I was near the end, so it was with considerable reluctance that I put down the book to go over the design plan one more time with Sean and Frank.

"Everything is in the garage," I told them after I had once more assured Frank I liked his design. "Are you sure you don't need me?"

"We can handle it, Dad." Sean looked tired, but I knew better than to comment on that. Other than asking how Alex and Rosie were doing this morning, I didn't inquire further.

Frank, after a quick sideways glance at Sean, said, "Laura and little Charlie have gone over there to visit while we're working here. Laura's going to help Alex catch up on laundry and a few things like that."

I nodded. "Sounds like a good plan."

Sean looked away. I gathered from his body language and his silence that he hadn't made any further headway in getting Alex to agree about hiring a nanny. I felt bad for Sean and Alex, and I prayed that this wasn't going to cause significant harm to their relationship. Surely Alex would see sense before much longer; otherwise she was going to end up in the hospital.

"I'll be in the den if you need me." I left them to get on with it and went back to my book.

Frank found me in the den two hours later, sound asleep on the couch. Once I'd finished the book, I had thought about getting the next one in the series. The couch had felt too comfortable, though, and before long I had dozed off.

Frank grinned as I sat up and blinked at him. "Sorry to disturb you, Charlie, but I want you to have a look at everything before Sean and I pack up and go home."

"I didn't mean to nap this long. I'm glad you woke me up. I don't know why I was so sleepy." I yawned and got off the couch.

As we passed by the living room, I stuck my head in to see that, while I napped, Haskell and Stewart had finished. There was no sign of them downstairs, and the kittens were now installed in their new corral. They were sleeping, and Diesel kept watch nearby. He chirped softly when he saw me, then went back to his vigil.

I followed Frank outside, and he led me to the street to get the full view. While we waited, Sean flipped the switch to turn on the lights. The effect wasn't the same, of course, in broad daylight, but I could see that the lights would be beautiful at night. Frank had created a simple forest scene with a few trees topped by stars and the words *Merry Christmas* strung across them. One star was larger than the rest, and I took it to be the North Star. The lights were set along the wall between the second and third floors.

They had also strung lights over the shrubbery, and I imagined that, in the dark of night, they would twinkle like stardust. Overall a simple but attractive effect, nothing overpowering, unlike what some of my neighbors chose to do.

I turned to Frank and smiled. "Perfect."

He looked relieved. "You said you wanted simple, not extravagant."

"That's what you've provided," I said. "Tasteful and lovely. Thank you."

"My pleasure, Charlie," he said. "Now, I'd better pack my tools so I can get Sean back to Alex. He's really worried about her."

"I am, too," I said. "I've talked to her, but until she's willing to accept help, I'm not sure what else anyone can do." We started for the garage, where Sean stood waiting for us.

"Laura was planning to talk to her," Frank said in an undertone as we neared Sean.

"Thanks for helping with this, son," I said. "I really appreciate it."

Sean shrugged. "Glad to do it, Dad. Feels good to be outside doing something physical, to tell you the truth. It's going to seem more like Christmas with the house decorated."

"Yes, it will. This will be the best Christmas we've had in a long time. Having Rosie and Charlie now makes it even more special," I said.

"I hope so," Sean said. "Look, I really need to get back home and check on Alex. Are you ready to go, Frank?"

"Soon as we get my tools back in the trunk," Frank said. "If you'll put the ladder back in the garage, I'll pack the rest away."

Sean nodded, and after thanking them both again, I went back into the house. I decided I might call Laura later this afternoon to find out how things had gone with Alex today.

I heard sounds coming from the direction of the kitchen. I headed there, hoping to find Haskell and Stewart. I wanted to thank them for their hard work and for transporting the kittens downstairs and installing them in their new habitat while I was napping.

Stewart had his head in the fridge, and Haskell occupied his usual place at the table. "There's some chicken salad left from the other night," Stewart said over his shoulder. "Oh, hi, Charlie, just foraging for lunch. Have you eaten yet?"

"No, I haven't," I replied. A glance at the clock informed me that it was almost one. "I was sound asleep in the den until Frank came and woke me up."

"Are they finished with the lights?" Haskell said.

"Yes, and they've done an excellent job," I replied. "I wanted to thank you both again for building that corral for the kittens *and* for toting everything back downstairs again. I'm so embarrassed that I slept through it all."

Haskell grinned. "Stewart looked in on you, but we decided not to wake you. You were sawing some serious logs."

"I'm not surprised," I said. "Look, why don't you two go out to lunch, on me, if you're feeling up to it. It's the least I can do. Anywhere you like."

Stewart shut the fridge. "Sounds good to me. How about the steakhouse?" He looked at Haskell. "I'm in the mood for a big, juicy steak and a baked potato stuffed with butter, sour cream, and cheese. My cholesterol can take an occasional hit."

"Works for me," Haskell said. "Why don't you come with us, Charlie?"

"Thanks, but I think I'll stay here with Diesel and the kittens. Y'all go on and enjoy yourselves." I pulled out my wallet and handed them four twenties.

"If you're sure you won't come," Stewart said, "I guess we'll head out. Be back in a couple hours."

Haskell followed him out the door into the garage, and soon I heard Stewart's car backing out.

I walked back to the living room. Diesel lay stretched out on his side, but he sat up when he heard me enter. The kittens had woken and started to play. They looked secure in their pen. The frames stood about seven feet high. I didn't think even Ramses would try to climb that high to escape.

"Time for lunch," I told Diesel after a glance assured me that the kittens had enough water and dry food to last them awhile. Diesel meowed and started for the door.

I was about to follow him when I heard loud voices outside. I moved over to the window and looked out, trying to locate the source of the noise.

I found it across the street at Gerry Albritton's house. Gerry and a man stood on her walk, only a couple of feet from the sidewalk, yelling and gesturing at each other. I couldn't make out the words, but from the tone I could tell that they were arguing. While I watched, the man whirled and headed for a car parked on the street in front of the next house. Gerry shot him the finger before she turned and stomped her way up the walk.

As he was getting in the car, the man turned in my direction, and I got a clear look at his face. He was familiar, but it took me a minute to place him. He was Billy Albritton, the city councilman—the man who told Melba he didn't know Gerry Albritton.

TEN

Over the weekend I thought about the argument I had witnessed. Billy Albritton had obviously lied to Melba about his knowing my neighbor. Surely he wouldn't engage in a loud argument with a woman he didn't know, particularly an argument that the neighbors could overhear. I thought about the cause for their quarrel. I could come up with any number of lurid reasons for it. One, for example, was that she was the first wife he had never gotten around to divorcing, and now she was threatening to expose him to his current wife and the town council.

I reckoned, however, that if Billy Albritton had been married before, Melba probably knew about it even though he was a good ten years older than either of us and had finished high school when we were still in elementary school. Melba collected information like some people collected stamps or coins. Luckily for the rest of us, she never used her knowledge in a malicious way; otherwise she probably would have been murdered for blackmail years ago.

I decided to wait until Monday, when I would see Melba at work, to tell her what I had observed across the street. For the rest of the weekend, I wanted to spend as little time as possible thinking about anything to do with my new neighbor. Her Christmas party loomed closer—this coming Tuesday, in fact. I dreaded it, but part of me was also curious to see what kind of party she threw. I had a feeling it would be memorable, one way or another.

On Monday morning, however, Melba did not come to work. At first puzzled by her absence, I finally remembered that she had planned to take the day off for her annual "well woman" checkup with her doctor. Diesel had come with me to work this morning, and I enjoyed having him with me again. I worked steadily until lunchtime, enjoying the end-of-semester quiet with no one else in the office. The graduate students would be back soon enough.

Diesel and I drove home for lunch, and as we approached our block, I saw that three large vans were parked in front of Gerry Albritton's house. Each van sported the logo of a local landscaping company, and I could see several men and women working in Gerry's front yard. This was an odd time of year to have landscaping work done, I thought. I realized, however, as I turned into my driveway, that the workers weren't engaged in the usual type of gardening work. Instead, they were busily installing Christmas decorations.

Given the amount of people at work in the yard, I suspected that the result would turn out to be a lavish display. They were still hard at it when I returned to work, without Diesel, after lunch. By the time I came home, later than usual from having run a couple of errands after work, they were gone. After I parked the car in the garage, I walked back outside and down the driveway to get a closer look at the landscapers' handiwork.

My first reaction was that I was glad I wouldn't be paying Gerry's electric bill. The second was that I wished I had blackout curtains on my bedroom windows since my bedroom faced the street. The glare from this display would be intolerable when I tried to go to sleep.

The walk to the front door bisected the yard evenly. The right section contained a mixture of inflatable elves, a couple of reindeer, and a toy shop strung about with lights. The left featured a stable with the Three Wise Men, the manger, a cradle, and figures kneeling beside it. I supposed they thought camels and a stray donkey or two would have made the scene too crowded. I wondered if the baby in the cradle was an inflatable, since the other figures all were. The landscapers had festooned the front of the house with enough lights to decorate half the houses on the block in a more tasteful fashion. If the effect Gerry was going for was gaudy and over-the-top, she had achieved it, and then some.

Shaking my head at the excess, I turned and walked back up the driveway and into the house. I awaited the coming of nightfall with a mixture of dread and curiosity, because only with the darkness would the true extent of the awfulness be apparent. Traffic would be terrible because the gawkers would come. I knew word of the display would spread rapidly, and half the town would drive down our street to see it. If Gerry had wanted to annoy her neighbors to distraction, she was going to succeed.

After greeting Azalea, I moved on to the living room

to see how Diesel and the kittens were doing. I found them all napping, no doubt reserving their energy for play later on. Cats were crepuscular creatures, I knew, most active at dawn and dusk. They weren't nocturnal, as many often thought they were. Diesel woke, sat up, and yawned. I reached down to rub his head, and he regarded me sleepily.

He followed me back into the kitchen, where we both sniffed appreciatively at the results of Azalea's labors at the stove and the oven.

"Smells great," I said. "What's for dinner?"

"Baked chicken, mashed potatoes, English peas with carrots, and caramel cake for dessert," Azalea replied. "I'll leave everything on the stove. Chicken should be ready in twenty minutes."

I thanked her, and she nodded.

"Have you seen what they've been putting up across the street at Gerry Albritton's house?" I asked.

"Haven't had the time," she responded. "What have they done?"

I gave her a description, and when I had finished, she shook her head. "Lord have mercy. I'm thankful I don't have to look at it. Why some people got to show off like that I just don't understand."

"I know what you mean," I said. "All this excess is beyond me. I'm not sure what point people are trying to make when they go so far overboard."

"I guess they reckon it's pretty," Azalea said, though her expression revealed her doubts about this.

"The good thing is, she waited until only a few days before Christmas to have it all put up," I said. "Hopefully it will all be coming down the day after."

Azalea nodded and turned back to the stove. I headed upstairs, Diesel beside me, to change out of my work clothes. At home, unless I was entertaining company, I preferred much more casual attire, usually sweatpants and a loose T-shirt. I wouldn't win any points for sartorial splendor, but I was comfortable.

After my delicious dinner I spent a quiet evening in the den. Diesel went back and forth between the den and the living room while I read. I had resisted the urge to look out the window at the horror across the street until I was ready to go to bed. I took one long look before I shut the blinds and pulled the curtains. They dimmed the glare considerably, but my bedroom was nowhere near as dark as I preferred when I slept.

The double-glazed windows helped with the noise from traffic on the street. During my nightly phone call with Helen Louise, we briefly discussed the party tomorrow night. I didn't have to tell her about the installation across the street. She saw it for herself when she drove home from the bistro after work.

Overwhelming was her word. "I really like what Frank and Sean did for your house, but I have to say I don't think most people will even notice it. They'll be too awestruck by what's across the street from you."

"Gerry's welcome to the attention, if that's what she wants," I said.

"I imagine that's exactly what she does want." Helen Louise chuckled. "Not everyone on your block has decorated outside, but those who have are more in line with your style. Her house will definitely stand out."

We chatted a few minutes more before we ended the call. I settled down to sleep. I tried to keep my mind clear of anything to do with Gerry Albritton and her decorations and was eventually able to drift off.

The next morning, I awoke around seven, half an hour later than usual, feeling refreshed. I had slept soundly, and whatever my dreams, I didn't recall them. The coffee was ready when I went downstairs. Diesel went straight to the living room. I prepared my cup and had a few sips before going to feed the kittens and clean their litter boxes.

With all that done, I went to fetch the newspaper. The sun was on its way up. I grabbed the paper and started to turn to go back into the house. Then I looked across the street at Gerry Albritton's house, not quite sure that I was seeing clearly.

I blinked and took several steps down the walk to get a closer look. No, I wasn't imagining things, I decided. During the night, vandals had wrecked Gerry's decorations.

ELEVEN

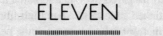

After the first shock of the mess in Gerry Albritton's yard began to wear off, I began to see that the decorations weren't wrecked so much as they were dismantled. The figures lay deflated on the dormant grass, and the lights hung drunkenly from a few spots on the façade.

No wonder I hadn't heard anything, I mused. Nothing was smashed or destroyed, as far as I could tell. But why not? This was not the work of typical vandals.

Maybe the person behind this wanted to delay the party or cause Gerry to cancel it. I suspected that neither of these would happen, that the party would go ahead as planned tonight.

I wondered whether I should go over and knock on the door to inform Gerry of what had happened. I couldn't see any signs that she or any other occupants of the house had stirred. The time couldn't be more than about seven fifteen or seven twenty. I stood, indecisive, for about thirty seconds, and then it occurred to me that I really wasn't dressed to go knocking on a woman's door at this hour. Especially not the door of Gerry Albritton. She might well misinterpret my attire—bathrobe over the shorts and shirt I slept in—as something I did not in the least intend.

No, better to call. Safer to converse with Gerry from a distance. I turned and walked back into the house. I had barely shut the front door, however, when I heard a scream of what sounded like outrage from the direction of Gerry's house. I moved into the living room to look out the front window. Sure enough, Gerry stood in the middle of her yard, surveying the damage.

I wouldn't mind playing the good neighbor and going out to talk to her, but I wasn't going to do it without being properly dressed. I hurried upstairs to change. Diesel seemed happy to be keeping an eye on the kittens, so I didn't have to worry about him.

Three or four minutes later I hurried down the walk and across the street. Gerry had a cell phone clamped to her ear and was speaking rapidly into it. I could see that a couple of neighbors must have heard the commotion and were in their yards, discreetly trying to see what was going on.

". . . get here within the hour and fix this mess." Gerry listened briefly. "I'll give you a bonus if you have everything set up again by noon." She listened again, then said "Fine" and ended the call.

Gerry wore a short, bright yellow, silken-looking robe that clung to her figure. She eyed me as if I were the enemy.

"Morning," I said. "So sorry about all this. Do you

have any idea who's responsible?" My breath misted in the chill air.

"I can think of several candidates." She scowled. "Did you hear or see anything last night?"

"No, not a thing. I was sound asleep by eleven, I think, and didn't get up until about half an hour ago."

Gerry shook her head. "I guess I ought to be grateful they didn't actually destroy anything. All they did was let the air out of the inflatables and pull the lights down. It could have been much worse."

I nodded. "Yes, but it's a bit strange, don't you think? Vandals usually are much more destructive."

"Who knows?" she replied. "Maybe they got scared off before they could do any worse damage."

"Possibly." I suspected, though, that she had a good idea why the damage wasn't more severe.

"Maybe it was an extreme kind of prank," I said.

"Maybe. It's not funny, to me anyway," Gerry said. "It will soon be fixed, and I can concentrate on the party."

"That's good," I said. "I gather that was the landscaping company you were talking to when I walked up."

"Yes, they're going to hustle and get it done by noon, if they know what's good for them," she said. "Look, why don't you come in for some coffee? I haven't even had my first cup yet."

I started to reply that I couldn't, that I had coffee waiting for me at home, but she had already turned away to go back inside—simply assuming that I wouldn't refuse the invitation, I reckoned. I wasn't thrilled to be going into her house this early, especially with neighbors watching, but I felt bad for her. She obviously wanted company. I followed her into the house, already considering how long it would be before everyone in the neighborhood thought we were having an affair.

Gerry walked down the hall to the back of the house and into her kitchen. I stopped in the doorway and gawked at the room. Everything was black, white, red, and chrome. The appliances were new, all maraschino-cherry red. The new floor sported a dizzying, swirling, asymmetrical pattern of black and white porcelain squares, and I found myself almost mesmerized by it. The kitchen table and chairs had a fifties-diner retro style, with the chair seats covered in fabric to match the appliances. A large island occupied a great deal of space, but the kitchen was big enough that it didn't seem crowded by the island.

Gerry stood in front of a coffeemaker far more complicated-looking and expensive than mine. The rich scent of the coffee tantalized me, and I couldn't wait to try it. Gerry poured a mug for me and then one for herself. "Cream, sugar, and sweeteners are on the table." She opened a nearby drawer and withdrew a spoon.

"Thanks." I accepted the spoon and followed her to the table.

She indicated the chair I should take, and once seated I helped myself to cream and sugar. She watched me intently as I took my first sip.

The coffee had much more of a bite to it than my usual brew, spicy and strong, though it wasn't unpleasant. The cream softened it enough to make it palatable to me.

I could see she was waiting for my comment, and I obliged her. "Delicious."

Gerry smiled. "Glad you like it. I like my coffee the way I like my men. Hot and strong." She drank more coffee.

My face reddened. I felt it. Even I wasn't dense enough to misunderstand her intent. I set my mug on the table and drew a breath while I tried to figure out how I was going to respond.

All at once it struck me as funny, and I started laughing. Gerry appeared startled, but after a moment she grinned and laughed along with me. When the laughter ceased, I said, "I beg your pardon."

Gerry held up a hand to forestall what I planned to say next. "No need to apologize. That was truly cornball." She snorted. "Hot and strong. What was I thinking?"

"Well, I *am* flattered," I replied, "but I'm happily involved in a relationship. I would never do anything to harm it."

"So I've heard," Gerry said. "Who is it? Do I know her?"

"I think you do," I replied. "Helen Louise Brady. She owns the French bistro on the square."

Gerry nodded. "I've been in there several times. Great food. Looks like she does a lot of business. Tell me, does she own the building?"

I had a sip of coffee before I answered. Why did she want to know? I wondered. Standard operating procedure for a Realtor, maybe. "Yes, she does." I could have told her that Helen Louise owned several of the buildings around the square. Her father had been a shrewd investor, buying up properties in high-demand areas, and he had left everything to Helen Louise, his only child.

"Good for her," Gerry said. I expected more, but she lapsed into silence, staring at some point on the wall beyond my head.

I decided to venture a question. "How long have you

been in real estate? I found your flyer, of course, and I've seen your sign up at several houses around here."

"A few years," she replied. "I don't suppose you're interested in selling your house, are you?"

"No. Not at all," I replied with a little more heat than I intended.

Gerry didn't seem to notice. "If you change your mind, let me know. What about your girlfriend? Will she be selling hers anytime soon?" She favored me with a slightly arch look.

"We're not planning to set up house together in the near future," I replied, taken aback by what I considered an intrusive question.

"Interesting," she said, eyeing me over the rim of her mug as she sipped her coffee. Before I could frame a response to that ambiguous comment, she continued. "I hope you're looking forward to tonight. I'm expecting a lot of people. I'm sure you'll know most of them."

"Probably," I said. "Everyone will be curious to see what you've done with this house."

Gerry's lip curled. "No doubt. That ought to bring them here, if nothing else does." She laughed. "They're in for a surprise or two."

Her tone had an edge to it, I thought, almost a combative one. What was she planning to do tonight?

"That should be interesting," I replied, hoping that she would elaborate without my asking a more pointed question.

She didn't. Instead, she laughed again. "We'll see." She glanced at her phone when it vibrated on the table. She picked it up. "Excuse me, a message I have to respond to."

I watched her as, head down over the phone, she tapped

on it with both thumbs the way I saw young people do. I had never mastered the trick, instead using one finger most of the time when I texted.

I drained my mug and set it on the table. Time for me to go home, I decided. When Gerry put her phone aside after a couple more rounds of texting, I said as much and stood to leave. To my relief she didn't insist that I stay for more coffee. She seemed more than happy for me to go.

Gerry led me to the front door. "See you tonight," she said.

I smiled and nodded. "Looking forward to it." She shut the door behind me, and I headed down the walk and across the street. As I neared my front door, I realized that I actually *was* looking forward to the party tonight. Gerry had piqued my curiosity over whatever surprises she planned to spring. If nothing else, I thought, the party certainly wouldn't be dull.

TWELVE

I was in the kitchen when Helen Louise arrived at ten minutes to seven. Diesel must have heard the key turn in the lock, because he darted out of the room. He escorted her into the kitchen, trilling and chirping—no doubt telling her how gorgeous she looked in her new dress.

I caught my breath looking at her. Her dress, she had told me during a phone conversation, was silk, but she hadn't shared the color. A brilliant emerald green, the dress had simple but elegant lines and reached to mid-calf. The fit was ideal for her statuesque figure, and the color complemented her lustrous black hair and dark eyes beautifully. Low-heeled black pumps, a black clutch purse, and a black jade-and-gold necklace completed the ensemble.

She stopped a couple of feet in front of me, awaiting my reaction. "Stunning," I said. "Every other woman at the party will be ready to claw your eyes out for making them pale in comparison."

Helen Louise laughed. "Thank you. That is exactly the effect I was going for." She moved closer to kiss me. Then she drew back and eyed me critically. "You look pretty stunning yourself. That black suit is my favorite, and how clever of you to wear a tie that complements my dress."

Startled, I glanced down at my tie. I didn't remember which one I had chosen. Then I laughed. The swirling pattern of emerald green and black did complement her dress. "We'll just have to let everyone think we coordinated our outfits."

Stewart walked into the kitchen along with Haskell. "Turn around and let me see the dress," Stewart said.

Helen Louise turned to face the two men, and Stewart whistled appreciatively. "Absolute knockout," he said. Haskell smiled broadly and nodded in agreement.

"You two look pretty spiffy yourselves," Helen Louise said. "Don't you agree, Charlie?"

Stewart and Haskell wore black suits similar to mine, with white shirts and brightly colored ties. I had to admit that, with their muscular frames and broad chests and shoulders, they looked more impressive in their well-fitted suits than I did in mine.

I laughed. "I do, although if the three of us stand around together at the party, the other guests are liable to think we're undertakers."

Haskell laughed, but Stewart shook a finger at me. "Don't even bring up any subject related to death," Stewart said. "No need to put those vibes into the ether."

"I didn't realize you were superstitious," Helen Louise said. "You can't taint the atmosphere by simply mentioning a subject."

"I'm not, particularly," Stewart said. "Superstitious,

that is. I simply don't want the notion planted in my brain. I'll have to flirt outrageously with all the attractive men and good-looking women at the party now to dislodge it."

Haskell snorted. "As if you needed an excuse."

Stewart ignored that sally. "Shall we saunter over? It's two minutes to seven."

"Do you want us to be the first ones there?" Helen Louise asked. "Isn't that a bit uncouth?" Her lips twitched.

"What if it is?" Stewart said. "I want to be able to watch as everyone else arrives."

"Whatever for?" I asked.

Haskell rolled his eyes. "So he can act like he's a reporter on the red carpet and comment on what they all look like in their party clothes."

Helen Louise linked her arm with Stewart's. "You can be Alice Roosevelt, and I'll be your best girlfriend."

Haskell looked puzzled, and I explained the reference. Alice Roosevelt was once supposed to have said that if you knew anything bad about someone, you should come sit next to her and share the dirt. He rolled his eyes again when I finished my explanation.

After a brief check on the kittens, we stopped in the hallway for Helen Louise to retrieve her coat. Haskell opened the door, and out we went. I had looked out the living room window earlier to see whether Gerry's decorations were back in place. They were. Alight, they looked as obnoxious as I anticipated. I wouldn't get the full effect, I was sure, until I was standing right in front of them.

Two cars occupied space in front of Gerry's house. Some neighbors would no doubt walk to the party. Two children, girls around nine or ten, stood on the sidewalk gawking. They squealed in excitement and pointed at various parts of the display as we walked past them and up the walk.

Gerry's assistant, Jincy—whose last name I had forgotten already—opened the door to us. She recognized me and nodded, and I quickly introduced the others. She stood aside and waved us in. "Down the hall and on the right at the back is the den," she said to Helen Louise. "You can leave your coat there."

Helen Louise thanked her, and I walked with her to deposit the coat on one of the chairs we found in the room. At least, I thought it was a chair. It looked horribly uncomfortable to me, an object shaped like the number five, but without the bar at the top.

Helen Louise and I looked at each other and shrugged. We walked back down the hall to rejoin Stewart and Haskell. The former, I noted, had placed himself beside the door to the living room. He faced the front door, so evidently Haskell hadn't been completely joking when he mentioned the red-carpet routine.

Haskell stood with Jincy near the front door, engaged in conversation with her. Helen Louise and I approached Stewart.

"Any arrivals while we were putting away my coat?" Helen Louise asked.

Stewart shook his head. "Shouldn't be long now, though."

There was still no sign of our hostess. I wondered about that, and then it dawned on me that she was probably either in the kitchen dealing with the catering staff or upstairs waiting until more people arrived. Then she would sweep down the stairs the way Loretta Young used to in her television show, smile benignly upon her suitably appreciative guests, and deign to converse with us.

Good grief. I'm starting to sound like Stewart. I had to suppress a chuckle at the thought. Later on, I would have to share that with him.

Helen Louise, Stewart, and I chatted while we waited for our hostess to put in an appearance and for more guests to arrive. Waiters came by with champagne and indicated that food awaited us in both the living and dining rooms. We each accepted a glass of champagne. I didn't have a refined enough palate to discern one champagne from another. After a sip—it went down smoothly—I looked to Helen Louise, who did have a refined palate.

"Bollinger," she said appreciatively. "Evidently our hostess has expensive tastes, or else she's out to impress."

"Provided," Stewart said with a grin, "that anyone else besides you tonight can tell Bollinger from the bargain bubbly most people serve at parties like this."

Helen Louise grinned and gestured toward the door. "Here comes someone who can tell."

Surprised, I glanced at the door to see Milton and Tammy Harville pause to talk to Jincy while Haskell moved to join us.

"Milton?" I said. "Or Tammy?"

"Milton," Helen Louise responded. "He's quite knowledgeable. We often talk about wines when he comes by the bistro. When Tammy isn't with him, of course." She sipped her champagne. "When they're together Milton hardly says a word, particularly not to me or any of my female staff."

"I didn't realize it was as bad as that," I said.

"That's why he tries to keep her out of the drugstore," Stewart said. "The woman is obsessed. He can hardly do

94

his job when she's there because she dogs him like you wouldn't believe." He shook his head. "I've seen it a few times, and it ain't pretty."

I looked at Tammy, glowering at Jincy while Milton conversed with her. A peroxide blonde, Tammy had a hard look about her. She seemed permanently disgruntled whenever I had the misfortune to run into her. Milton served as the target for all her discontent. He couldn't seem to measure up to what she required, no matter how he tried. She ran him down all the time, even right in front of him. I wondered why he didn't seek a divorce on the grounds of mental cruelty.

We continued to watch the trio near the door. From what I could tell, Milton was making an effort to end the conversation with Jincy. He kept darting sideways glances at his wife. Tammy continued to glower. Finally, she seemed to have reached her boiling point. She grabbed Milton's arm and towed him away from the door, leaving Jincy open-mouthed and Milton beet red.

Tammy pulled her husband into the living room without any acknowledgment of the four of us by the door. Milton glanced at us, his expression a sad mixture of apology and shame.

Stewart sighed. "Did you see what Tammy was wearing? I swear, I don't think I've ever seen a woman with a knack for always picking out the most unflattering outfit she can find."

I hadn't paid any particular attention to what Tammy was wearing myself. I had been too busy watching her face. Helen Louise had noted the outfit, however. "Can't argue with you, Stewart," she said. "Her skin looks like leather from all those hours in the tanning bed. Wearing gray with blonde hair and a complexion like that makes her look so much older than she really is."

I had to agree, now that I took a more critical look at Tammy, that the combination of gray dress, bleached hair, and tanned skin made her look way older than Milton.

"Enough of that. I don't know about y'all," Helen Louise said, "but I'm ready to sample the food. I'm curious to find out who did the catering."

"I'm ready, too," I said. "Excuse us, guys, unless you want to join us."

Stewart shook his head, his gaze intent on the front door as new guests continued to arrive. Haskell sighed. "I'm coming with you. I've had enough red carpet for one night."

The three of us stepped around Stewart and into the living room. As I gazed around the space, I noted that some pieces had been shifted to accommodate two tables full of food. The holiday decorations were on the minimalist side, as they had been in the hall, I now realized. I wondered why Gerry hadn't attempted to make the rooms more festive when she had gone overboard in decorating the exterior of the house. Anything in the holiday mode that might jibe with the industrial feel of the room, however, was hard to imagine.

I followed Helen Louise and Haskell to the end of one of the tables. They picked up plates, napkins, and forks and began to move down either side. I could tell from my partner's expression that what she saw laid out did not impress her. I had to agree. Given the money Gerry had spent on the champagne, I somehow thought the food would be more than what one could get at the local discount warehouse. Mini-quiches, a variety of cheeses and crackers, sliced apples and grapes, and sliced ham and turkey—all no doubt tasty enough, but nothing out of the ordinary. We loaded our plates and moved on.

The second table replicated the first, we discovered. "Perhaps the dessert-type items are in the dining room," I said.

Helen Louise shrugged and cut a mini-quiche in half. "Probably those little cheesecake squares and chocolate-covered cherries." She chewed the piece of quiche. "Not bad," she said when she finished it. "Not great, but not bad." She ate the other half.

"Not near as good as your food," Haskell said. "But I'm not going to turn it down."

I finished a cracker with mozzarella and a couple of red grapes. I loved cheese, and the mozzarella tasted fine. I might have to go back for more of it, I decided.

We moved out of the way of other guests who had drifted toward the tables, and found a corner across the room from the one currently occupied by Milton and the still-haranguing Tammy. While we ate, I couldn't stop watching the unhappy couple. Milton looked like he wished the floor would swallow him, but other than simply walking out on his wife, I doubted there was any way he could cut off the flood of vituperation. I couldn't hear the words, but the tone was obvious, even fifteen or more feet away.

Haskell spotted a man he wanted to talk to, excused himself, and left us.

I recognized most of the people in the room now, four couples and three singles. The guests started to mingle, once they had loaded their plates. We began to circulate to chat with them. Most of them knew Helen Louise because of the bistro. I glanced toward the door to see Stewart still avidly watching the arrivals. A couple paused to talk to him, and a few more guests wandered into the room, evidently in search of food. They headed straight for the tables.

"Quite a good turnout," said Betty Camden, a retired schoolteacher who lived at the end of the block on my side. "I know I, for one, have been dying to see the inside of this house." She laughed. "Particularly after seeing the outside. Talk about over-the-top."

"Yes, it's pretty extravagant," Helen Louise said. "And so is the champagne."

"Can't say the same for the food." Betty cast a critical eye over the contents of her plate, then glanced around the room. "Her decorating style is not my taste at all, I must say. Way too modern."

Chip, Betty's husband, said, "Looks like the inside of a factory to me." I didn't know him or his wife well, only saying hello if I encountered them somewhere. "I'm dying to meet our hostess," Betty said. "I've seen her two or three times out and about in town, and once when I drove by here, but that's it. Have you gotten to know her any, Charlie?"

"I hear she's attractive," said Chip, and Betty flashed him a look of irritation.

"Nobody asked you." Betty turned back to me.

"I've chatted with her a few times," I said. "Briefly. She did tell me she grew up here, but I'd never met her before, and she seems to be about my age. If we'd gone to school together, I think I would remember her."

Betty nearly spit out a mouthful of champagne. "Don't

let her fool you, at least about her age. I got a good look once at her face and her neck. She's closer to my age, I'd swear to it. I grew up in Athena, too, and I don't recall her, either. Definitely some kind of mystery there."

"You ought to be able to figure it out." Chip, a lawyer often rumored to have political ambitions, nodded at me. "You like solving mysteries, right?"

I laughed. "I do, but I'm not sure this is one I want to solve."

"Don't encourage him," Helen Louise said.

A sudden commotion in the hall interrupted us. Nearly as one, the guests in the living room surged toward the door. Helen Louise and I set down our plates on a small table against the wall before we followed. We ended up next to Stewart. He grinned at us and said, "Fasten your seat belts. It's going to be a bumpy night."

I almost didn't hear him because of the screeching going on right in front of us. Tammy Harville and Gerry Albritton faced each other at the bottom of the stairs. Gerry stood silent, her expression one of bored contempt as she listened to Tammy.

All conversation had ceased by then, and everyone had no trouble hearing Tammy's next words.

"I'm telling you for the last time, you whore. Stay away from my husband, or you won't live to regret it."

THIRTEEN

I watched, fascinated, as Gerry remained cool in the face of Tammy's wild anger. Poor Milton suddenly stepped forward from wherever he had been lurking and grabbed Tammy's arm. He jerked her around to face him. She stumbled and nearly fell, but Milton's tight grip kept her upright.

"That's enough, do you hear me?" Milton's face evinced both his embarrassment and his rage. "You're completely out of control. I swear if you don't stop this, I'll get you committed to Whitfield if it's the last thing I do."

Whitfield was the state mental health facility near Jackson. Tammy appeared so out of control that she probably needed the kind of help Whitfield provided. This was not normal behavior.

Tammy, now faced with a husband who had finally found his snapping point after the Lord only knew how much provocation, appeared stunned.

"Would you mind removing this lunatic from my house?" Gerry asked, her tone still calm. "I won't tolerate this kind of behavior from anyone."

"We're going." Milton tugged Tammy toward the door, and she provided no resistance. I thought even she had realized how far over the line she had stepped.

Jincy hurried to open the door for them, and Milton pushed his wife out of the house. I had never seen him angry, let alone in a rage like this. Jincy closed the door, and after a few beats of silence, conversation erupted. Gerry began to move among her guests, and from her manner, no one would ever imagine she had just endured a highly emotional confrontation.

"Poor Milton," Helen Louise said. I hadn't known she was behind me, and I turned and nodded.

"She needs help," I said. "I wonder, do you think she has an addiction problem? Could drugs or alcohol be making her act this way?"

"Possibly," Helen Louise said. "She's been erratic as long as I've known her, though, so if she is an addict, it's been going on for years."

"Maybe now that Milton has had enough," Stewart said, "Tammy will change her ways. *If* Milton doesn't back down, that is."

"For their sakes, let's hope he doesn't," I said. Then I thought of a question for Stewart. "Remember what you said to me about a bumpy night? That sounded familiar."

He laughed. "Yes, it's a direct quote from *All About Eve*."

"That's it," I said. "Bette Davis."

"My favorite," Helen Louise said. "That's exactly who Gerry reminded me of during that scene with Tammy. Gerry's a tough broad, too."

Stewart stepped away from his position at the living room door. "I don't know about you two, but that kind of drama makes me long for more champagne." He went off in search of more bubbly.

I leaned close to Helen Louise and whispered, "How long do we have to stay to be polite? I'm already feeling too warm with all these people around us."

Helen Louise responded in a firm tone. "Longer than we've been here so far. The champagne probably warmed you up. You finished the first glass already. You usually make one glass last for half an hour, at least."

Before I could respond, Helen Louise nodded in the direction of the front door and said, "Look who's here now. I wasn't sure she would actually grace us with her presence."

I turned to see who it was. Deirdre Thompson. Doyenne of the neighborhood, second only to my friends the Ducote sisters in what passed for the aristocracy in Athena. Her forebears had settled in Athena at roughly the same time as the Ducote clan and had contributed greatly to the civic life of the town for nearly two hundred years.

Unlike the Ducote sisters, Deirdre had married, and more than once. When the latest husband died, she resumed the surname of her first husband, Cedric Thompson, but she kept everything else from the subsequent marriages.

She arrived alone. She acknowledged Jincy's greeting but moved on quickly. Chip and Betty Camden approached her and led her toward us. Deirdre nodded and vouchsafed a brief smile as the trio moved past us into the living room.

"Deirdre looks to be in a good mood tonight," Helen Louise said. "I didn't realize she was so friendly with Chip and Betty, though. Ever since she parted ways with Chip's law firm, anyway."

"Must have been an amicable split, from the look of things," I said. Deirdre continued to smile pleasantly as we watched her move along the table, the Camdens almost on her heels. "Maybe Chip is trying to woo her back."

"Good evening." Gerry Albritton's cool voice came from behind. Helen Louise and I turned to greet our hostess.

"So glad you could come," Gerry said in response to our comments on the party. She held a large snifter in one hand, not a champagne glass like everyone else. I found that odd. She had a sip of what looked like brandy. "I hope you're enjoying yourselves, *despite* the ridiculous drama that deranged woman caused." She smiled. "Why on earth she would imagine I have any interest whatsoever in her poor husband, I don't have the least idea. I do shop in his drugstore, and we may have passed the time of day a few times, but that's all."

"Most everyone in town knows Tammy," Helen Louise said. "She has cried wolf over Milton so many times I doubt anyone here took her seriously. There's no need for you to even think about it." She waved a hand in a dismissive gesture.

I nodded. "Helen Louise is right. Most people steer clear of Tammy if they can. Everyone knows what she's like."

"If she sets foot on my property again, I'll sue her for trespassing." Gerry grimaced. "If you *can* sue someone for that. I doubt she'll have the guts to show up here again anytime soon."

"I'm sure you've seen the last of her," Helen Louise said in a soothing tone. "Don't give her another thought."

Gerry smiled. "If I feel like I need protection, I can always yell for help from Charlie, since he's only across the street from me." She laid a hand on my arm and let it rest there for a few seconds before pulling it away.

Helen Louise did not find that amusing, and frankly, neither did I. Surely the woman wasn't flirting with me right under my partner's nose. I looked sharply at Gerry but couldn't detect any hint of irony or humor in her manner.

"You'd do better to call the police department," I said in as polite a tone as I could muster. "I'm not much good at heroics, like chasing burglars or stopping would-be attackers."

Gerry's attention appeared to be drawn somewhere else at that moment. She murmured "Excuse me" and walked away from Helen Louise and me.

"What is with her? Rudeness on top of that blatant flirting," Helen Louise said, an irritated glint in her eye. "I'm not going to put up with any more of that behavior."

"Don't get too annoyed. She was probably joking with us," I said, although I didn't think my protest sounded even partially convincing.

Helen Louise slipped her arm through mine and pulled me closer. "Maybe, but if she was, it was in extremely poor taste."

"Granted," I said, "but you've seen that living room and that horrendous display in her front yard. Would you call either of them tasteful?"

"Point taken," Helen Louise replied. "Let's find more champagne and see if there are any sweets to be had."

We found the dining room, along with more champagne and, as Helen Louise had predicted, small cheesecake squares. There were also morsels of chocolate, peppermints, and several types of cookies. No chocolate-covered cherries, however.

Before long, as we encountered various people to converse with, we ended up in different rooms. I found myself back in the living room, having accompanied Stewart and a colleague of his from the college chemistry department on a quest for more mini-quiche. I didn't know Stewart's colleague, a jovial man about my age who lived a couple of streets behind me. His name was Gary Fenstermacher, and I discovered that he, like me, was an avid mystery reader. We discussed our favorite writers. He turned out to be a fan of serial killer novels and international intrigue thrillers, neither of which appealed to me all that much. I had read many of the late Helen MacInnes's novels, however, and he turned out to be a huge fan. We were discussing her, with Stewart listening patiently but not contributing to the conversation, when I became aware of a new arrival.

What was Melba doing here?

She didn't live in the neighborhood, but she might have wrangled an invitation from Gerry. I thought that unlikely, however, after Melba's attempt to question Gerry and find out about her past. Melba turned to smile at a man who approached her, and I recognized him. He was Jared Carter, a widower who lived next door to Gerry on the north side. I had heard Melba mention Jared a couple of times recently, but I hadn't thought much about it. He was a well-known, successful dentist, and she might have been to see him professionally. She chattered about all sorts of people, and—rude though it might have been—I didn't always pay close attention.

I couldn't recall the context in which Melba had brought up Jared's name, whether professionally or personally, but from the playful look she was giving him right then—and the indulgent smile he wore in return—I would have to say it must have been personal. They were obviously interested in each other. I didn't think Melba would feign interest in a man simply to attend a party, no matter how deep her curiosity about its hostess.

I became aware that Gary was waiting for a reply from me, but I had no idea what he had said or asked. I smiled ruefully. "I'm sorry, Gary, I got distracted when I saw a good friend of mine over there." I tilted my head in Melba's direction.

Gary and Stewart followed my gaze. Gary laughed. "Melba Gilley, I see. She's definitely distracting. Who's that she's with?"

"A neighbor of mine," I said. "In fact, he lives next door to this house. Jared Carter. I hope you'll pardon me, but I must go speak to Melba and Jared."

"Sure, go ahead," Gary replied. "Stewart and I can gossip about the chemistry department. Have you heard the latest about the chairman's oldest son?"

I left the two men deep in discussion of some youthful peccadillo and walked over to where Melba and Jared stood talking. Melba saw me approach and smiled. Jared nodded to acknowledge me.

"Good evening," I said. "Jared, it's nice to see you. It's been a while."

"Haven't been out much," he replied, and I recalled

that he had lost his wife not quite a year ago. "Melba is getting me out now, though, and I'm enjoying myself." He smiled down at her.

Jared stood a good six five, I reckoned, and Melba was probably five nine or so in high heels. They made an attractive couple despite the noticeable disparity in height. Jared sported a thick head of gray hair and distinguished features in addition to his lean height. Melba was vivacious, attractive, and always knew how to dress in a flattering style. Jared, I judged, had to be in his midsixties. I vaguely remembered that he had graduated from high school in Athena about a decade before Melba and me.

"Jared took me out for an early dinner," Melba said. "When we finished, he suggested that we drop by the party since Gerry is his next-door neighbor."

"I thought it was the neighborly thing to do," Jared said. "I've talked to her a couple of times, and she made a special point of insisting that I show up." He appeared suddenly a bit uncomfortable, and I had little doubt that Gerry had come on strong with him. She might not appreciate seeing him here with Melba, I thought.

I was about to find out, because I spotted Gerry making her way toward us from behind Melba. "Here comes our hostess now," I said in an undertone.

Jared turned toward Gerry, but Melba remained facing me, a wicked glint in her eye. *Watch this*, her expression seemed to say.

"Good evening, Jared," Gerry said brightly. "I'm so glad you could come tonight. I would have been *so* disappointed if you hadn't." She looked up into his face and offered a coquettish smile.

"Good evening, Gerry," he said. "Looks like a big turnout."

"Yes, even better than I hoped." She frowned at Melba's back. "Am I interrupting you?"

This was perhaps the cue Melba had been waiting for, because she turned to face Gerry. "Good evening," Melba said.

Gerry's mask of hospitality slipped ever so briefly, and I could read the irritation in her eyes. Then she became the consummate hostess again. "How nice to see you again. Mildred, isn't it?"

Melba laughed. "No, it's Melba, honey. Nice to see you again, too." She slipped her arm through Jared's and hugged it to her side. "I didn't realize until tonight that you and Jared were neighbors. He was telling me about it over the most delicious dinner I've had in I don't know how long."

"How charming for you," Gerry said, her drawl at its most exaggerated on the word *charming*. "Would you mind if I stole Jared away for just one little minute? I have something I really need to say to him."

I felt Melba stiffen beside me at Gerry's request. By then I had moved to stand on Melba's other side, where Gerry could easily see me. She flicked a glance in my direction but otherwise didn't acknowledge my presence.

"Of course not, honey," Melba said sweetly. "Just remember where you got him, all right? I'm sure Charlie will be glad to keep me company for a minute or two." She relinquished Jared's arm, and he moved a few feet away from us with Gerry. He threw Melba a glance of apology as he went.

"Enjoying yourself?" I asked as soon as the others were out of earshot.

"Sure am," Melba said. "Why shouldn't I?"

"What are you up to? And since when did you and Jared become such good friends?" I said.

Melba sounded exasperated when she replied. "If you actually listened to me instead of only pretending to half the time, you'd know that Jared and I have been going out together for about three weeks now."

"Sorry." I felt chagrined. I really ought to pay more attention when she talked, but sometimes I couldn't help my mind drifting onto something else. "I've always thought he was a nice guy."

"He is," Melba replied simply. "The nicest one I've known in a long time."

"Is it serious?" I asked.

Melba shrugged. "Too soon to say, but so far I like him a lot. We'll have to see whether it goes anywhere."

Melba had been on her own for a long time, and she certainly deserved to have a good man in her life, if that was what she really wanted.

We both watched the conversation between Jared and our hostess. We couldn't hear it with so much chatter around us, but it seemed to me that Gerry stood much closer to Jared than was necessary.

Melba evidently agreed with me. I heard the thinly repressed anger in her voice when she said, "She'd better back off, or I'm about to go over there and remove every single one of those dyed red hairs on her head and laugh the whole time I'm doing it."

FOURTEEN

||||||||||||||||||||||||||||||||||||||||||||||||||||||||||

"You don't really want to cause a scene, do you?" I asked, made more than a little uneasy by Melba's tone.

"I wouldn't give her the satisfaction," Melba said. "She knows I'm watching her, and she's doing it deliberately. Trying to goad me into embarrassing myself, but I'm not going to let her."

Relieved, I said, "Good for you. What *are* you going to do?" Because I knew Melba well enough to realize that she would retaliate somehow.

She looked at me and smiled. "I'm going to chat with her guests, and I'm going to find out if anybody here knows anything about her. Who she really is, where she came from, and what she's up to. She's no Albritton, that's one thing for sure."

This was the first time today that I had seen Melba, and I realized that I still hadn't told her about overhearing a shouting match between Gerry and Billy Albritton on Sunday.

"I've been meaning to tell you something," I said in an undertone. "You may have to change your mind about her being an Albritton. On Saturday your friend Billy came to see her, and they ended up having a really loud argument."

"And you're only just now telling me about this?" Melba frowned at me.

"You weren't at work yesterday," I reminded her, "and I wasn't there today. I figured I'd wait until I saw you at work tomorrow. I didn't think it qualified as news that had to be shared immediately."

"Tell me about it now, then," Melba said.

I shared with her what I knew about the quarrel, and that wasn't much, only that they were shouting at each other loud enough that I heard the noise from inside my house.

"But you couldn't hear what they were saying?" Melba asked.

"No, I couldn't," I replied. "I thought the fact that they were arguing would be of sufficient interest to you. If they were complete strangers to each other, I can't imagine they would carry on like that where the neighbors could hear."

Melba looked thoughtful. "I wonder if Jared heard them. I'll have to ask him, but not right out. I don't want him to think I'm nosy."

"He'll find that out soon enough," I said.

Melba ignored my little dig. "Time to break this up."

I watched her move in on Jared and Gerry. The latter quickly found herself detached from Jared, and Melba bore him off to another part of the room, where they started chatting with another couple. I didn't know the people, but I supposed either Melba or Jared did.

I looked around for Helen Louise. I had had enough of the crowd now and was ready to go home. If Helen Louise was intent on staying, though, I wouldn't make an issue of it. She worked hard and deserved the chance to enjoy herself at a party, if that's what she wanted. I didn't see her in this room. With her height, she was generally easy to spot.

The hall held a crush of people, and I worked my way through it to the dining room. I went around one side, trying to maneuver where the path seemed a bit more open. When I reached the wall, I turned to survey the room. I spotted Helen Louise moving toward the door. Slightly aggravated, I retraced my steps, but by the time I reached the door, I couldn't see Helen Louise.

I chanced to glance down the hall toward the room where she had left her coat. There she was, making her way toward the back of the house. I set off once more in pursuit, muttering "excuse me" repeatedly as I squeezed between and around couples and groups.

I caught up with her at the door of the den and started to speak, but she held up a hand to silence me. Then she nodded toward the partially open door. I thought I heard voices coming from inside the room. I moved closer to her, and together we peered into the room.

A heated exchange was in progress, between Gerry and Deirdre Thompson. The issue seemed to be the flyer that Gerry or her minion had left at Deirdre's house.

". . . ask you not to bother sticking such things on my door," Deirdre said, each word enunciated and dripping with disdain. "I don't like trash left at my house. Why you ever thought I would be interested in selling a home that's been in the family for four generations, I'll never understand."

Gerry shrugged. "Nothing ventured, nothing gained. Isn't that the way the saying goes? Besides, if I remember correctly, the house is only about seventy-five years old, if that much—your father bought it, so don't give me that four-generation crap. Looks it, too, from what I can see on the outside. That's why I thought you might be interested in selling it. If you're going to keep it, you ought to do something to improve it."

Helen Louise leaned close to whisper in my ear. "She's not kidding. Deirdre is so tight with her money, she hardly ever spends it. Just look at that dress. Must have belonged to her grandmother." Now that she mentioned it, I thought Deirdre's dress did seem old-fashioned. I remembered seeing my grandmother in a similar style. I even think we buried her in a dress like it. I hadn't known that Deirdre had a reputation as a skinflint. Rumor had it that she was rich enough to buy Memphis two times over and have change left.

Gerry was still talking. ". . . going to fall in if you're not careful." She laughed. "You'll end up buried in the rubble when the whole thing crashes down around you. Let go of a few bucks, why don't you? I'm sure your father left you a lot of them as his heiress, right?"

Deirdre's hands clenched and unclenched repeatedly. I thought she might be struggling not to slap Gerry or punch her right in the face. Gerry didn't appear to be concerned about any potential attack from Deirdre. After all, women like Deirdre were reared to remember the first tenet of Southern genteel womanhood: *Thou shalt at all times behave like a lady.*

That probably explained why Deirdre hadn't fired back a response yet. These old codes of behavior are difficult to break sometimes, and I watched with great curiosity to see if Deirdre reached the snapping point.

All at once Deirdre's hands relaxed, and she smiled. "You are probably the most remarkably ill-bred person I have ever encountered. You've made the entire neighborhood a laughingstock with that completely tasteless display in front of this house. By putting that up for all and sundry to gape at, you've shown us all just how *little* class you have always had. Then you go and serve expensive champagne to your guests and pair it with the cheapest food you could find that's halfway edible. I decided to come here tonight on the vague chance that you were someone worth acknowledging. I was wrong to do so, because you're obviously not."

Deirdre shot Gerry a look of haughty triumph and began to walk away. Gerry stared at Deirdre's retreating back, and if Deirdre had burst into flame from Gerry's gaze, I don't think I would have been surprised.

"Not so fast, Deirdre dear," Gerry said, more coolly than I would have thought possible. "You don't want to make an enemy of me, I promise you. I know a lot about you, don't forget that. Some people think they're so much better than anyone else when they really aren't. Think about how your society friends would react if they knew some of the things I do. Wouldn't do to let some of those things get around, now would it?"

Deirdre whirled around, her face white. "Don't try to threaten me. My *society friends* wouldn't listen to a word you say about me. I couldn't care less what you've heard from the type of people *you* probably know intimately." Her lip curled. "*Too* intimately, I imagine."

Gerry's expression hardened. "Why don't we test my little theory, Deirdre? Introduce me to some of your society friends. If you play nice with me, maybe I won't destroy your reputation after all."

"You can go to hell."

With that, she turned and came toward the door.

Helen Louise and I were frozen to the spot for a moment, but before we could decide what to do, Gerry's mocking laughter halted Deirdre in her progress.

"If you know what's good for you, Deirdre darling, you won't leave the room until I've finished what I have to say to you." After a brief pause, during which Deirdre didn't move, Gerry continued. "I have a proposition for you, and it's to both our advantage, so listen up."

Helen Louise and I exchanged glances. I knew we were both thinking that we should have walked away before now. This was none of our business. Accordingly, we both stepped back from the door and turned toward the front of the house. I could see Stewart still making his way through the crowd in the hallway, evidently intent on reaching us. We moved forward to meet him.

"Finally," he said, when he stood only a couple of feet from us. "I've been looking for you two *and* for our hostess for the past five minutes or so."

"Is there a problem?" I asked.

"No," Stewart said. "Haskell has to be up early in the morning, and we're going home. Thought you should know, and of course, I wanted to thank Gerry for inviting us."

Helen Louise responded hurriedly. "I think Gerry's pretty busy at the moment with another guest. We're not ready to leave yet, and we'll be happy to express your thanks to her. You can always write her a note later." She smiled.

Stewart's gaze narrowed as he regarded us. "Okay, you two, what's going on? You can't fool me. What have you heard?"

"Nothing to worry about," I said in a firm tone. "Y'all go on home. We won't be far behind you."

A voice from behind us gave me a start. "Would you mind moving out of the way? You're blocking the hall."

"Sorry," I said, and moved aside.

Deirdre Thompson brushed past me, her face set in angry lines. She continued to push her way through the hall.

Stewart stared after her briefly, then turned back to Helen Louise and me. "Whatever it was must have involved Deirdre. Who was she talking to that you overheard?" Then he appeared startled. In a low voice he said, "Never mind. Here comes Gerry."

I turned, as did Helen Louise. Gerry came up to us, her hostess's smile in place. "I hope you're enjoying yourselves this evening. Be sure to have more champagne. There's plenty of it." She nodded and walked on past us.

"She looks pretty satisfied with herself," Helen Louise said. "You wait here. I'm going to the restroom." She headed back toward the den and the bathroom connected to it.

"Why does Gerry look satisfied with herself?" Stewart demanded. "Were she and Deirdre having an argument?"

I knew Stewart would continue to pester me, so I might as well go ahead and tell him now. I gave him a short summary of what Helen Louise and I had witnessed.

Feeling guilty at my behavior, I concluded by saying, "We should have walked away immediately, of course. It was a breach of good manners to stand there and watch, but the temptation was too great to resist, I guess."

"Yes, it was." Stewart winked at me. "But life would be pretty dull if no one ever eavesdropped. I wonder what on earth Gerry knows about Deirdre that's blackmail-worthy. Fascinating idea."

Over Stewart's shoulder I saw Haskell coming our way. Not far beyond him, headed toward the front door, was a man who looked like Billy Albritton from the brief glimpse I had. He disappeared through the door, and then I wasn't sure I had seen the councilman after all. Probably someone who looked a little like him.

Haskell tapped Stewart on the shoulder. "Where have you been? I've been waiting at the door, and I saw Gerry go by, into the dining room. Did you speak to her?"

"No, I didn't," Stewart replied. "It doesn't matter. Charlie and Helen Louise will express our thanks. Let's go home. See you in the morning," he said to me.

They disappeared into the crowd, and I turned to watch for Helen Louise. At least two more minutes passed before she returned. She had not brought her coat, and I interpreted that correctly to mean that she wasn't ready to leave the party. I suppressed a sigh and followed her back to join the festivities. I gave a fleeting thought to taking refuge in the den, but Helen Louise wouldn't let me get away with that.

Helen Louise accepted another glass of champagne, but I refused. I asked the waiter instead if there was bottled water available, and he assured me there was. He promised to return soon with one for me. While I waited, I stood next to Helen Louise and listened with half an ear to her conversation with a woman I vaguely recognized as a resident of my street. I gathered that she and Helen Louise had worked on a church committee together last year, and they were discussing the results of their efforts.

The waiter returned promptly with my water, and while I sipped at it, grateful that it was cold, I surveyed the room. I spotted Deirdre Thompson once again talking to Betty and Chip Camden. Deirdre evinced no signs now of her acrimonious argument with Gerry earlier. I wondered idly what it was that Gerry had demanded of her.

Melba and her escort, Jared, stood a few feet away from me. Upon seeing me, Melba waved me over. I glanced at Helen Louise, but she was too involved in her conversation with her church friend for me to interrupt. I joined Melba and Jared.

"Looks like a successful party to me," Melba said. "Lot of people here, so that must make Gerry happy. How nice for her." She smiled at Jared, who smiled benignly back.

It took me a moment, but I got it. Melba wasn't about to let Jared know how she really felt about our hostess. I had to suppress a chuckle. Jared probably had no idea that the women loathed each other, and I didn't plan to be the man who enlightened him.

"Yes, it is nice, isn't it?" I said. "Jared, what do you think?"

"Nice," he said. "Definitely."

A loud crash sounded somewhere behind me. Women screamed. I turned around, seeking the source of the noise, but I couldn't see anything at first. There were too many people in the way. So I moved forward, and someone stepped aside.

Then I caught a glimpse of Gerry Albritton on the floor, surrounded by serving dishes and food scattered about.

Our hostess lay prone on the floor. She wasn't moving.

FIFTEEN

Had she suffered a heart attack or a stroke? Or had she simply fainted? Like everyone else, I stood where I was, not moving, stunned by what I was seeing, focused on Gerry lying on the floor.

I glanced up and saw Helen Louise standing a couple of feet to the left of where Gerry had fallen. There were two women close to her, Deirdre Thompson and Betty Camden. Melba and Jared Carter stood not far away from me, but they were facing the other direction.

Suddenly Helen Louise was on her knees beside Gerry, and I pushed through the people in front of me to help her. Helen Louise was trained in CPR.

"Someone call an ambulance," I said harshly. I knelt and helped Helen Louise turn Gerry on her back. Helen Louise quickly positioned Gerry's head and began blowing air into her mouth. In my days as a library manager I had learned CPR, too, though it had been quite a few years since I had had to make use of my skills. I helped with the chest compressions.

Helen Louise and I worked on Gerry until an ambulance crew arrived to take over. I helped Helen Louise to her feet, and we moved out of the way.

"It's no use," Helen Louise said softly. "She's gone."

Her dress now splotched from the food scattered on the floor when Gerry fell, Helen Louise looked tired and shaken. I glanced down and saw that my knees and lower trouser legs were stained as well.

I slipped my arm around Helen Louise's waist, and we watched as the EMTs worked on Gerry a few minutes more. Then one of them called a halt, and they stood back.

Police arrived on the scene and began clearing the room. They moved us into the dining room, and I could tell that many people had left. Only the curious had remained, it seemed. Deirdre Thompson was not one of them, I noticed. I didn't see Betty Camden, either, although Chip was still there.

Melba and Jared came over to us. "Your beautiful dress," Melba said in tones of sorrow.

Helen Louise looked down. I don't think she had noticed until now. "Couldn't be helped," she said.

"You were terrific," I said. "You did everything you could."

She smiled faintly. "So did you. Thanks for helping."

"What do you think happened?" Melba asked. "Looked like maybe she had a heart attack. I didn't actually see her fall, though."

"I don't know," Helen Louise said wearily. "She had walked by me moments before, and then I guess she stumbled and fell. I was talking to someone and didn't pay much attention until I heard the crash. I looked down, and there she was on the floor."

"You two were nearby," I said to Melba and Jared. "Did you see anything?"

Jared shook his head. "No, I don't think so."

Melba frowned. "I saw her go by us. I think she had come from the hall, or at least, she seemed to be moving from that direction."

A low buzz of conversation filled the room as those remaining no doubt discussed Gerry's sudden and tragic collapse. I wasn't sure whether everyone realized yet that she was dead, though I doubted it would take long for word to spread.

"How long should we stay?" Jared asked. "I don't really see what the point is for all of us standing around here. There's nothing we can do for her now."

"The police will want to question anyone who saw her fall," I said. "In cases of sudden death like this, they usually do, even if it's from natural causes."

"Do you think it's not natural?" Helen Louise asked, her tone sharp.

"How do I know?" I said. "I didn't mean that I think it isn't, only that the police are bound to ask questions anyway."

Helen Louise still looked troubled, and I figured she was recalling the conversation we had overheard less than half an hour ago. Not to mention that confrontation earlier in the evening with Tammy Harville. Tammy, at least, had been taken home, but Deirdre Thompson had still been present. *And standing not too far from where Gerry collapsed.* I couldn't suppress that thought. It was pretty coincidental that Gerry died not long after that conversation with Deirdre.

Melba leaned toward me and spoke in a low tone. "Are you thinking she was murdered?"

Jared recoiled from her. "What are you talking about?" he asked.

Melba smiled sweetly. "I've known Charlie most of my life, and I can read him without even trying. He's thinking Gerry could have been murdered."

Helen Louise, Jared, and Melba stared at me. Melba had indeed read me all too easily. I couldn't put my finger on it, but there was simply something too convenient about Gerry's dying like that after two nasty episodes with women who loathed her.

"Well?" Jared said.

I shrugged. "It's probably not likely, but you can't dismiss it completely as a possibility."

Melba looked smug. "I knew it. I'll bet Tammy Harville sneaked away from Milton and got in here somehow and poisoned Gerry's drink."

"Keep your voice down." Helen Louise shot Melba a quelling look. "That's how ugly rumors get started."

Melba did not take quelling at all well, and she glowered at Helen Louise. Normally they got along fine, but we were all on edge tonight. I didn't want to make things worse by saying the wrong thing, but I couldn't stand there mute.

"Let's reserve any speculation for another place and time," I said. "Until we hear the official verdict on Gerry's cause of death, we'd only be wasting time and mental energy."

"I guess you're right," Melba said grudgingly.

"I'm ready to get out of here," Jared said. "I'm tired, and I resent having to stand around waiting. I'm going to ask someone if I can leave." He stepped away and headed for the door.

Melba didn't appear pleased by his petulance or his actions. Jared's use of the first-person pronoun had been all too obvious, I thought. He wasn't thinking about Melba, and she had picked up on it.

Helen Louise moved closer and leaned against me. I slipped an arm around her waist. "What a horrible end to a party," she said. "I was enjoying myself, for the most part, but now I'm tired, my feet hurt, and I want to go home and get out of this dress."

"I know, sweetheart," I said.

Melba eyed the dress critically. "The cleaners might be able to save it. But I wouldn't count on it."

Jared returned. The angry set to his mouth indicated to me that he hadn't received the answer he wanted.

"What did they say?" Melba asked, her tone none too cordial.

Jared didn't appear to register her irritation, being evidently too wrapped up in his own. "They're waiting for somebody from the sheriff's department. They wouldn't say who, but an officer told me everyone had to remain until the deputy arrived and assessed the situation."

I felt Helen Louise stiffen beside me, and I knew why. We both reckoned that the deputy we had to wait for was none other than Chief Deputy Kanesha Berry. Kanesha, Azalea's daughter, investigated homicides in Athena and in the county. Our police force didn't have a homicide detective, so the county handled murders and unexplained deaths. Any that the county couldn't handle got turned over to the MBI, the Mississippi Bureau of Investigation.

If the police here at the scene called in Kanesha, that meant they considered Gerry's death suspicious. I wondered what they had discovered to make them suspect foul play.

Jared glanced from one to another of the three of us in turn before he spoke. "Obviously y'all know something I don't. I guess calling in the sheriff's department is significant somehow."

Didn't the man ever read the newspaper or watch a cop show on television?

I suppressed the spurt of irritation I felt at Jared's naiveté. "Yes, it is significant," I said. "There must be something suspicious about Gerry's death."

I could see from Jared's expression of increasing unease that he finally understood the gravity of the situation.

Two police officers began to circulate through the room, taking down names, addresses, and phone numbers. While our foursome waited for one of the officers to reach us, we remained silent.

Our turn came about ten minutes later, though it seemed longer. The officer who took our details had moved on to the next group when a voice called for our attention. I recognized that voice. Kanesha had arrived.

Everyone turned to face the deputy. Kanesha surveyed the room, and I thought I saw her grimace slightly when she caught sight of me. Then she began to speak.

"Sorry to hold y'all up when I'm sure you're ready to go home," Kanesha said, "but we've got some questions about what happened. We also have to follow procedures, and I'm sure y'all understand that we want to do everything by the book. I need to talk to anyone who saw or spoke to Ms. Albritton in the fifteen minutes or so before she collapsed. If those of you who did would move to your left and those who did not will move to your right, that will be a big help."

At first no one moved at all. Kanesha frowned. "Come on now, folks. Some of you saw or spoke to her, I'm sure. I will make this as quick as I can, but nobody's leaving until I get some cooperation."

After that, people began to move. Helen Louise sighed and began to move to the left. Melba went with her. I thought it had been more than a quarter hour since I had seen Gerry before she collapsed, but given the argument Helen Louise and I had heard, I knew I might as well go ahead and talk to Kanesha tonight. I felt her eyes on me—though I probably imagined it—as I followed Helen Louise and Melba. Jared, I noticed, went the other way.

"Thank you," Kanesha said when the two groups were finally separated. "Those of you who moved to the right can go, unless you need to wait for someone in the other group. My deputies will be in here to answer questions and help you if you need anything."

Haskell stepped into the room, now in uniform. Kanesha must have called him in. He was her staunchest supporter in the sheriff's department. I wasn't too surprised that she would want him to be part of this investigation.

Haskell spotted Melba, Helen Louise, and me and nodded to acknowledge us. He and his fellow deputy watched as a few people filed out of the room. Jared Carter made a move as if to leave, but then subsided. His resigned expression as he glanced at Melba made me wonder about their budding relationship and whether it would survive the stress of this night.

Kanesha left the room but was back in about two minutes. She held notebook pages, and she glanced through them. Then she looked up, and her eyes met mine.

"Mr. Harris and Ms. Brady, I'd appreciate it if you would come with me." Kanesha indicated that we should follow her, and she led us to the dining room.

I felt Helen Louise stiffen beside me when we entered the room, and I knew she was thinking the same thing I was. Neither of us wanted to see poor Gerry Albritton still lying on the floor.

I was relieved to see, however, that the body had been removed. The table and the spilled food, however, had not been touched.

Helen Louise stopped and stared at the area where Gerry had lain. She wore a puzzled expression.

Kanesha drew us toward three dining room chairs arranged about ten feet away from the spot where Gerry died. Helen Louise and I occupied the two chairs that faced the one Kanesha took. The deputy took out a notebook and pen. She stared at Helen Louise and me for a moment, and then she addressed Helen Louise.

"Ms. Brady, when you stopped to look just now at the place where Ms. Albritton fell, it looked like something was bothering you. What was it?"

Helen Louise frowned. "Something is missing," she said slowly. "The brandy snifter. What happened to her brandy snifter?"

SIXTEEN

I concentrated on recalling the scene. Had there been a snifter? I wasn't sure. I didn't remember it.

"Snifter?" Kanesha asked. "That's a kind of glass, isn't it?"

"Yes, it's stemware with a wide bottom and a narrower top," Helen Louise said. "Used for brandy, port, that kind of thing."

"And Ms. Albritton had one?" Kanesha said. "In her hand when she collapsed?"

Helen Louise frowned. "I'm pretty sure she did."

"It didn't break?" Kanesha said.

"No, the carpet is thick enough that it wouldn't, and the snifter looked like good crystal," Helen Louise said. "There might be a stain in the carpet. Although . . ." She hesitated. "She may have drained the glass before she fell. I'm not sure."

"Excuse me a moment." Kanesha got up and went to talk to the other officers. Two of them began to examine the carpet carefully while Kanesha came back to resume questioning us.

"I understand you performed CPR on Ms. Albritton," Kanesha said. "Tell me everything you did." She looked at Helen Louise.

"All right." Helen Louise drew a deep breath, then exhaled slowly. "I had just started talking to Deirdre Thompson and Betty Camden when I saw Gerry moving in our direction. Next thing I knew, she stumbled into the table and knocked it over. I'm pretty sure she had the snifter in her hand. She went down with the table and was lying prone beside it."

"Did you see her take a drink from the snifter?" Kanesha asked.

"Yes, during the couple of seconds, at the most, that I looked at her," Helen Louise said.

"Did she choke or cough?" Kanesha asked.

Helen Louise considered the question. "No, I don't think so. Like I said, it was a really brief glance."

"Okay then, please continue," Kanesha said.

"After she fell, I think everyone froze for a few seconds, we were all so shocked. I could see she wasn't moving. I thought at first she'd only been stunned by the fall, but then I realized she might need help. I knelt beside her. I had to turn her over, of course. Charlie helped."

"Take a moment and visualize the scene," Kanesha said. "Do you remember seeing the snifter then?"

Helen Louise nodded slowly. "Yes, it had rolled several feet away, I think. But I barely noticed it. I was concentrating on Gerry and getting her turned so I could do CPR. Once we had her in position, I started. Charlie did chest compressions."

Kanesha turned to me. "How about you? Do you recall seeing the snifter?"

"No, I don't," I said. "I didn't actually see Gerry fall. I heard the noise she made when the table toppled over, but by the time I saw her, she was on the floor. If the snifter rolled several feet away like Helen Louise said, it was probably out of my line of sight."

Kanesha nodded. "How long do you think you worked on her?"

"I can't really say," Helen Louise replied. "Five minutes, maybe as many as ten. We worked on her until the EMTs arrived, so however long it took for them to get here."

"Were people standing close to you while you performed CPR?" Kanesha asked.

"I think so," Helen Louise said. "You know what people are like when something happens, nobody wants to miss anything. But I was focused on what I was doing, so I didn't think much about it."

"I agree," I said. "I was aware of the people crowded around us, but I didn't have time to think about it. I didn't waste energy on trying to get them to move back. I had to focus on what I was doing, because it's been years since I performed CPR on anyone."

"So anyone could have picked up the snifter and taken it away while everyone else was watching the two of you trying to revive the deceased," Kanesha said.

"Wouldn't someone have noticed the snifter being carried away?" I asked. "A champagne flute would be much easier to conceal under a jacket. A snifter would cause at least a small bulge."

"People were distracted," Kanesha said. "The person who removed it counted on that."

"Probably so," I replied. "Since the snifter disappeared, it must be important. Why steal it unless Gerry was poisoned? Right?"

Kanesha nodded reluctantly. "Poison is certainly a possibility, although we won't know for sure until the toxicology report."

"When could someone have put poison in the snifter?" Helen Louise asked.

"That's what I have to try to find out," Kanesha said. "I'll be questioning everyone, and I want to find moments when she might have set it down somewhere, and if she did, for how long."

"And who was in the room when she did," I said.

Kanesha nodded. "I want you both to think back to the times you saw her tonight and whether she had the snifter with her."

"We will." Helen Louise and I exchanged a look. We were both thinking, I was certain, that we needed to tell Kanesha about the confrontations that Gerry had with Tammy Harville and Deirdre Thompson. I didn't like bearing tales, but if it turned out that one of these women murdered Gerry Albritton, she should be held accountable. I didn't see how Tammy could be responsible, though, unless she sneaked away from Milton and came back to the party without his being aware of it.

"We think there are some incidents at the party tonight that you need to know about," I said.

"Because they could have some bearing on Gerry's death," Helen Louise added.

"Okay, I'm listening," Kanesha said.

Helen Louise looked at me, and I interpreted that as her wish for me to do the talking, at least initially.

"Do you know Milton and Tammy Harville?" I asked.

Kanesha's expression turned grim. "Yes, I do."

"If you know much about them," I said, trying to choose my words as diplomatically as possible, "you know that Tammy is really possessive of Milton. She is always suspicious of interactions he has with other women."

"I'm aware of that, yes," Kanesha said. "Go on."

"Tammy made a nasty scene tonight when Gerry came downstairs to the party," I said. "In front of many witnesses, so I'm sure you'll hear about it from other people." I paused briefly. "She called Gerry a whore and told her to say away from Milton. Otherwise she wouldn't live to regret it."

"I see. How did Ms. Albritton react?" Kanesha asked.

"Completely cool and collected," Helen Louise said. "She asked Milton to remove Tammy from her house. Actually, Milton got really angry first and told Tammy she had to stop this kind of behavior. He threatened her with Whitfield."

"Did either Mr. or Mrs. Harville return, to your knowledge?" Kanesha looked from Helen Louise to me.

"No," I said, and Helen Louise answered the same.

Kanesha wrote in her notebook, but whatever she noted didn't take long. She looked up when she finished. "You said *some incidents* occurred. How many?"

"Two," Helen Louise replied. "There is a den at the back of the house on the right side of the hall where guests left their coats. There is also a bathroom attached to the den. I went back there—sometime after the incident with Tammy and Gerry—but as I neared the door I could hear two voices from inside the room. The door was open about a foot, maybe a little more."

"I had been trying to find her in the crowd," I said, nodding toward Helen Louise. "I saw her heading down the hall and followed her. We both stood in the hall and listened. We shouldn't have eavesdropped, but I think we were both so surprised by the conversation we simply stood there and didn't move."

"Did you see who was talking in the den?" Kanesha asked.

"Gerry and Deirdre Thompson." Helen Louise paused, looking uncomfortable.

Kanesha prompted her. "And what were they saying that could have a bearing on Ms. Albritton's death?"

Helen Louise looked at me. I nodded, and she continued. "Deirdre Thompson was complaining to Gerry about the flyers that Gerry had put—or had someone put—on every front door in the neighborhood. Gerry was advertising that she was looking to buy houses in the neighborhood."

"She was a real estate agent?" Kanesha asked.

"Yes, had her own agency, I think. Though I'd never heard of her or her agency until she moved into the neighborhood a couple of months ago after coming back to Athena after some time away. I've seen two or three for-sale signs in the neighborhood with her name on them."

"So apparently she was looking for houses to sell, as well as to buy," Kanesha said. "Go on—Mrs. Thompson was complaining, you said."

"Yes, she was pretty unpleasant about it," I said, taking over from Helen Louise, "but Gerry gave back as good as she got. Gerry didn't seem at all intimidated by Deirdre Thompson. In fact, toward the end of what we heard, it sounded to me like Gerry was threatening Deirdre."

"Yes, Gerry made it sound as if she knew things about Deirdre's past that Deirdre wouldn't want getting around," Helen Louise said.

"Right after that is when we walked away," I said. "So if Gerry told Deirdre what she knew about her, we didn't hear it."

"We met Stewart, who was looking for Gerry, to thank her for the invitation to the party. He and Haskell were heading home because Haskell had to be up early tomorrow," Helen Louise said.

"While we were talking to him," I said, "Deirdre came down the hall behind us and ordered us out of her way."

Kanesha made more notes while Helen Louise and I waited. I clasped Helen Louise's hand in mine and gave it a gentle squeeze. We were both tired and ready to be out of this house. I hoped Kanesha didn't have many more questions for us.

"Did you speak to Ms. Albritton at any point after that incident?" Kanesha asked.

"Yes," I said. "She came down the hall not long after Deirdre did. Stewart had left, and Gerry came up to us and asked if we were enjoying the party. She encouraged us to have more champagne."

"She didn't appear upset or anything by the scene with Deirdre," Helen Louise said. "Cool as cool could be."

"Did she have the brandy snifter with her then?" Kanesha asked.

Helen Louise and I exchanged glances of inquiry. I shook my head. "I don't think so, but I really can't say for sure. She might have."

"I don't think she did, either," Helen Louise said.

"She must have left it somewhere while she was in the den," I said.

"Or she could have had it with her in the den, left it, and then went back for it," Helen Louise said.

"If she left it unattended in the living room or the dining room," I said, "anyone could have slipped poison into it."

"Yes, I had already figured that out." Kanesha's tart tone reminded me that I didn't need to state the obvious around her. She resumed questioning us. "Did you at any time see any other person tonight drinking anything from a snifter?"

"No, all I saw was champagne flutes," Helen Louise said.

"I asked for a bottle of water at one point," I said. "I think I saw a few more of those, but no glasses besides the champagne glasses."

"The catering staff would know more about that anyway," Helen Louise said.

Kanesha nodded. I noticed, with slightly bitter amusement, that Kanesha did not inform Helen Louise that she had already figured out that obvious point. Evidently the deputy reserved such remarks for me.

"One more question for now," Kanesha said. "I might have others later. Tell me this, did either of you see Ms. Albritton again, before she collapsed?"

"No," Helen Louise and I said in unison.

Kanesha stood. "All right, then. Thank you. You can leave now."

Helen Louise and I rose tiredly from our chairs. "We need to retrieve Helen Louise's coat from the den," I said. "Is that all right?"

"I'll send Haskell for it," Kanesha said. "I assume he would know which one it is."

"He would," Helen Louise replied. "Thank you. We'll be waiting near the front door. Okay, Charlie?"

"Yes. Good night, Deputy Berry," I said.

Kanesha nodded, and Helen Louise and I left the room. We didn't have to wait long before Haskell brought the coat. I helped Helen Louise into it, and we thanked Haskell and bade him good night.

The temperature had dropped since we entered the house, and we hurried across the street to escape the chill. Helen Louise stopped at her car.

"Would you like to come in for a few minutes? Maybe have some coffee?" I said.

"No, thank you, sweetheart," Helen Louise said. "I want to go home and get this dress off. I'm going to take something to help me sleep, and hopefully I'll conk out quickly and not dream about this awful night."

I hugged her and kissed her good night. "Drive carefully," I said as I opened her door.

"I will," she said. "Good night, love."

I watched her back out and drive down the street. I had one last look at Gerry's garish decorations before I went into the house. I hoped someone turned them off. I didn't think I could bear looking at them again.

SEVENTEEN

After a restless night, during which bad dreams fractured my sleep, I woke with a dull headache and a stiff neck. I rubbed a pain-relieving lotion onto my neck and took a couple of aspirin for the headache. Diesel watched me attending to my neck, and his nose twitched. I didn't think he cared for the aromatic scent of the lotion.

Downstairs, I poured a cup of coffee, added cream and sugar, and slowly began to sip at it. I was doing my best not to think about the disastrous party and the death—perhaps murder—of the hostess. It had dawned on me belatedly last night that, if Gerry had been poisoned, Helen Louise might have risked being poisoned herself by performing CPR. I supposed it depended on the type of poison used, whether there would be any residue on Gerry's lips that could affect anyone else.

I had texted Helen Louise after that alarming thought had occurred to me and waited anxiously for an answer.

I'd been on the point of calling her when I received her reply. She was fine and felt no ill effects. That had relieved me, but it hadn't stopped my subconscious from fretting over it during the night, hence the bad dreams.

After a few more sips of coffee, I felt up to checking on the kittens. They would be ready for breakfast, I had no doubt. Diesel was already in the living room, sitting next to the cage and watching them. Upon seeing me they all crowded against the wall of the cage, meowing and batting at the wire mesh.

"Good morning, boys and girls," I said. "Never fear, you're not going to starve. I'm going to feed you, I promise." I had to watch them carefully when I opened the door to slip inside and out again. Ramses wasn't the only talented escape artist among them.

Somehow I managed to get in and out with the empty food dishes. When I returned with the food, they were too interested in eating to try to escape from the cage. They stayed engrossed in their breakfast long enough for me to freshen their water. When that was done I cleaned the two litter boxes, and then I stood outside and watched the kittens for several minutes. Their mischievous innocence provided the tonic I needed. I could so easily get used to having them around, I knew.

At least, my heart knew that, but my head knew that six cats in the house, even one as large as this, were five too many. Or maybe only four too many. Diesel might like to have a little companion.

Stop that, I told myself sternly. It would be time to think about that only once I found out where the kittens came from and whether they were truly in danger if they went back there.

Diesel came with me when I left the living room. I retrieved the paper from the walk, and I noticed that the Christmas display at Gerry's house was no longer lit. Then I went back inside. The longer I stared at the house, the more my thoughts would turn to the events of last night. This was one unexplained death in which I did not want to be involved, other than as a witness. I knew Kanesha would come back with more questions before long, but once I answered them, I wouldn't do anything more.

Right, the little voice in my head said sarcastically, but I banished it and went into the kitchen to drink coffee and read the paper. Diesel went to the utility room to eat his own breakfast. Azalea would arrive momentarily, and mine would soon be ready, too.

Later, after I dressed for my day at work, Diesel announced his intention to accompany me by standing at the door to the garage and meowing. After bidding good-bye to Azalea, I led Diesel to the car, and we headed for the library administration building, which was located in an antebellum house that had belonged to the college for nearly a century.

Melba hailed us right after we entered the building, and Diesel and I went into her office to wish her good morning. "How are you?" I asked. "Were you able to sleep last night?"

Melba, busy petting and cooing over Diesel, didn't respond right away. Finally, she said, "I slept okay. Doesn't look like you did, though. Bad dreams?"

I nodded. "Bad, and strange. I was restless most of the night. Gerry's death really bothered me."

"You got to leave before I did, though," Melba said without rancor. "Must have been another hour before

Kanesha was finally through asking me questions. When I was done, I halfway expected that Jared would have gone, and I'd have to ask the police to take me home. Or come and wake you up to do it."

"Did he wait for you?" I asked.

"He did," Melba said, not sounding altogether pleased by that fact. "He drove me home, but he whined about it. Not so much about seeing me home but having to hang around that house until I was able to leave. Gerry's death really bothered him, too. I didn't think he knew her well enough to be grief-stricken over her."

"I don't imagine he did," I said. "I think you're forgetting that it hasn't been all that long since his wife died. When someone that close to you dies, you become more sensitive to death. I know I did. The worst of it goes away eventually. I imagine Gerry's death brought back painful memories."

Melba sighed. "You're right. I should have thought of that myself. I was a little frosty to him last night, so I guess I probably should call him and apologize. I was too tired last night to think much about it."

Diesel meowed, as if in sympathy, and Melba chuckled. "That's right, sweet boy. I was so tired, I think I fell asleep the second my head hit the pillow."

"I wish I could fall asleep like that," I said. "Did Kanesha learn anything interesting from what you had to tell her?"

"Who can tell with her? That poker face she's got." Melba shook her head. "She wanted to know about when and where I had seen Gerry at the party and if I noticed anyone behaving oddly." She paused to think. "Oh, and

she asked about a brandy snifter and whether I had seen
Gerry with it. And if she put it down anywhere."

"Did you see her with it?"

"Once, I think," Melba said. "I know I saw it on the
sideboard in the dining room once. It was sitting beside one
of those bizarre candlesticks she had. Did you see them?"

I shook my head. "No, I don't remember noticing the
sideboard, actually."

"The candlesticks were copper, pipes actually, fitted
together in a crooked pattern." She shrugged. "Not my
taste. Anyway, I saw a snifter sitting next to one of them
at some point. After you told me about Billy Albritton, I
think."

Hearing the councilman's name brought back the
memory of the moment I thought I saw him leaving Gerry's house last night. It was only a fleeting glimpse, and I
couldn't be sure it was really him. I didn't see him full-
face, after all. Should I have told Kanesha about it?

"What is it?" Melba asked. "Looks like you just remembered something."

I shrugged. "I caught a glimpse, a very brief glimpse,
of a man last night leaving the house. I thought it might
be Billy Albritton."

"I wonder if anyone told Kanesha about the argument
you saw him having with Gerry," Melba said.

"I never thought about it last night," I said. "Other
neighbors might have seen it, too. Gerry and Billy were
certainly loud enough. I suppose I should probably tell
Kanesha, though. Surely Billy didn't sneak into the house
last night to kill Gerry."

"I've never thought of him as that kind of man," Melba

said. "For a politician, he's always been reasonably honest, but you never know what can drive someone to kill. How did she die, anyway? There must have been something suspicious about it, since Kanesha was asking all those questions."

"Poison, I think," I replied. "But that's only a guess on my part. Kanesha wouldn't say for sure that's what she suspected. Only the usual line about waiting for the test results."

Melba looked thoughtful. "That's why she was so interested in the snifter. I didn't see anyone else last night with one. Did you?"

"No, all I saw were champagne glasses, or flutes, as Helen Louise calls them."

"I looked up *snifter* online this morning before I came to work," Melba said. "I only had a vague idea what one looked like. They're really different from the flutes, so there's no mistaking one for the other."

"If Gerry did leave the snifter unattended at some point, or at more than one point, anyone there last night could have added poison to the brandy," I said.

"That means the person brought the poison to the party." Melba shivered. "Talk about cold-blooded."

"Yes," I said. "Makes you a little sick to the stomach to think someone was roaming around last night with poison."

"How could the killer be sure that only Gerry would get poisoned?" Melba asked suddenly. "Did he know that she wouldn't drink champagne last night? Did she only ever have brandy?"

"Excellent point," I said. "I hadn't gotten that far yet, but you're right. In a way it was lucky for the killer, if he didn't know about it beforehand."

"Otherwise he'd have had to take a chance on putting the poison in the right champagne glass," Melba said. "I don't like that. I'd prefer to think he knew about the brandy snifter."

"I agree," I said. "Simply goes to show you, though, how vulnerable you are in a crowd like that. He could easily have killed someone else by mistake."

"Thinking about that is enough to give me nightmares," Melba said. Diesel chirped and Melba stroked his head fondly. "Sweet boy."

"This was premeditated," I said, thinking about the implications. "The poisoner must have felt he—or she—had a problem to solve, and killing Gerry was the best, or only, solution to it."

"Who *was* Gerry?" Melba said. "That's what gets me. Who knew her before she moved in to your neighborhood? Seems to me she popped up out of nowhere, but she had a past. Somewhere."

"Neither of us can say for absolute certain that she hadn't always lived in Athena," I said. "The fact that *you* didn't know her is strange, I'll admit, but even you don't know everybody."

Melba shrugged. "No, I know that, but given her age, you'd have thought we might have known her from school. She couldn't have been that much older than us."

I remembered what Betty Camden said last night and repeated it to Melba.

"She could be right," Melba said. "I did think that, when I saw her up close last night and the other day, she'd had some work done on her face."

"Really?" I said. "How could you tell?"

Melba rolled her eyes at me. "At your age, surely you've

seen other women, and even men, who've had plastic surgery."

"I probably have," I said, "but it's not something I give a lot of thought to. You really think Gerry'd had work done?"

"Yes, I do," Melba replied. "The skin on her face looked pretty tight to me, and that's not natural in a woman her age. She's not like some women I've seen, who've had their faces lifted so many times they can barely open their mouths wide enough to eat." She shook her head. "At that point it's so obvious, and to me that would kind of defeat the purpose."

"Gerry didn't look like *that*," I said.

"No, she didn't," Melba said. "But she'd had plastic surgery at some point, I'll bet you. That nose of hers was a little too perfect, if you ask me."

"People don't have plastic surgery just to improve their appearance," I said slowly, as a new thought struck me. "They also have it to alter their appearance and change their identity."

EIGHTEEN

||||||||||||||||||||||||||||||||||||||||||||||||||||||

Throughout the day, I returned to that particular idea—
that Gerry Albritton might have had plastic surgery at
some point in order to change the way she looked, perhaps
significantly. That might be why Melba didn't recognize
her yet thought there was something about her that
seemed familiar.

What about the name, though? If she'd changed her
appearance to look a lot different, would she also have
changed her name, taken on a fresh identity?

I kept telling myself that Gerry's true identity was not
my problem. Kanesha was the one who would have to
figure it out. I needed to mind my own business this time
and not get involved.

The puzzle intrigued me, though, the same way it did
in the mysteries I read. I always tried to figure them out
before the author revealed everything at the end of the
book. That was why I enjoyed classic detective-story

writers like Agatha Christie and Margery Allingham so much. I wanted to be able to analyze the clues for myself, put all the evidence together, and come up with the answer. In this case, however, I would not be privy to enough of the evidence to be able to figure it out myself. Kanesha would be perfectly happy, I was certain, *not* to have the benefit of my amateur sleuthing.

Despite not being able to banish thoughts about Gerry's death for very long periods of time, I managed to get my work done. Having Diesel as company during the morning improved my mood. We went home for lunch, and he wanted to stay there to watch the kittens when I was ready to come back to the office. I let him into the cage with them and reminded Azalea to let him out at some point before I got home.

Gerry's sudden death had pushed thoughts of the kittens' owner out of my mind. I thought about that briefly on the way back to work for the afternoon, but I soon found myself back to ruminating over the manner of her death. There were times I wished that my mind had switches on various compartments so that I could turn those compartments on and off. Especially the compartment that had trouble letting go of puzzles like the death of Gerry Albritton.

For a while I managed pretty well to keep to the task of cataloging, with only a couple of minor distractions. The first distraction came in the form of a text message from Melba to inform me that she was leaving the office early today and would see me tomorrow. I responded with a simple *OK*. An e-mail message marked *Urgent* provided the second one. A researcher at a university in Alabama was asking about one of the archival collections, and I was able to answer the questions easily and quickly.

By the time I was ready to close up shop, I felt satisfied with my productivity, and that put me in a good mood for the short drive home.

When I reached my block, I averted my gaze from Gerry's house. Christmas was only a few days away, and I didn't want to be depressed by looking at that sad display in her yard. The less I allowed myself to think about her and her odd death, the better for my peace of mind. Or so I told myself.

Diesel did not meet me at the kitchen door when I came in from the garage. I greeted Azalea, and she informed me that Mr. Cat, as she called him, was in the living room watching over the kittens.

"I'll go say hello," I said.

"Before you go you might want to take a look at what I found on the front door this morning." Azalea pointed toward a grubby-looking envelope on the table.

"What is it?" I went to the table and picked it up. I saw my name written in childish block capitals: *MR. HARRIS*. The envelope contained something with a little weight to it. I suspected coins.

"Went out to sweep the doorstep," Azalea said. "It was pinned to the door."

"You didn't see any sign of whoever left it there, I guess."

"No, I didn't. It was around ten when I went to sweep."

The envelope had seen better days. To judge by the outside, it had been dropped in dirt, perhaps more than once—although the child who left it had made some efforts to reduce the staining. I turned it over and saw that it was sealed.

I took care as I opened it not to let the contents spill. I extracted a small piece of paper, along with a five-dollar bill, a quarter, a dime, and two pennies. In the same block capitals, the child had written: *FOR THEIR FOOD*. I showed the note and the money to Azalea.

"That child at least has a notion of what responsibility is," she said.

"Yes, this isn't something I expected. I suppose she had to wait for her allowance." The gesture touched me, and I felt sad that the poor girl had had to give up the kittens she obviously loved. I had to find her and figure out a way for her to keep them, if that's what she wanted.

I put the money and the note back into the envelope and took it to the den, where I placed it in a desk drawer. I had no intention of spending the money. I hoped I would be able to return it soon. If I could only figure out how to find the child. That was proving difficult.

Then I remembered Melba's idea about setting up a camera to record activity at the front door. I doubted that today's note would be the last time I would hear from the child, so there should be opportunities to get her on video. I resolved to talk to Frank this evening, if he had time, to solicit his advice and find out what equipment I would need and how much it might cost.

I headed for the living room to check on Diesel and the kittens. Diesel would have heard me when I came home and was probably wondering where I was. When I walked into the room he looked up at me and meowed loudly. I greeted him and scratched his head, and he meowed again, but this time he sounded happier.

The kittens were quiet when I first entered the room, all napping in the back corner. But the sound of my voice woke them. They yawned and stretched, then scampered over toward me, mewing and making noises similar to Diesel's trilling. Ramses was the loudest, as usual. He seemed to be demanding to be released from prison.

"No, you little miscreant," I said firmly, pointing a finger at him. "I'm not going to let you loose in the house. Heaven only knows what you would get into if I did."

Ramses paid no attention to me or my admonitory finger. Instead he started trying to climb the side of the cage. Probably to put himself on eye level with me, I thought, the little hardhead. He managed to climb about three feet before his determination seemed to falter, and he hung there, continuing to meow.

The other boys, Fred and George, emulated Ramses and started climbing. The girls appeared to have no interest in climbing. They took the opportunity, while the boys were otherwise engaged, to head to the food bowls and have a snack.

I stayed and watched them for a good ten minutes. Diesel went up to the cage three times and batted at the boys' front paws, trying to encourage them to get down, I figured. Fred and George gave up, but Ramses hung there until I thought I was going to have to go inside the cage to get him down. Finally, however, he must have tired of the contest of wills, because he turned and jumped off.

I had to admire the kitten's force of will. Whoever ended up with him would have a battle royal on his or her hands. The name I had given him suited him all too well.

"I'll be back a little later," I said, "when it's dinnertime.

Come on, Diesel." He followed me out of the room and back to the den.

I checked the time. Almost ten minutes after four. I decided to call Frank to ask about the video setup.

He answered promptly, and after we exchanged the usual pleasantries—and information on the status of the world's most wonderful grandson—I explained what I wanted to do.

"I can rig that up for you," Frank said. "Won't take me long. I can probably do it first thing tomorrow morning, since I've finished grading finals. Is that soon enough?"

"Yes," I said, "but will I be able to find the equipment you'll need by then?"

Frank chuckled. "You don't need to buy anything. I think I can manage with what I have. If you decide at some later point that you want a permanent camera on the front door, then you can look into buying what you need."

"I really appreciate this." I knew better than to offer to pay him for his time and effort. Instead I would buy a couple of bottles of the wine he and Laura liked. They rarely bought it for themselves because of the expense. The bottles could be part of the Christmas presents I had already found for them.

"You know I don't ever mind helping you out," Frank said. "I'll be there before you leave for the library in the morning."

I thanked him again and ended the call. With that camera installed—if it did the job properly—I might soon have an answer to the question of the child's identity.

One thought did strike me, however. The child had lurked around the living room windows, probably more than once, to see how the kittens were faring. I had to hope she wouldn't be doing that tomorrow morning while Frank was here. I thought she was probably smart enough to figure out what he was doing, and that might scare her away.

Feeling better now that I had a plan to solve this one riddle, I found my mind irresistibly drawn toward another one. Who was Gerry Albritton? I would have accepted her at face value had it not been for Melba's dogged insistence that Gerry was not really a part of the extended Albritton clan. According to Melba, it was a large clan, and I suspected there could be offshoots that Melba knew little about. Gerry could have belonged to one of those.

For some reason I suddenly thought of property records. They were public, available through the tax collector's office. Even better, they were online, and I could easily search them to see whose name was on the deed to Gerry Albritton's house. If Albritton was not her legal name, only an assumed one, then her legal one would be on the deed.

I grabbed my laptop and turned it on. Diesel stretched out on the sofa beside me, and I stroked him while I waited for the computer to boot up fully.

I typed in the URL for the county website and followed the links to the property database. Options for searching included the owner's name, street address, and lot number. I used the street address. I certainly had no idea what the lot number was, and I didn't know what name was on the deed.

The record popped up on the screen, and I scanned it quickly. My eyes focused on the name of the owner.

Well, looks like Melba was right after all.

The owner's name was listed as Ronni Halliburton.

NINETEEN
||||||||||||||||||||||||||||||||||||||||||||||||||

I wondered if Melba knew any Halliburtons in the Athena
area. I would ask her later. At the moment I was wondering what to do with this information. Should I communi-
cate with Kanesha and tell her what I had discovered? Or
was this something she would have checked on herself?

Let's take it a step or two further.

I opened a genealogy database and searched for Ronni
Halliburton. I found many, many more results than I had
expected, and I started going through the list. There were
variant spellings for the surname: *Haliburton* and *Halybur-
ton.* I found Janes, Janas, and even Johns. The exact matches
on the name *Ronni Halliburton* didn't jibe with what I knew
of Gerry Albritton's age.

That was not an encouraging start. Next, I searched for
Geraldine Albritton, and once I narrowed down the results to search for the exact name, I was left with only a
few from which to choose. Again, none of the birth dates

worked for the woman I had known. She would have had to have been in her seventies or eighties to match these entries, and even if she'd had extensive plastic surgery, as had been suggested, I didn't think any surgery could take twenty to thirty years off someone's age.

Who was Ronni Halliburton then?

Was there a third, as-yet-undiscovered name for this woman?

Kanesha could get fingerprints and use those, I supposed, to find out whether the dead woman had a police record. That might yield her real name, but that was information I doubted Kanesha would share readily.

Next, I searched the name *Halliburton* on the Internet in conjunction with *Athena*. Turned out there was a Halliburton or two in the county, but not anyone I knew. Melba might know them, of course.

Recalling Gerry's interest in buying houses in my neighborhood, I went back to the county property site and did a search using *Ronni Halliburton* as the owner. This search yielded four results: the house across the street, two other houses in my neighborhood, and a house in another part of town.

I set the laptop aside and got up to retrieve a pen and a notebook from my desk. I jotted down the addresses, and when I had done so, I stared at the page. Now that I had this information, what was I going to do with it? I had adjured myself last night to stay out of this investigation, but I had allowed my curiosity to pull me in, at least this far. I revisited the question of whether I should share with Kanesha the information I'd found.

Another possibility occurred to me. What if Ronni Halliburton and Geraldine Albritton were two different people? Maybe Halliburton had the money and Albritton did the buying. That was certainly possible—not the first time the money person chose to stay in the background.

If they were two different people, though, it was odd that I couldn't find either of them, with any certainty, in the genealogical database. Surely there was a birth certificate—or two—somewhere. Not all birth and death records in Mississippi had yet been digitized. I knew because I had searched for my own online and came up with nothing. The records existed, no doubt. They simply weren't available online. I had no legal authority to obtain copies from the state Department of Health office. Kanesha could do that, I imagined, and would if necessary.

As if she knew I was thinking about her, I received a text from the chief deputy. She had more questions for me, the text said, and wanted to know when I was available to meet with her. I responded to let her know that I was at her disposal, and she answered that she would come to my house within the next half hour.

I checked the time. Nearly five o'clock. Azalea would be leaving soon, and that was just as well. Mother and daughter strongly disagreed over Azalea's continuing to work for me, particularly since Azalea could retire whenever she wanted. She didn't appear to want to, and that was fine with me. Considering the fact that they were almost exactly alike when it came to temperament and stubbornness, I didn't think this was a battle either would ever win. I didn't enjoy being caught in the middle. I certainly wasn't going to fire Azalea to make Kanesha happy, and I wasn't going to ask Azalea to tell Kanesha to back off. As long as they managed to maintain a truce, I would be happy.

"Come on, boy," I said to Diesel. "Let's go see if Azalea is still here. Then we need to give the little monsters their dinner."

Azalea was about to walk out the back door when we strolled into the kitchen. "Roast in the Crock-Pot," she said. "It's been cooking since first thing this morning. Give it another hour, and it should be ready." She nodded in the direction of the stove. "Mashed potatoes, green beans, and cornbread ready to be warmed up."

"Thank you," I told her. Azalea's pot roast was always a treat. "Have a good evening."

Azalea nodded. "See you in the morning. Bye, Mr. Cat." She headed out the door.

Diesel supervised while I prepared dinner for the kittens. He continued his supervision while I went into and out of the cage to exchange dirty dishes for clean ones filled with food, and then to freshen their water. The five of them ate like they hadn't had food in three days, though their round little bellies belied that.

We watched them eat for a couple of minutes. "Okay, Diesel, your turn," I said. He followed me back to the kitchen and into the utility room, watching closely, rubbing against my legs a few times, while I prepared his dinner and refreshed his water bowl. There were always stray hairs in the water when I refreshed it. I wished I could keep them out, but unless I changed the water every couple of hours, that was a useless wish.

Stewart entered through the back door from the garage and called out, "Hello, Charlie, where are you?"

"Right here." I stepped out of the utility room. Diesel remained there to scarf down his dinner.

"Have you figured out who murdered Gerry Albritton

yet?" Stewart opened the refrigerator and rummaged in it until he brought out a can of diet cola.

"Very funny," I said. "I don't even know for sure yet that she *was* murdered. It could have been natural causes."

"Do you really believe that?" Stewart popped the top on his can and took a long draught of soda.

"Well, no," I said. "I don't think it *was* natural, but I'm trying not to let myself get too involved in it."

"And how is that working for you?" Stewart cocked an eyebrow, and his lips twitched.

"Not well," I admitted. "So you can let up on the ragging. I can't help but be curious about what happened." I glanced at the clock. Kanesha would be here in a few minutes. I shared that news with Stewart.

He grimaced. "Unless she specifically wants to talk to me, I'd just as soon stay out of her way. I'm not in the mood to feel like a butterfly pinned on a board tonight. I'd better get upstairs anyway and get Dante ready for his walk. See you later."

He hurried out of the kitchen, and moments later I heard him running up the stairs. I looked down at Diesel, who had joined me in the kitchen. "Guess we'll have to talk to Kanesha alone." The cat warbled. He and Kanesha had warmed toward each other a little, but Kanesha still wasn't a big fan. Neither was the cat, although he didn't disdain her presence as he did with some people he didn't like.

I poured myself a glass of sweet tea from the fridge and settled down in my usual spot at the table to await Kanesha's arrival. The front doorbell rang about five minutes later, and Diesel accompanied me to let her in.

"Would you like something to drink?" I asked on the

way back to the kitchen. "Sweet tea? Diet cola? Or I can make some coffee. Won't take long."

"No, thank you, I'm fine." Kanesha took the chair to my right. Diesel trotted off to the living room, evidently preferring the kittens' company.

"If you change your mind, let me know," I said. "Now, I know you said you have questions for me, but I also have some information for you that could be potentially useful." I watched her intently for signs of her reaction.

Other than a slight quirk of her left eyebrow, she gave no other overt sign of irritation. "What kind of information?" She pulled out her notebook and pen and flipped through the pages.

"Melba Gilley no doubt told you last night that she was suspicious from the get-go about Geraldine Albritton not being who she claimed. Melba knows the Albrittons, and she insists there isn't a Geraldine among them."

Kanesha nodded. "Yes, she told me. Go on."

"Gerry put out flyers around the neighborhood, telling the owners that she was ready to buy their houses if they wanted to sell. I was curious about that. I was also curious to find out whether *Geraldine Albritton* was her real name."

"Let me guess," Kanesha said, a slight edge to her tone. "You searched the county property records and came across the name *Ronni Halliburton*."

I nodded. "I figured you already had the information, but in case you hadn't, I wanted to share it."

"I appreciate your interest," Kanesha replied, "but you don't have to feel compelled to help, you know."

"I know," I said, "but I'm fascinated by the question of who Gerry really was. If Albritton wasn't her name, was it Ronni Halliburton? I searched both names in a genealogical database and couldn't come up with a match for either. At least not a match to the right age."

"According to her driver's license—in the Albritton name—she was fifty-nine back in April," Kanesha said.

"If that's the case, then none of the records I found would fit her," I replied. "Who do *you* think she was?"

"For now I'm working on the assumption that she was Geraldine Albritton," Kanesha said, "unless and until I find evidence that the name was an alias."

"She told me she had lived in Athena all her life, but Melba is sure she was lying about that. I don't remember her, either, from when I grew up here. She was about four to five years older, so she was probably out of high school before I got there." Talking about high school gave me another idea. The public library had copies of the high school yearbook going back decades, certainly well before the time that Geraldine Albritton would have graduated. I would look through the appropriate years to see if I could find her under either name.

"You're going to check the old yearbooks at the public library," Kanesha said. "Aren't you?"

Was I that readable? I wondered. It was uncanny the way her mind and mine were synching. "Yes," I said.

"Don't bother. I'd really like to find some trace of her as soon as possible, so I'll put a deputy on it," Kanesha said.

"You don't know anything much about her, do you?" I asked, a little surprised.

"No, I don't," Kanesha said. "She just turned up in Athena one day, it seems. No roots, no checkable background, but she seemed to have plenty of money. If I can find out who she really was, I'll be able to find out who poisoned her, and why."

TWENTY

"That's really strange," I said. "She has a driver's license, though."

"Yes, but I don't quite know how she got one," Kanesha replied. "You have to have your birth certificate, two proofs of residence, and your Social Security card."

"Have you found a Social Security card or a birth certificate among her effects?" I asked.

"Not so far," Kanesha said. "If she has them, they're well hidden. They might be in a safe deposit box at a bank."

"Did you find any kind of legal documents?" I asked.

Kanesha shook her head. "We're still searching the house. I think something's surely bound to turn up before too much longer."

"Unless she paid cash for that house and the three others she bought, wouldn't there be some kind of bank trail?"

"Another angle we're looking into," Kanesha said. "This could be a tough one to crack, I have to say. No emergency contact information that I could find, other than that assistant of hers, Jincy Bruce."

"Does she know anything?" I asked.

"If she does, she's hiding it well," Kanesha said. "I'm going to be questioning her again, though. She must know something, even if she doesn't think it's important."

"For your sake, I hope so," I said. "You said you had some questions for me when you texted earlier."

"Right." Kanesha consulted her notebook. "First, have you remembered anything else about last night, some detail you might have overlooked?"

I hesitated. This was the point when I needed to tell her about the argument I had witnessed between Gerry and Billy Albritton—plus the fact that I thought I saw him leaving her house last night.

"There are two things," I replied. "First, there was an argument I overheard between Gerry and Councilman Albritton." I gave the few details I had to share, and she frowned.

"I wasn't aware that he knew her," Kanesha said.

"Melba talked to him about Gerry, and he swore up and down that he didn't know who she was," I said. "If he *wasn't* lying about that, then what was he doing having an argument with her? It wasn't too smart of him to let the neighbors see him with her if he's trying to deny that he knows her."

Kanesha snorted. "He's got a short fuse. In my experience, he usually acts before he thinks about the consequences. If he was really angry with her about something, he probably didn't stop to think about it."

"I don't know much about him," I said. "He doesn't represent this area."

"Count yourself lucky," Kanesha said. "You mentioned two things. What's the other one?"

"I think he—Billy, that is—might have been in the house last night during the party."

Kanesha's eyes narrowed. "When did you see him?"

"I saw him not too long before Gerry collapsed," I said. "Stewart and Haskell were ready to leave. I was standing in the hall with Stewart, and I looked over his shoulder to see Haskell coming toward us. Behind him, going out the front door, was a man I thought was Billy Albritton."

"Are you sure it was Billy?" Kanesha asked.

"No," I said with some reluctance. "I'm not prepared to swear to it. It was only a quick glimpse, and I don't really know him. I simply thought the man looked like him."

"Okay, let's think about this. Earlier during the party, did you ever see a man you thought looked like him?"

I thought about that, and I could tell that Kanesha was getting restless by the time I replied. "No, I can't say that I did. I mean, I circulated a fair bit, I suppose, and saw a lot of people, but no man who looked like that."

"Then it's possible you really did see Billy Albritton," Kanesha said. "And you saw him leave not too long before Gerry Albritton collapsed and died."

"Yes," I said. Now I was concerned that she was going to fasten on the councilman as her chief suspect. I had to admit that she had grounds for her suspicions, but she would have to have more evidence to go on than what I had provided.

"Haskell didn't mention seeing him," Kanesha said,

"though it sounds like he could have, if Billy had to pass by him to go out the door."

"I couldn't say," I replied. "You'll have to go into that with Haskell. He was ready to go home, and he may not have been paying attention. He was concentrating on finding Stewart, I think."

"Melba didn't mention him, either, when I questioned her," Kanesha said. "Are they friends?"

I shrugged. "Friendly, at least. I don't know that they're particularly *good* friends. You know Melba, she seems to know everyone. You're not thinking she could be protecting him by not telling you he was there, are you?"

Kanesha responded with a question of her own. "Did she know about the argument you overheard?"

"Yes," I said. "I told her about it earlier, during the party. That was my first opportunity to talk to her about it in person."

"Did she seem upset by it?"

"No, not at all," I said. "Simply curious, like me. She told me she would talk to him again, though, and try to worm the truth out of him."

A faint smile creased Kanesha's lips. "If anyone can, Melba can. It's a good thing she never went to law school. I wouldn't want to face her in court."

I had to laugh at that. "I wouldn't, either, and she's one of my closest friends."

"I'll have to talk to him," Kanesha said. "Even if you can't swear to it, it's a possibility I have to explore. If he was there, he had the opportunity to poison her drink."

Kanesha seemed to be in a cooperative mood, and as long as it lasted, I would try to find out what I could. "Did your deputies or the police ever find that snifter?" I asked.

"No. Whoever picked it up—and it had to be the killer, I think—managed to get it out of there without anyone noticing."

"Do you think the killer left the party then?" I asked. "Surely he wouldn't hang around."

"It would have been the smart thing to do," Kanesha replied. "I gathered from Ms. Bruce that guests were coming and going pretty steadily."

"Unless," I said slowly, "it would have looked odd if he was gone when the police arrived."

"How do you mean?" Kanesha asked.

I thought about that briefly. "Okay, here's a scenario. The killer has poisoned Gerry's brandy. He could have left right after he managed to do it, but he might have wanted to stay and watch. Have the satisfaction of seeing her die." *Horrible thought. So cold-blooded.* "If he did stay, he might have been having a conversation with a person or several people, and if he disappeared when Gerry collapsed, they might remember that and tell the police. It would look suspicious, wouldn't it?"

"To me it would," Kanesha said. "Good points. I'm going to be questioning a number of the guests for a second time, and I'm going to work that in. It might spark a memory."

"I have to confess that I have done my best *not* to think about last night," I said. "I wasn't totally successful, of course, but I didn't run through the events in my mind. I'll do that, though, and if I come up with anything else that might be pertinent, I'll let you know."

"Thank you," Kanesha replied. After scanning a couple of pages in her notebook, she stood. "I think that's all for now. You've given me a promising new lead, and I'm going to follow that up."

"Anything to help," I said as I saw her to the front door. I called to Diesel once the door was shut. "She's gone now, boy."

Diesel emerged from the living room and trilled. He followed me into the kitchen, where I checked the clock. Enough time had passed since Azalea left, I decided. The roast should be ready by now.

Diesel watched me closely while I ate. I knew he wanted bites of the roast beef, but he couldn't have any because of the onions Azalea put in the pot with the beef. Instead, I gave him an occasional green bean, and he made do with those. I really needed to stop feeding him from the table, but it was difficult to break the habit. Besides, he could put on the most pitiful look when he wanted something, and I felt powerless to resist.

After I cleaned up the kitchen and put away the leftovers, I thought about calling Melba to tell her about my conversation with Kanesha. Then I realized that Kanesha probably would not want me to do that. She might have already talked to Melba, but I figured if she had, Melba might have called me by now. I wished I could talk to Helen Louise, but this was one of her nights to close down the bistro. I wouldn't be able to talk to her until around ten or ten thirty.

I decided to spend time with the kittens. They needed more interaction with people, and I probably hadn't been giving them enough of that. I couldn't let all of them out at once because I might be up all night long trying to find them once they got loose. Instead I settled on bringing two of them at a time out of the cage and playing with them. Two I could manage, and Diesel played with them, too.

Two hours passed before I was aware of it, and I was

ready to turn out the lights and head upstairs. I left the hall light on for Haskell and Stewart. The latter had come back in with Dante and then had gone out again while I was talking to Kanesha. Diesel, after a visit to his litter box, came upstairs and joined me on the bed.

I picked up my current book and settled down to read. I had chosen an old favorite by Margery Allingham, *The Tiger in the Smoke*. I had read it at least twice already, but I've always thought that my favorites were worth reread-ing, and more than once. In a way, I considered it spend-ing time with a good friend. By doing this on a regular basis, I knew I was missing opportunities to read new books and perhaps discover new favorites, but the pull of old friends was irresistible.

I drifted off at some point. When my cell phone rang, my book lay atop my chest and my neck felt a little stiff. I grabbed the cell phone, vaguely noticing that the time read a few minutes past ten.

To my surprise, the voice on the other end was not the one I expected. Sean said, "Dad, sorry if I woke you, but I need to talk to you."

"What's wrong?" I came fully awake, terrified that something had happened to Alex and baby Rosie.

"There's no emergency," Sean said. "Only this is the first time today I've had time to myself long enough to call you."

I could hear the exhaustion and stress in his tone. "Alex isn't doing any better?"

"No," he replied. "I've been trying to talk to her about a nanny, but she says she won't listen and starts crying and saying I think she's a terrible mother. I just don't know what to do. I'm not sleeping, I'm up to my eyeballs in work with no end in sight, and I can't deal with Alex anymore. What should I do to help her? We can't go on like this much longer."

I had feared that the situation might come to a crisis point like this. Alex desperately needed help, but the poor child was so wrapped up in misery she was pushing away any attempt to help her. Always a high-achiever in everything she did, she couldn't cope with a situation she wasn't able to control. Her loved ones were going to have to intervene to solve the problem.

The question was, how?

TWENTY-ONE

I overslept the next morning by nearly three hours. Having been up until about two a.m., I couldn't drag myself out of bed at the usual time.

During my conversation with Sean last night I had suggested he call Alex's best friend, Caroline, right away and ask her to come to the house to talk to Alex. They had known each other since the fifth grade and had been like sisters ever since. I went over as well. Stewart was in the kitchen when I left, and I hurriedly explained where I was going and why.

At the last minute I decided to take Diesel with me. He was fond of Alex, and she of him. I thought his presence might help somehow.

Caroline was there when I arrived. She already had the situation in hand, as I expected she would. She was deeply shocked by Alex's condition. Alex hadn't said anything to her about her struggles. Caroline's husband's sister-in-law,

Anne Marie, was a therapist. Caroline had called Anne Marie to assist, and she arrived not long after I did. While I looked after Sean and baby Rosie, the two women took care of Alex. Diesel stayed with them for half an hour or so; then he came to find me and baby Rosie.

Much of the time I spent with my son was spent listening to his self-recriminations. Sean insisted on blaming himself for not having asked Caroline for help sooner. I didn't try to argue with him. Once he'd had a chance to rest and could see things more clearly, I would talk to him.

Anne Marie turned out to be a godsend. As Caroline told us later, the therapist dealt kindly but firmly with Alex and got her to agree to go to the hospital. Alex was badly run down and at the point of complete collapse. Around one thirty Sean and Anne Marie took Alex to the emergency room, and Caroline stayed with Rosie. She insisted that I go home, and knowing how capable Caroline was, I didn't argue.

The hospital planned to keep Alex overnight for observation and to also get her rehydrated; then they would let her go home. In the meantime there was stored breast milk at home for Rosie, along with formula if needed.

I felt depressed when I got up late the next morning. Christmas would be upon us soon, and Alex might not feel up to being with a large group of people. To celebrate without her seemed wrong somehow, but I knew she would feel guilty if she found out that we didn't because of her. I would figure something out. We could hardly all crowd into her bedroom to have a party.

I had completely forgotten that Frank was due this morning to install the video camera to monitor the front door. By the time I remembered and hurried downstairs to see if he was there, he was finishing the setup. I found him in the living room. The kittens were playing noisily, and Diesel lay beside the cage watching them. I rubbed his head briefly before addressing my son-in-law.

"Frank, I'm so sorry, I completely forgot you were coming," I said. "I didn't get to bed until two this morning."

He held up his hand. "It's okay, Charlie, you don't have to explain. Sean called Laura this morning to let her know what was going on." He shook his head. "Alex has been needing help, and it sounds like she's getting it. I feel bad for her and Sean. I feel incredibly lucky that Laura didn't go through this."

"Yes, it's been such a difficult time for everyone concerned," I said. "I hope Sean didn't stay all night at the hospital and then try to go to work."

"He came home for a while this morning. He told Laura that he didn't care if the office burned to the ground. He was going back to the hospital as soon as Azalea's cousin's daughter could get there to start looking after Rosie. Caroline has gone home but is planning to come back later."

"Then I won't call him. I'll wait until he calls me," I said. "He looked like he was at the point of collapse himself last night. I was afraid he might end up in the hospital with Alex."

"Now that Alex is getting the help she needs," Frank said, "I'm sure he'll bounce back pretty quickly. One thing I've learned about him and Laura is how resilient they both are." He smiled. "I think they take after you in that regard."

"Yes, they are resilient," I said. "Whether they take

after me is another matter." I decided to change the subject. "Everything is set with the video camera now?"

"Almost," Frank said. "We need to download an app to your phone and install it on your laptop, or the desktop if you prefer."

"Phone and laptop will be sufficient, I think." I gave him my phone.

While he downloaded the app, I retrieved my laptop from the den. Once he finished with the laptop, he showed me how to access any video from both devices.

"Pretty simple," I said. "At least this part is, anyway."

"It was an easy job," Frank said. "The camera is motion-activated, so it won't record unless movement triggers it. It will keep recording as long as there is some activity. There are actually two cameras. One is hidden in the wreath on the door. The other one is sitting in one of the shrubs, aimed at the living room windows."

"That's great," I said. "I hope the object of all this didn't see what you were doing."

"I don't think so," Frank replied. "I never saw anyone, and it took me only about three minutes to place the cameras outside."

"What about wires?" I said. "Are they visible?"

Frank grinned. "No, I used invisible wire."

If I hadn't still been so tired, I would have picked up on his meaning right away. As it was, I think I stared blankly at him until he said, "They're wireless, Charlie."

"Right," I said. "Sorry, I'm slow on the uptake this morning."

"Understood." Frank grabbed his tool bag and another bag that I presumed had contained the equipment he brought. "If you have any problems or questions, let me know. I need to get to my office at school to pick up something, and then I'm heading home to take care of Number One Son while Laura goes to the grocery store."

I thanked him again and let him out the front door. Diesel meowed at me, rather insistently, and I wondered what he was trying to tell me. Then I realized what it was. The kittens were overdue to be fed. I checked the time: nearly nine forty-five.

Azalea greeted me when the cat and I entered the kitchen. I apologized for being late, but she shook her head. "No need. I know what's going on."

Of course she did, I realized. Her cousin's daughter, whose name I couldn't recall at the moment, was now taking care of my granddaughter.

"You sit right down there and have some breakfast," Azalea said in her no-nonsense tone. "It's ready, and I know if you don't have your coffee soon, you won't be fit to talk to."

"I have to feed the kittens first," I said.

"I did that already," Azalea replied. "Didn't clean out those boxes, but you can do that after breakfast. Won't hurt them to wait a little longer."

Diesel meowed loudly at that, and I supposed he was seconding Azalea. I wondered why he had meowed so insistently a few minutes ago then. Perhaps he'd wanted me to get to the table because he knew he might receive a few bites of bacon, one of his favorite treats.

"All right, no arguing with that," I said. "Besides, I need coffee. I've got a good start on a caffeine-withdrawal headache."

Azalea set a full mug on the table in front of me, and I quickly added cream and sugar. That first sip went down like nectar—hot, reviving nectar. Next came a plate of scrambled eggs, grits, bacon, and toast. I ate like I hadn't eaten in three days, occasionally pausing only to dole out a little bacon to the cat.

When Azalea refilled my coffee, she said, "I called your work and told them you might not be in. Seems to me you could stand to take the day off and rest."

"Work." I groaned. "Thank you, Azalea, I completely forgot I was supposed to be at work today." I thought about staying home. Sean might need me for something—to talk, if nothing else. Until he called me, though, I wasn't going to risk calling him and disturbing his rest.

I might as well go to work, I decided. Even though I no longer worked full-time, I did stay busy enough that on days when I didn't work I sometimes felt at loose ends. Now that Helen Louise had cut back her work schedule, at least she was sometimes available and we could do things together. Today, however, she was working so that one of her full-time staff could take care of medical appointments for her child.

Accordingly, after I cleaned the litter boxes, I hurried up to the shower and got ready for work. Diesel wanted to stay home, and I let him in with the kittens. Azalea promised to let him out when he was ready. During the drive to work, I left a message on Helen Louise's cell phone, giving her a quick update on what I knew.

I made it to my office a few minutes after eleven. Melba was not at her desk when I entered the building. I would text her to let her know I had arrived, and I knew she would appear in my office sometime soon after that. I wondered if Kanesha had questioned her yet. I would take my cue from Melba. If she didn't mention that she had an interview with the chief deputy, I wouldn't talk about mine, either.

Text message sent, I settled down to work, firmly resolved to keep my mind focused on the tasks at hand and not to let it wander over anything else.

Melba appeared in my office a few minutes after noon, when her lunch hour began, and made herself comfortable in the chair across the desk from me. She held up a paper bag and a bottle of water, saying, "Mind if I eat while we talk?" Without waiting for a response, she pulled a sandwich from the bag and unwrapped it.

"No, go right ahead," I said a bit dryly. "How are you today?"

"Just peachy," Melba replied after swallowing a bite of her sandwich. "How about *you*? How come you're so late today?"

Azalea obviously hadn't shared the news about the late-night vigil and Alex's condition, although I had little doubt that Melba had tried to prize it out of her.

I gave her a brief summary of the situation, and her eyes filled with tears. "Poor Alex," she said. "I can't imagine what she's going through. This has to be tearing her apart. Sean, too." She dabbed at her eyes with her napkin. "If there's anything I can do, please let me know."

"Thank you. I know they'll both appreciate your concern. For now, I think we have to wait and let the doctors and nurses do what they can to help her get her physical strength back, and Anne Marie, I have no doubt, will be able to help her with her state of mind."

"Who did you say this Anne Marie is?" Melba asked. "I don't think I know her."

"She is the sister-in-law of Alex's best friend's husband.

His brother's wife, I believe. You know Caroline Pitcairn, right?"

Melba nodded and took a bite of her sandwich. When she swallowed, she said, "Used to be Caroline Jamison. I know the family."

"I was sure you would." I smiled. "I may leave early today, I don't know yet. Depends on when I hear from Sean."

"Heaven knows there's nothing urgent here," Melba said. "Andrea"—the library director and our boss—"left this morning for Texas. She's spending Christmas with her family."

"Safe travels to her," I said. "Are you still planning to join us for Christmas dinner?"

"Around one o'clock, right?"

I nodded.

"I'll be there, but if you change your plans because of what's going on with Alex, I'll understand," Melba said.

"At the moment we're not changing anything," I said. "That reminds me, though. I want to call Caroline in a little while to find out how things are going."

Melba, having finished her sandwich, delved into her lunch bag and brought out a slim tube of cheese encased in plastic. She swore it tasted good, but I remained dubious of processed cheese. Helen Louise, with her gourmet's tastes and knowledge, had weaned me off it.

"If Andrea is gone for the holidays," I said, "what are you going to do? Are you taking any time off?"

"Yes, the week between Christmas and New Year's," Melba replied. "By the way, this afternoon I have to be at the sheriff's department at one thirty. Kanesha wants to ask me more questions. To tell the truth, I'm not real anxious to talk to her and answer any more questions."

"Why not?" I asked. "You certainly don't have anything to hide."

Melba looked uncomfortable. "That's the whole point. I *do* have something to hide."

I couldn't believe I'd heard Melba correctly. What on earth was she afraid to tell Kanesha?

TWENTY-TWO

||||||||||||||||||||||||||||||||||||||||||||||||||||||||||||||||||||

"Can you tell me what it is?" I asked.

"It's about Jared," Melba said. "I think he knows more about Gerry than he ever let on."

"Why do you think that?"

Melba hesitated. "Something I overheard the other night made me a little suspicious. It was when she wanted to talk to him and pulled him away from me. Remember?"

I nodded. Melba hadn't been pleased with Gerry's behavior.

"You also remember I went over to them when I got tired of waiting for her to get done talking," Melba said. "I heard him give a little laugh and say, *Sure thing, honey.* Do you think that's her real name? Or was he just getting friendly? If it is her real name, he surely knows more about her."

"Are you sure *honey* was what he called her?" I asked.

"I thought it was," Melba said, "but it could have been

Lonnie or *Ronnie*, maybe. Why do you ask? What do you know?"

"I found the name *Ronni Halliburton* in the county property tax records as the owner of Gerry's house. Ronni Halliburton also owns three other houses in town."

Melba appeared dumbstruck by this information, and that—all humor aside—rarely ever happened.

"Look," I said, "if Jared knew the name *Ronni*, then he obviously does know something about Gerry's business, if nothing else. He knows that Gerry *was* Ronni. I know you like him, but if he's in any way connected to Gerry's death, you don't want to get involved with him. You have to tell Kanesha what you heard."

"You're right," Melba said. "I know that. It's just that I'm sure he'll know I'm the one who told Kanesha."

I understood how she felt, but she hadn't known this man very long at all. I thought she was being overly scrupulous. I told her that.

Melba heaved a large sigh. "I'll tell Kanesha what I heard. I can't believe Jared killed her, but you're right, I don't know him well enough yet."

"Are you going to see him again while the investigation is going on?" I asked.

"I don't know," Melba replied. "I'll have to think about that." She stood. "I'd better get downstairs. I have a few things to take care of before I go over to the sheriff's department. I'll text you when I leave."

"Okay, good luck." I watched her go. She was walking slowly and not with her usual energy. I hated that this was weighing so heavily on her, and I was concerned that the man she was so evidently interested in could be somehow involved in Gerry's death.

Melba's recounting of what she had heard prompted memories of the night of the party. Jared had seemed particularly unhappy about remaining in the house after the arrival of the sheriff's department. At the time I hadn't thought too much about the source of his unease. Simply figured that he was antsy staying in the same house with a dead woman, still deeply affected by the death of his own wife.

Now, however, I considered his behavior in the light of this fresh knowledge. Could he have killed Gerry and thus was uneasy about having to deal with the police and sheriff's deputies? I found it hard to reconcile this, however, with the cold calculation it took for someone to slip poison in Gerry's brandy and later steal the snifter to get rid of it.

That snifter was the sticking point. If Jared had taken it, what had he done with it? Unless he had slipped out of the house to stow it and then came back, I didn't see how he could have hidden the thing. He couldn't put it under his jacket. There would be no way to disguise the bulge the snifter would make. Ditto with his pants pockets. I should have thought to ask Melba whether he was gone from her side for any length of time after the murder occurred. Now was not the time to ask her that, I thought, when she was obviously so worried. I would wait.

I went back to my work and also back to doing my best to suppress any thoughts of the murder. I had Alex and Sean to worry about instead. As the minutes and hours passed, I wondered why I hadn't heard from Sean. At two o'clock I picked up my phone to call but, after a moment, put it down again. No, I didn't want to take the chance of waking him up. During his teenage years he could sleep twelve hours, sometimes more. He probably needed that much rest now.

I worked a little later than usual today, and thus it was a quarter after four when I locked my office and headed down the stairs. My phone rang as I was unlocking the car. I checked the caller ID. Sean. Hurriedly I slid into the car and shut the door against the chill wind.

"Hello, Dad." Sean sounded more himself. "Sorry I'm so late in calling, but I slept until about thirty minutes ago. I came home to have a shower and change clothes before heading back to the hospital. Caroline's gone home for now."

"I don't know what we would have done without her," I said. "You're feeling better?"

"Everyone is doing better. Cherelle is doing great with Rosie. She's agreed to move into the guest bedroom until Alex is back on her feet. We're hoping Alex will be home from the hospital sometime early this evening. In the meantime, Cherelle can be here for Rosie around the clock."

"That's great," I said. "A huge worry off my mind. Now, how is Alex?"

"I'm heading to the hospital in a minute. They've had her sedated, but she's supposed to be awake by the time I get there. She was obviously even more sleep-deprived than I've been. Resting and sleeping will help, plus getting the proper nutrition. I'll call you after I've seen her and give you an update."

"Give her my love and tell her I'll come see her soon, if they're allowing visitors."

"Will do," Sean said. "Thanks, Dad. I don't know what I'd do without you sometimes."

"That's what I'm here for," I said. "Go see Alex."

I ended the call, reflecting on the change in my relationship with my son. Since he'd suddenly appeared in Athena a couple of years ago, announcing that he had quit his job as a corporate lawyer in Houston and wanted to stay with me for a while, we had regained the closeness we'd had before his mother died. My son had shed the last vestiges of adolescence, and I had shaken off the isolation in which I had cocooned myself after my wife's death.

My phone pinged—a sound I didn't recall having heard it make before. Then I remembered Frank mentioned that he had set the video app to alert me whenever there was fresh footage to view.

I tapped the icon to open the app and stared at the screen, trying to remember what to do next. I tapped another icon, and a video opened. I saw a hand move in to rest on the sill. Then slowly a second hand joined it. In a jerky movement a head popped up quickly, but the head was covered by a black hood. All I could see was the hood. Evidently the child had it pulled close around her face, almost as if she knew she was being filmed.

The head remained in view for about twenty seconds before it withdrew. I waited to see if there was more, but the video stopped after another thirty seconds or so. I replayed the video, trying to discern any potential clues to the child's identity. All I discovered was that the child was a fingernail-biter. Every nail that I could see had been chewed on to various degrees.

I put down my phone in frustration. Either the child had seen Frank installing the cameras and took pains to hide her face, or she was extremely bright and had suspected all along that there might be a video camera installed for security purposes. Either way, it looked like I might not get any satisfaction from Frank's efforts.

Unless, I thought suddenly, I set a trap for her. I would give that some thought. I needed to find out where the kittens came from. They were old enough to be adopted out, if necessary, but if the child was able to take them home again, I wanted her to have that option.

The simplest trap I could set, I realized, was to leave another note on the door. I needed to place it so that the child might look into the camera on the door without realizing it. I closed my eyes and visualized the scene in my mind. I saw the child reaching for the note and snatching it from a crouching position.

No, that wouldn't work. I had to get the child to stand taller in order to get her face as close as possible to the camera. I would have to place the note higher up. I also needed to estimate the child's height. When I got home I could measure the height of the living room windows, watch the video again to get a reference point from the child's actions, and go from there.

As I was about to pull out of my parking space, my cell phone announced a new text message. I glanced at it and saw that it was from the pharmacy. My high blood pressure medicine had been refilled and was ready for pickup. I sighed. I hated having to take this medicine, even though it was a low dose. If I could only follow my doctor's advice and lose a bit of weight—and cut out some of the food I loved best—I probably wouldn't have to take it. I hadn't been on the medicine long, only for two months. I was due back in the doctor's office in another month for a check on my blood pressure to determine whether the dose was effective.

I debated picking the prescription up tomorrow or the next day. I had at least two more pills, as I recalled, for the once-daily dose. I might as well pick it up today, I decided, in case I forgot and woke up on Christmas morning to find myself without any.

Instead of turning the car toward home, I had to drive in another direction, toward the town square. Milton Harville's pharmacy occupied space across the square from Helen Louise's bistro and the independent bookstore, the Athenaeum. After a short drive, I counted myself lucky to find an open parking space directly in front of the pharmacy. Unlike many other small towns around the country, Athena had a thriving downtown area, and parking was often at a premium at this hour.

Two people waited in line ahead of me at the pharmacy counter, and the first of them, an elderly man, querulously demanded to know why the price of his medication had gone up. Jenny Harville, Milton's daughter, patiently explained the reason for the change—a matter of seventy-five cents, from what I managed to overhear. Finally, the man paid and left. The person right in front of me made no objection about the price of her several prescriptions and paid quickly. I stood at the counter next.

"Mr. Harris, how are you?" Jenny smiled. "And how is that gorgeous kitty of yours?"

"I'm doing fine, Jenny," I replied. "Diesel is doing fine, too, spoiled as ever."

"As he should be," Jenny said. "Why else do we exist, other than to serve our feline masters?" She laughed. Jenny, I knew, had a couple of cats of her own, both Siamese, and she doted on them.

"You have one to pick up," Jenny said, and I nodded.

While she retrieved my prescription, I looked around for her father. He appeared from behind a shelf in the dispensing area, staring at a bottle in his hand. When he looked up, he happened to glance my way. He came toward the counter.

"Charlie, have you got a minute? I really need to talk to you." Milton looked even more stressed than usual, and I wondered if Tammy had been in the store within the last hour. She always had this effect on him.

He obviously needed to talk, and though I was eager to get home, I knew I couldn't put him off. "Sure," I said. "Let me pay for my drugs, and we can talk."

Jenny shot a glance filled with suspicion at her father as she returned to the counter. From this I guessed that she didn't know what was worrying him. She rang me up, I paid, and then Milton motioned for me to come around the counter. He led me through the shelves to the small office he shared with Jenny at the back of the store.

As soon as we were in the room, I asked him what was going on. "I can tell you're worried about something."

Milton leaned against his desk and rubbed a hand across his eyes. He took a deep breath before he spoke. Then his words came out in a rush.

"I'm terrified, Charlie, so sick I don't know what to do."

"Why? What happened?"

He looked me in the eye, and I could see the fear.

"When we got home the other night after the party, I shut myself up in my den to try to cool off. Stayed in there a couple of hours before I felt like I could talk to Tammy without wringing her neck." He paused for another deep breath. "I couldn't find her anywhere in the house. I'm afraid she went back to the party and killed Gerry Albritton."

TWENTY-THREE

I nearly dropped my bag, I was so shocked by Milton's revelation. Could Tammy have come back into Gerry's house without anyone seeing her? If she had, surely someone would have informed Gerry, if Gerry hadn't seen Tammy for herself.

I had seen Milton often enough worried about, or angry with, his wife, but this was far more serious. He stared at me with such fear and agony in his expression, I wasn't sure I could do or say anything to help him.

Taking him by the arm, I led him around the desk to his chair. "Sit," I said gently, and he obeyed. He now seemed to be in a near-catatonic state as his gaze focused on the desk.

I perched on a corner of the desk after I pushed a wire inbox out of the way.

"Milton." He looked up at me. "Did you ask Tammy where she went?"

He nodded. "She refused to tell me."

"Do you have any idea when she left the house or how long she was gone?"

"Don't know when she left," he said. "Didn't come back for about half an hour after I came out of the den."

If Tammy had left immediately after Milton took refuge in his den, she could have been gone nearly two and a half hours.

"Why do you think she went back to Gerry's house?" I asked. "Maybe she went for a drive or to a bar until she thought you had cooled off. Maybe to a friend's house."

Milton shook his head. "She doesn't have that kind of friend. When she came back, she was wearing one of her wigs. Brown hair. And she'd changed her dress."

Another shock. That sounded really bad. If Tammy had taken the time to disguise herself, she might have been intent on getting back into the house, hoping no one would recognize her.

"She refused to tell you where she'd been?" I said.

"Yes."

"Did you ask her if she had gone back to the party?"

"Yes," he replied. "She still wouldn't answer. She just went to the bedroom and locked herself in. We haven't talked since. The last I saw of her, she yelled at me to get the hell out of the house and stay out."

"Does Jenny know any of this?" I asked.

Milton shook his head. "She knows I'm upset with her mother, but that's nothing unusual. I don't think she suspects how bad it is."

Poor Jenny. I couldn't imagine what it was like having to deal with her parents' contentious relationship.

"What are you going to do?" I asked.

"Besides talk to a divorce lawyer?" Milton said bitterly. "I meant it, you know, what I said to her after she attacked Gerry. She can't go on this way. She's got to get help, or I'm going to leave her."

"Is she an addict?" I asked, knowing that it was a horribly intrusive question. But Milton needed a friend. Looked like I had been elected.

Milton didn't appear offended by my question. "Yes, she is. Painkillers, mostly, but sometimes she drinks along with it. She hurt her back pretty bad doing yard work a few years ago, and ever since, she's been taking painkillers." His eyes met mine. "She's not getting the pills here, Charlie. Neither Jenny nor I would let her have any. She's not stealing them, either."

"I'm sorry that you and Jenny are dealing with this," I said. "Tammy has refused to get help?"

"Yes, no matter what Jenny and I do or say," Milton said. "She's been taking the pills so long, I think she's terrified of trying to live without them." He snorted derisively. "As if she has any kind of life living like this. I sure as hell don't."

Milton was a good man for sticking by Tammy this long, I supposed. I knew it was hard to get self-destructive people to change, and sometimes all you could do was walk away, if you wanted to preserve your own health and peace of mind. I thought Milton had reached that point, though he might not have fully realized it yet. I wished I knew what to say to him about this. Stating it outright would come across as brutal at the moment, and I hesitated to do it. I didn't think he was wanting that kind of advice from me.

I addressed another point instead. "Are you going to tell the authorities about this?"

"It's my duty, isn't it?" he said. "Even if she is my wife." He rubbed his eyes. "Maybe this is what it will take to get her to do something about those damn pills."

I didn't envy him the decision he had to make. I knew that he should tell Kanesha. I could do it for him, but I felt uncomfortable even at the thought. This was Milton's battle, and I suspected he would talk, or else force Tammy into admitting it to Kanesha herself.

"It might," I said. "There's another point, though, that could affect all this. You weren't there when Gerry collapsed, of course, but from the little bit I've been able to glean from Kanesha Berry—and my own observations—Gerry was poisoned by something that killed her almost instantly. If Tammy killed her, how did she obtain anything that lethal?"

Milton laughed suddenly, a little wildly. He sobered quickly. "From the garden shed," he said. "When she isn't strung out on pills, Tammy is out in the garden. That's why she has such a dark tan. People in the neighborhood consult her a lot, because she knows so much about chemicals. She has all kinds of hazardous stuff in that shed. Including sodium cyanide."

"Good grief, where does she get the cyanide?" I asked, remembering another situation where cyanide had come into play.

"She distills it herself," Milton said. "You probably don't remember this, but she has a degree in chemistry. Worked for a big company in Memphis for almost five years after we first got married."

I didn't think Milton needed me to tell him how bad things looked for Tammy. She went out of the house disguised, knew how to make a deadly, fast-acting poison, and had had a nasty confrontation with the dead woman. The circumstantial evidence was highly suggestive.

"You understand now why I'm so terrified," Milton said.

"Yes," I said, still stunned by the latest revelation. Could there be another explanation for why Tammy had disguised herself when she left the house? I thought of a sordid one, but there could be other, less sordid ones.

"Was this the first time, to your knowledge, that Tammy went out disguised like that?" I asked.

"No," Milton replied. "I've caught her doing it three or four times in the past few years. I think it has something to do with her sources for the pills."

That was the sordid explanation that had occurred to me. "Then isn't it possible that's what she did Tuesday night? Went out because she needed more pills?"

"I've thought about that myself," Milton said, "but I know for a fact that she got a fresh supply on Saturday." He sighed. "She thinks I don't know where she hides them, but I do. I've been tempted so many times to dispose of them, but I know that wouldn't stop it."

In the length of the time she had been gone from home on Tuesday night, she could have driven to Holly Springs or another good-sized town not far away. If Tammy hadn't needed pills, though, then she wouldn't need to don her disguise in order to meet a dealer or go to another pharmacy.

Back to the scenario with Tammy as the murderer.

"Doesn't look good, does it?" Milton said in a despairing tone.

"No, it doesn't," I replied. "If you told me all this because you wanted my advice—"

Milton interrupted me. "I do."

"Then my advice to you is to talk to Kanesha Berry. She's intelligent, and she's fair. If she isn't absolutely sure that Tammy is responsible for Gerry's murder, then she won't arrest her. But she needs to know about this."

"I know," Milton said. "Besides, somebody there might have recognized her, and for all I know, they've already informed Deputy Berry."

"Yes." I got up from the desk and placed a hand on Milton's shoulder. I squeezed it lightly. "This is really rough, I know, and I hate that you're having to go through all this. You're a good man, Milton, and you deserve better."

The look of gratitude Milton gave me touched me deeply. He looked more peaceful now. He had undoubtedly needed to unburden himself, and though I was not happy to know all the things about Tammy that I knew now, I *was* happy that I could help my friend by listening.

"Thank you, Charlie," Milton said, his voice husky from emotion. "You're a good man, too."

"I'm going home now," I said. "If you need to talk again, let me know."

"Thanks, I will," Milton said.

I looked back at him before I stepped through the door. He sat staring at the telephone on his desk. I turned and walked away, saying a prayer for him as I went.

When I left the store, I stopped beside my car while my eyes adjusted to the bright afternoon sun. Though the air chilled me, the sun was warm on my face. I took time to glance around the square, surveying the holiday decorations. The town council and the square merchants worked together every year to put up a beautiful Christmas display, and this year the square was as beautiful as ever.

Colorful metallic garlands wrapped around light poles, and oversized ornaments dangled from trees and light poles alike. Storefronts were also strung with garlands and festooned with holly. At night, multicolored lights would suffuse the square with a magical glow. In the middle of the square itself stood a stable, surrounded by the Three Wise Men, their camels, and assorted stable animals. I knew that inside the stable there stood a crèche in which the holy infant rested, while on either side of him his earthly parents knelt in prayer.

When I was a small child growing up in Athena, the displays weren't quite so lavish, but I remembered the excitement I felt when my parents would bring me to the square on Christmas Eve. We would walk around the square and check out the displays in each store window. After we made one circuit, my father would put me on his shoulders so that I could see over the crowd of other families who had also come to enjoy the sights.

Thanks to recent events, my Christmas spirit had retreated. I had too many worries on my mind to let the joy of the season work its usual magic. Now, however, with the vista spread before me, I started to catch the spirit again. I vowed that my family would have a joyous holiday, Alex included.

A loud voice and a quick toot on a horn roused me from my daydreaming. I glanced toward the street, where I saw a man in his car trying to attract my attention.

"Are you coming or going?" he asked in an easygoing tone. "If you're going, I could really use that parking space."

"Sorry, yes, I'm going." I smiled before I got in the car,

thankful that he hadn't been rude. As it was, I felt guilty enough for tying up the parking space longer than was strictly necessary. I backed out, and I saw in my rearview mirror that he moved right in. I focused on the street ahead of me.

Traffic was heavy around the square, and cars moved slowly through the four-way stops at each corner. While I waited for the cars ahead of me to move, I continued to glance around the square. Up ahead to my left I spotted the building that housed Jared Carter's dental practice and a couple of lawyer's offices. The young woman emerging from the building looked familiar, and as the cars began to move, I drew closer to where she stood by a parked car, talking on her phone.

She glanced my way, and I recognized her and waved. Startled, she waved back, as if by reflex, then turned away. I wondered if Jincy Bruce, Gerry's assistant, had been consulting one of the lawyers or if she had been to see the dentist. Given the fact that Jared had possibly known the identity of Ronni Halliburton, I suspected she might have been to see Jared. She had an expression similar to one I often sported after a session with my dentist— extreme discomfort.

Was it only a simple visit to the dentist, though? Maybe Jincy knew more about this whole situation than I had thought.

That idea led me to another one. Was Jared somehow involved in Gerry Albritton's real estate schemes?

TWENTY-FOUR

||||||||||||||||||||||||||||||||||||||||||||||||||||||||||||||||||||||||||||||||||

That constituted a rather big leap in logic, I told myself—
going from a chance, overheard remark at the party to a
connection between a prominent dentist and a secretive
real estate scheme.

If Melba had heard correctly, however, then Jared
Carter obviously knew something about *Ronni*. Was it
really a person's name? Or perhaps it was simply a code
word. There might not be a Ronni Halliburton at all, at
least in this case.

Kanesha had the resources to trace the true identity of
Gerry Albritton. I had no access to databases used by law
enforcement agencies, and presumably one of Kanesha's
deputies had checked the yearbooks by now. If Kanesha
couldn't turn up anything through her sources, though,
the mystery might never be solved. I needed to let go of
my curiosity over this investigation and stay out of Kanesha's way. I couldn't help but wonder, though, whether

Milton had picked up the phone and called her. Not my business, I reminded myself sharply, and concentrated on driving.

Finally, I got clear of the slow-moving traffic around the square and made my way home. The kittens would be clamoring for their dinner, no doubt convinced they would never eat again. I grinned as I pictured them. I had to admit that I was quickly growing attached to them, one in particular. But I reminded myself that I did not need six cats in the house. Two, maybe, but not six. Diesel had tolerated them all so far, even seemed fond of them, but he might not take to the idea of having them become part of the family.

Azalea had departed by the time I got home. I found a note on the fridge. She had already fed the kittens. I would have to thank her especially for helping with them. I suspected that she was fonder of them than she would be willing to admit. There was a tender heart protected by the gruff personality she presented to the world.

Diesel appeared quickly, and I listened to him meow and warble as he told me all about the kittens. If only I could understand him, I was sure I would be highly amused by what he had to say. I wondered if he was tiring of his self-imposed babysitting duties. Perhaps he was telling me that he wished I would hurry up and find out where the kittens belonged, so he could have the house to himself again.

After some stroking and a few comments from me, he ceased his vocalizing and trotted off to the utility room. I finished reading Azalea's note. She had left a shepherd's pie in the oven, and there was a fresh salad in the fridge. She had also made a lemon icebox pie, one of my favorites.

Was it any wonder I had high blood pressure and a

weight problem? I really should sit down with Azalea and have a talk with her about making some changes in the food she prepared for me.

Or I could stop being a slug and join the gym. Stewart periodically raised the subject, and I always put him off. I couldn't see myself working out in the gym, but I also hadn't had much success exercising on my own at home. Maybe I should let Stewart work with me. I'd think about it, but I wasn't going to do anything until after the holidays.

I wasn't quite ready for my dinner. I wandered into the living room to check on the kittens. I took them out of the cage by turns and spent half an hour playing with them and talking to them. While I did that, I also thought about the note I wanted to write and leave on the door for the mysterious child.

What if I took a direct approach and asked the child to talk to me? Would she be willing to do that? I would be perfectly happy to let her visit the kittens. If she happened to confide in me the identity of the man she'd referred to in her original note, I would promise to help her talk to him about the kittens.

Worth a shot, I decided. I put Ramses back in the cage with his siblings. Not for the first time I wondered how many different fathers had sired this litter. Perhaps two? I knew it wasn't unusual for litters to have multiple fathers. Since three of them were orange tabbies and the other two were dark gray, I thought two fathers was a reasonable guess. I had no idea what their mother looked like, so perhaps some of the kittens had her coloring while the others had the father's. Feline genetics was not one of my areas of expertise.

Back at the kitchen table, pen in hand, I composed the note that I would put on the door. I kept it simple. *I'm sure you would like to see the kittens and play with them. Can we talk? I want to help however I can. Thank you for the money, too.*

I read it through a couple of times. Simple, but to the point, I hoped. I made some calculations based on the height of the living room windows on the outside, then watched the video again to get some idea of how tall the child was. From these two factors I decided on how high to place the note.

With note, thumbtack, and yardstick in hand, I went to the front door and opened it. Diesel came with me and watched, curious as to what I was doing. I stood on the stoop and pulled the door nearly shut. I measured with the yardstick, and as I had anticipated, the point where I calculated the note should be was in the center of the large wreath, itself hung several inches above the center of the door.

I tacked the note in place and stood back to look at it. Unless I'd known where to search, I don't think I would have spotted the small camera hidden in the greenery of the wreath. I went back inside the house, and half a minute or so later my phone pinged to announce the availability of a new video.

I watched it once, amused to see that the camera had captured close-ups of my chest. Not so amused, however, to see the size and shape of said chest. Toned, I was not.

Half an hour later, finished with dinner, I was cleaning up after myself in the kitchen when my cell phone rang. After hastily wiping my hands on a dish towel, I grabbed the phone off the table and read the caller ID.

"Hi, son, how is Alex?" I said.

"Doing better. She's home," Sean said. "She's slept for over twelve hours, and even though she's a bit disoriented from some of the meds, I think she's a little better mentally."

"That's great," I said. "Do you think she's in any condition to have visitors?"

"Maybe by tomorrow evening," Sean replied. "Right now, they're keeping her calm with medication while we try to build her up again. I guess I hadn't realized how much weight she'd lost. She hadn't reached the point of malnutrition yet, but she was too close."

I had noticed the weight loss, and it had worried me, but recently Alex had taken to brushing off any inquiries about her appetite and her general state of well-being. I could only be thankful that she was now getting the care she needed.

"You need to catch up on your sleep, too, you know."

"I'm going to after dinner," Sean said. "Cherelle wants to make a run home to pick up some clothes and a few other things, so I'm going to take care of Rosie while she does that. I'm going to cook myself a steak, microwave a big potato, load it up with sour cream, butter, and cheese, and have a feast. Have you had dinner yet?"

"Yes, and as good as it was, yours sounds better," I said with a laugh. "Enjoy your meal, and give my beautiful Rosie a few kisses from her old grandpa."

"Will do, Grandpa," Sean said. "I'll call you sometime in the morning with another update."

"Thanks. I'll be praying for more good news. Good night." I ended the call.

Satisfied that I had properly tidied the kitchen, I turned

out the light and went to the living room to have a look at the kittens. Diesel and I watched for a few minutes while they tumbled and tussled with one another. They seemed perfectly happy in their corral.

In the den I settled on the sofa with Diesel stretched out beside me. I had recorded a program from one of the cable channels that I wanted to watch. I hoped a documentary on recent archaeological discoveries in Egypt would interest me enough to help me keep my mind off worries about Alex, concern for Milton and Tammy, and my interest in the murder case. Thanks to the writer Elizabeth Peters, I had become fascinated with ancient Egypt years ago.

I became engrossed in the documentary, and time slipped by. I checked my phone a couple of times, but no new video appeared. Perhaps the child wouldn't come to check on the kittens until the morning. She ought to be home getting ready for bed. It was nearly nine o'clock.

Helen Louise called at nine thirty. The documentary had ended a few minutes before, and I was surprised that she called earlier than usual. When I mentioned this, she explained that two of her evening staff were closing the bistro tonight.

"I'm glad you got away early," I said. "I know you're tired."

"About the same as usual," Helen Louise replied. "Do you have any update on Alex? I've been praying that whatever treatment they're doing is already making a difference."

"I talked to Sean a few hours ago," I said. "Alex is home now. Sean seems to think she has improved. She slept for over twelve hours, he said."

"I'm so glad," Helen Louise said. "I've been so worried about her. I tried talking to her one day last week, but she got upset, almost hysterical, and it was all I could do to calm her down again. She kept talking about Rosie being colicky. She seemed so worried that the baby wasn't getting enough to eat. It's a good thing Sean acted when he did."

"I've been worried, too. I would never tell Sean this, of course, but I had hoped he would do it sooner, before Alex got quite this bad," I said. "But I think she finally frightened him badly enough he did what had to be done."

"To be fair, I don't know that Sean was thinking all that clearly himself," Helen Louise said. "From what I gathered, he wasn't getting more than a few hours' sleep a night. That kind of sleep deprivation can wreak havoc with your thinking processes."

"Yes, you're right," I said. "He was not in the best shape himself last night when I got there. Thank the Lord that Azalea's cousin's daughter Cherelle was looking for a job. Sean says she's great with Rosie."

"I believe that's Lurene's daughter," Helen Louise said. "She worked for me for one summer a few years ago, and I was sorry when she left. Hard worker, always on time, learned quickly. But she left when school started again. She had saved enough money to get her through the school year, and she wanted to concentrate on her education."

"She seems to have a way with babies," I said, "and for that I'm powerfully grateful."

"Change of subject here," Helen Louise said. "What's the latest on Gerry Albritton's murder? I've been itching to call you all day, but we were too busy."

I brought her up-to-date on my discovery of Gerry's

house purchases, my conversations with Kanesha and Melba, and my spotting Jincy Bruce coming out of the building where Jared Carter had his dental practice. I did not mention my conversation with Milton Harville. He had spoken to me in confidence, and I didn't feel comfortable sharing that with anyone, not even Helen Louise, until Milton either told Kanesha about it or gave me permission to tell her.

If Milton had talked to Kanesha, the investigation might soon end. *If* Kanesha determined that Tammy was the killer, that is. I hoped Milton had made the call, but I had no way of knowing unless he told me himself or Kanesha shared the news. I considered going by the pharmacy the next day to check in on Milton. He would surely tell me then, unless he was afraid to face me after his confession today.

What would I do if I found out he hadn't called Kanesha?

TWENTY-FIVE

<!-- ||||||||||||||||||||||||||||||||||||||||||||||||||| -->

Wrestling with that question and the ethical dilemma it posed kept me tossing and turning in the bed for a couple of hours. Diesel, disturbed by my restlessness, meowed a few times and sat by my shoulder. Finally, he jumped off the bed and trotted out of the room. I figured he was going downstairs to visit the kittens and give me time to settle down.

I didn't want to violate Milton's confidence, although he had never asked me not to tell anyone else. If Tammy *hadn't* killed Gerry, then what she did that night was none of my business. That was a matter for her and Milton to work out. If, however, Tammy *had* killed Gerry, she should be arrested, and the due process of the law would follow. At least the court might take her long history of addiction issues into account during the trial and particularly the punishment phase.

I finally decided that I would go see Milton again in

the morning and talk to him. If he hadn't called Kanesha, I would urge him to do so. If he refused, then I would have to tell him that I felt I had no choice but to talk to her myself. Unless she told me that she had solved the case and was confident that she had identified the murderer, I would have to reveal what I knew about Tammy.

With that decision made, I was finally able to settle down and go to sleep. When the alarm went off at the usual time the next morning, I woke with a slight head-ache from the tension in my neck and shoulders. Diesel had returned sometime during the night. He regarded me sleepily when I sat up and turned on the bedside light.

I checked my phone to see if I had missed an an-nouncement for a new video, but I had not. Perhaps the child would appear this morning. I wondered if the app could be set to ping when it started recording, not only when it finished. I would text Frank later to ask. I should have thought of it sooner. If it pinged when it started re-cording, and I was home, I might be able to get to the door in time to see the child directly.

I could take my time this morning. Normally I would have to get ready for my volunteer day at the Athena Pub-lic Library. The library was closed today until after Christmas, however, so I had a free day. I had a few last-minute errands to run, in addition to a stop by the phar-macy to talk to Milton, but I didn't have to rush out the door as early as I usually did on a Friday.

I pulled on a robe over my gym shorts and T-shirt and headed downstairs for coffee. Azalea would arrive soon to cook breakfast. Besides coffee, I wanted to feed the kittens and take care of their litter boxes right away. Thankful for automatic coffeemakers, I poured myself a mug and doctored it with the usual mix. After a few sips I felt able to face the kittens and their litter boxes.

Ten minutes later I was done with kitten care. Diesel refused to come out of the cage when I finished. I left him with the playful quintet and went to fetch the newspaper. The note I had left last evening remained in place. Back in the kitchen, mug in hand, I ignored the ping from my phone. I was in no hurry to see a video of my bathrobe-clad self.

Azalea arrived soon after, while I was still engrossed in the newspaper—the comics, actually. I was one of the dinosaurs who still enjoyed reading the newspaper in print every morning. I discovered that Azalea already knew about Alex's progress in the hospital. Sean had told Cherelle, Cherelle had told her mother, and Lurene had told Azalea. The small-town grapevine at work.

Azalea, knowing that I wasn't working today, made biscuits for breakfast. By the time they were ready, Stewart and Haskell, fresh from the gym, joined me at the breakfast table. I asked Haskell how the investigation was progressing. I knew any information he shared would be only whatever Kanesha approved. I was intrigued when he mentioned that they had a new lead.

"Someone called yesterday to give information that might be pertinent to the case," Haskell said. "Kanesha will be following up on it today." He regarded me blandly, and I wondered whether he was referring to Milton Harville, who might have told Kanesha he had talked to me before calling.

"That's good," I said. "I hope it will lead to an arrest, if it's really pertinent."

"You know my boss," Haskell said. "She doesn't get

excited over anything. This new lead could be a blind alley. Until she has the autopsy and toxicology reports, she can only do so much."

"Once she knows how Gerry was killed," I said, "that should narrow down the suspects, I should think. It would be a matter of who had access to the particular poison used, right?"

Haskell nodded. "We can make an educated guess. A couple of witnesses saw her take the last drink from the glass and her reaction. Whatever it was, it hit her fast."

Haskell probably knew more than he was telling, but I wouldn't press for details. If Kanesha hadn't wanted me to know even as much as he had shared a moment ago, he wouldn't have told me. My heart sank, however, because it sounded to me like cyanide poisoning, and I remembered Milton's confession that Tammy knew how to make it herself. Looked to me like the evidence was piling up strongly against her.

Haskell drained his coffee and pushed back his chair from the table. "Thanks for breakfast, Azalea," he said. "I'm ready to face the day at work now." Azalea acknowledged his thanks with a brief smile, and Haskell headed upstairs to dress.

"What's on your agenda today, Charlie?" Stewart asked.

"I have a few errands to run, last-minute stuff for Christmas," I said. "Is there something I can do for you?"

"No, I'm good," Stewart said. "I'm not planning to get out of the house today, except maybe a quick run to campus to pick up something in my office. I'll be happy to keep an eye on Diesel, if you're not planning to take him. The kittens, too, of course."

"Diesel will be staying here. Thanks, I appreciate that,"

I said. "I'm sure Azalea will be pleased, too. One less thing I have to burden her with."

"The Lord knows I surely don't mind checking on those babies from time to time," Azalea said on her way out of the kitchen to head upstairs.

Stewart grinned at me. "Lo, how the mighty have fallen. I'd be willing to bet she'll adopt one of those kittens."

"That's a sucker bet." I smiled back at him. "I won't be gone more than about an hour and a half, I think, so you won't be on duty all that long."

"No problem," Stewart said. "Take as long as you want. When are you going?"

"Not for a while," I said. "The stores won't be open until nine. I want to get in and out as quickly as I can. I'm sure things will be chaotic because of other last-minute shoppers like me."

"Tomorrow will be much worse," Stewart said. "Be thankful you don't have to enter a mall to do your shopping. It will be hard enough to find parking spaces on and around the square today and tomorrow."

"Yes, it will." I grimaced. "I don't know why I put myself through this every year. You'd think I'd have learned by now to get things done sooner so that I didn't have to deal with the crowds and parking issues."

"There's always next year." Stewart laughed and pushed back his chair. "Shoot me a text when you get ready to leave. I'll be upstairs until then."

"Will do," I said. By force of habit I got up and started to clear the table. Then I realized I should stop. When Azalea was in the house, the kitchen especially was her domain. Any cleaning to be done, she insisted on doing. Though it pained me not to pick up after myself, I knew better than to cross Azalea. I couldn't bear that one expression she had that made me feel like a no-good ten-year-old who's just been caught stealing from the cookie jar.

By five after nine I was ready to sally forth. I texted Stewart to let him know I was leaving, told Azalea I should be back in plenty of time for lunch, gave Diesel a few scratches on the chin, and then made for the car.

My first stop took me to the square and the independent bookstore, the Athenaeum. The owner, Jordan Thompson, had notified me by e-mail that the books I had ordered had come in. Since they were intended as Christmas presents, I had to pick them up today if I wanted to get them all wrapped and ready to go under the tree tomorrow. Luckily I found an empty parking spot near the bookstore.

I spent an enjoyable half hour in the Athenaeum. I chatted with Jordan when she wasn't helping other customers, and as usual, I left with more in my bags than I had intended to buy. Jordan always had such excellent suggestions, and I almost always succumbed. She hadn't steered me wrong yet.

Among the purchases in the two large bags I took out of the store were board books for my grandchildren. Neither was even a year old yet—they were only a few months old, in fact—but I believed it was never too early to start reading to your children. My wife and I had read to Sean and Laura when they were infants and well after the time they were able to read for themselves. Books were important to us, and our children loved books and reading, also. Both were excellent students in school, graduating near the top of their respective classes, and I was convinced that being lifelong readers had played a big part in that success.

Next I went to the pet supply store, where I spent another half hour, if not slightly more, browsing for cat toys for Diesel and the kittens. I knew some would think me foolish for buying Christmas presents for the cats, but I probably wouldn't like those people anyway.

I had intended my final stop to be a department store, where I could purchase perfume for Helen Louise. I knew her favorites, and I knew the department store would have them. I decided to go to the pharmacy instead because Milton carried similar stock. The perfume purchase would serve as a good reason for my going there.

This stop brought me back to the square. My parking luck had run out. I finally found a spot on one of the side streets, a good five-minute walk from the square. I put my purchases in the trunk, a habit acquired long ago in Houston, where you didn't dare leave things in plain sight. I hadn't heard reports of car break-ins during the holidays in Athena, but I didn't want to have to report one on my own behalf.

The pharmacy wasn't crowded, but there were a good dozen other shoppers roaming the aisles. I located the two fragrances that I knew Helen Louise preferred, chose the bottles, and took them to the pharmacy counter to pay, instead of the counter near the front door. Jenny Harville waved to me from the dispensing area, and an assistant rang up my purchases. From what I could see, Jenny had a strained look, as if she hadn't slept well. I didn't see Milton anywhere.

After I paid the assistant for my purchases, I stepped to one side to let the next customer take my place. I observed Jenny for a moment. I hated to interrupt her, but if Milton was here, I wanted to talk to him. I called to Jenny, and she looked up inquiringly.

"Is Milton here this morning?" I asked.

"No, he's not." Jenny came from the dispensing area and moved a few steps toward the counter. "Is there anything I can help you with?"

"No, it's your father I really need to talk to. Do you know when he'll be in?"

"I'm not sure." Jenny regarded me for a moment, then seemed to come to a decision. She walked all the way to the counter, then toward the end, away from the cash register. I moved down.

Jenny spoke in a low voice. "I think Dad must have told you about my mother."

I nodded. "He confided in me yesterday."

"He's at the sheriff's department with her. He told her she had to go with him, or he would call the police to come to the house and pick her up." Jenny looked suddenly miserable. "I can't let myself believe that Mother would deliberately poison somebody, but she has these rages, and we can't do anything with her. I'm afraid she's going to jail."

"I'm so sorry, Jenny," I said, my heart aching for her. "I know this is tough, but your father really had no choice. I don't want to believe that Tammy killed anyone, either. If she didn't do it, Kanesha will not hold her responsible.

This experience might scare your mother enough to do something about her problem."

"Lord, I hope it will," she said. "Dad and I are so numb from years of dealing with her that we can't take much more."

She looked ready to start crying, and I knew she wouldn't want to break down in front of the customers.

"Try to focus on your work for now," I said, "and pray for your mother. It's out of your hands, so concentrate on being there for your dad and taking care of your customers and making sure they get the medicines they need. That's important."

Jenny smiled. "Thank you, Mr. Harris. I will do that."

On the way to my car, my cell phone sounded. I pulled it out and found a text message from Kanesha. She had new information and wanted to talk to me. She also asked if I could come to her office sometime in the next thirty or forty minutes.

I responded to say I would be there in less than ten.

I hurried to the car, put my newest purchases in the trunk, then drove to the sheriff's department a few blocks away.

By now the deputies and personnel at the front desk knew me, and the deputy on duty today simply waved me on to Kanesha's office. I headed down the hall.

Kanesha's door was open, but I knocked to alert her to my presence. She seemed engrossed in her computer. She turned toward the door, frowning. The frown didn't go away, but she motioned me in and asked me to shut the door.

"You'd better sit down," she said. "What I've got to tell you is pretty shocking. Threw me for a loop, I can tell you."

Alarmed, I almost stumbled into the chair and sank into it. I had never heard Kanesha say anything like this. "What is it?"

Kanesha said, "Got a short prelim report from the autopsy. Minimal information, but one significant thing. Gerry Albritton was born a male."

TWENTY-SIX

▮▮▮

Looking back, I felt grateful that Kanesha had warned me to sit before she shared her news. I didn't know when I had been more shocked than I was at hearing that Gerry was evidently transgender. My mind began to clear, however, and questions occurred to me.

"She must have had surgery, correct?" I asked.

Kanesha nodded. "The information is only preliminary, like I said, but the pathologist estimates that it was done at least twenty years ago, probably longer."

"I would never have guessed," I said.

"In addition, she'd had plastic surgery on her face, but it's difficult to say how extensive it was."

"Maybe that's why Melba thought she looked familiar. She might have known Gerry as a man, but she would never think to link the man she knew with Gerry."

"For the moment, I don't want this to go any further," Kanesha said. "That's a good point, though, about Melba.

I might consult her on this to see if she can come up with potential names for me to check on."

"I won't say anything to Melba," I said, "or to anyone else, though I don't think I've ever sat on information this sensational before."

"It's a twist I would never have expected," Kanesha said. "I'm still trying to wrap my head around it and figure out all the implications for her murder."

"It will certainly add to the list of potential motives, I should think," I said.

"*If* the killer knew it," Kanesha said.

I felt chagrined. "Of course. I wonder if anyone involved in the case knew anything about her past."

"So far no one has admitted to it," Kanesha replied. "Finding out who this woman used to be may be an impossible task."

"There must be a link *some*where," I said. "Unless she systematically destroyed everything that could provide that link."

"It's possible she did," Kanesha said. "I never met the woman when she was alive, so I really don't have a grasp yet on her personality. Give me your take on her."

"Let me think a minute." I recalled my meetings with Gerry and tried to put together some cogent thoughts to share with Kanesha. What had Gerry's personality really been like?

"The first thing I'll say," I told Kanesha, "is that Gerry was hard to read. She came across as brazen." I gave a short description of the first time I met the woman. "At the time I was a bit freaked out, I guess, at her flirting. It's not anything I'm used to. That put me off, I have to say, and I tried to stay away from her after that."

"Did you see her again before the party?" Kanesha asked.

"A few times when I was out with Diesel, walking to work," I said. "I always made the excuse of needing to get to work, though, so I could keep the conversations short. She wasn't as flirtatious at those meetings." I thought for a moment. "I also saw her the morning of the party. Someone had destroyed her decorations, and she was outside looking at the damage. I walked over to talk to her."

"Did she have any idea who had caused the damage?" Kanesha asked.

"She said she had a few ideas, but she didn't mention any names," I said. "She asked me a few questions, like whether I was interested in selling my house and whether Helen Louise owned her building. Then she got a text message, and not long after that I left."

"Before you went to the party, how would you have summed her up?" Kanesha asked.

"Forceful. Determined. Attractive. Intelligent." I grimaced. "I didn't think a lot of her taste in interior—or exterior—decoration. The inside of her house is way too modern for my taste, and that Christmas display is unbelievably tacky."

"I agree with you on that," Kanesha said. "Do you think that was deliberate?"

"I don't know for sure, but I suspect it was," I said. "I think she liked being provocative. She obviously had courage, too."

"Why do you say that? About courage," Kanesha said.

I took a moment to think about how to express what I meant. "I don't completely understand what brings a person to the realization that she or he was born in the wrong body, so to speak. I haven't experienced it myself, and no one that I'm really close to has, either. But I think to act on that realization, especially to face the necessary surgeries and other treatments, takes a lot of courage. If Gerry faced all that successfully, I don't think she'd balk at much else, do you?"

"No, I think you're right," Kanesha said. "I hadn't thought about it that way, frankly."

"I have a question for you now," I said.

"Go ahead," Kanesha replied.

"Why did you share this particular bit of information with me?" I said. "You're not always forthcoming on the details of the cases you're working on when I'm around."

"No, I'm not," Kanesha said. "This case is so different from any other I've worked. I'm great at solving problems and pulling together and interpreting evidence. Intricate police work is what I'm really good at, but sometimes you make these imaginative leaps that pull things together into a picture I hadn't quite grasped yet. Do you understand what I mean?"

"I do, and I'm extremely flattered," I said. "I'll be honest with you: Everything seems jumbled most of the time, but then suddenly the pieces shift, and I can see everything in a different way. It's hard to explain, but it just happens."

Kanesha smiled tiredly. "I wish I could get it to happen. The thing is, I'm hoping you'll be able to do that in this case. I need every bit of help I can get if I'm to have any hope of solving it."

"All I can say is, I'll do my best," I replied. "Whatever information you do have about her life, I'll need to see, however."

"I believe you now know pretty much everything I

know at this point," Kanesha said, "but I'll put together a summary for you and e-mail it later. How's that?"

"Sounds good," I said. "Are you still working on the assumption that she was killed by poison put into her snifter of brandy?"

"Yes," Kanesha said. "I have a deputy working on compiling statements from witnesses. I want to be able to track her movements and those of the snifter during the party, but that's going to take some time. Before I forget, I want to thank you for encouraging Mr. Harville to bring his wife in. That was an interesting story they told."

"I'm relieved that Milton realized how important it was to tell you, and that Tammy agreed to come with him. Is Tammy still a suspect?" I asked.

"She claims to have an alibi for the time she was absent from her home—an alibi that also allegedly explains her use of a disguise. I'm considering her a suspect until her alibi can be corroborated. Plus, we're going through statements from witnesses at the party to see if anyone mentions seeing her or a woman fitting the description of the disguise she was wearing. All this is going to take some time, given some of the details I'm not at liberty to share."

"What about Tammy's expertise in chemistry?" I asked, not quite ready to move on. "According to Milton, she knows how to make her own cyanide for use in gardening."

"They told me that as well," Kanesha replied. "It is an extremely important point, but if her alibi pans out, well, it becomes moot."

I figured I wouldn't get any more out of her about Tammy, at least for now. I wondered whether Tammy's alibi had anything to do with her procuring more pills. Unless Milton or Tammy herself enlightened me, I probably wasn't destined to know.

"I presume you've been through Gerry's papers," I said. "Did you find anything that could shed light on this?"

"We're still going through all her effects, including her papers," Kanesha said. "We haven't found a will. We don't know yet who her lawyer was. She had to have one for the real estate deals, but the odd thing is, in searching her home, we haven't found any contracts, deeds, mortgage documents, leases, or anything else that relates to real estate."

"That is very strange. I've been curious about the source of the money she used to buy four houses," I said. "The three in my neighborhood, for example. None of them is a mansion, but they're all on decent-sized lots and two of them are three stories. According to the values I found on the county property tax website, those three are worth, collectively, over six hundred thousand dollars. The other house isn't in as good a neighborhood, as far as real estate values go. I think it is valued at about a hundred and five thousand."

"Close to three-quarters of a million total," Kanesha said. "If she bought them outright, without mortgages, that's a lot of money to throw down in a short space of time." She shrugged. "But she might have made down payments and planned to pay the mortgages every month until they sold."

"The fact that you haven't found any kind of paper trail for her real estate deals has given me an idea, and it has probably already occurred to you," I said.

Kanesha nodded. "Yes. Someone else supplied the money and stayed in the background, while Ms. Albritton made the deals."

"Exactly," I replied. "I've had an idea about who that could be. Did Melba tell you what she overheard Jared Carter say to Gerry at the party?"

"When Ms. Albritton pulled him aside?" Kanesha said. "She did, but I'd have to dig out my notebook to see exactly what she told me. Right now I'm drawing a blank."

"It's not much to go on," I said, now feeling uncertain about my hunch. It was really nothing more than that.

"That's okay," Kanesha said. "In the past your *not much to go on* has usually turned out to be on the mark."

"All right. Melba heard Jared say, *Sure thing, Ronni.* Now, Melba heard the word as *honey*, but the room was full of people talking pretty loud. I think Jared must have said *Ronni*, as in *Ronni Halliburton*, the name on those deeds. If he knew that name, maybe he knows a lot more about the real estate transactions."

"I think you're onto something," Kanesha said. "At least it's a potential lead. One more than I had before."

My cell phone chose that moment to ping, startling me and causing Kanesha to frown.

"What was that?" she asked.

I pulled the phone out of my pocket and held it up for her to see. "That noise is a signal that I have a new video from the surveillance cameras Frank installed at my house."

"Surveillance cameras?" Kanesha said, obviously puzzled. "Why do you need to surveil anything?"

"The kittens," I said, busy locating the app on my phone. Once I found it and opened it, I pulled up the video and played it.

"You're recording the kittens?" Kanesha asked, beginning to sound irritated.

"No, not the kittens themselves," I said as I watched the video. "Cameras are set up on the front door and in the shrubs under the living room windows."

"Trying to get video of the kid who left the kittens, in other words," Kanesha said. "That makes more sense."

The video showed the same dark hood pulled close around the child's face. Her head came up out of the shrubbery so she could see the kittens in their cage through the window. She stayed in that position for nearly a minute, according to the video timer. Then the head disappeared briefly. It reappeared in front of the door. I was excited. Maybe now I could see the child's face.

The face inside the hood was that of a horrible gremlin.

TWENTY-SEVEN

I must have groaned. Kanesha asked, "What's the matter?"

The leering face of the gremlin moved upward as the child reached for the envelope. Then the child darted back into the shrubs. The video continued for another thirty seconds, but the child did not reappear.

Kanesha repeated her question, and this time I responded.

"That child is a lot cleverer than I expected." I told Kanesha what I had seen. "I thought the whole idea of the video cameras was clever, but this child is smarter than I am. Or more devious, perhaps."

"No clues at all?" Kanesha asked.

"See for yourself." I handed her my phone and told her how to start the video.

She watched it all the way through. It was about three minutes long. Then she watched it again before she returned the phone. "Frustrating," was her only comment.

"I didn't see anything that I could use to identify her."

"You think the kid's a girl?" Kanesha said.

"Yes. Gut feeling, more than anything, though I think the handwriting in her notes looks like a girl's," I said. "It reminds me of Laura's handwriting at that age."

"I wish you good luck in finding out who the kid is," Kanesha said. "I'll be in touch if I dig up anything more."

That was my cue to leave. "And if I come up with any potentially helpful information, I'll let you know." I nodded, turned, and left her office.

On the way to the car, I realized I had been gone a good half hour longer than I had intended. I should have texted Stewart to let him know I was going to be late. I texted him then, saying I'd been delayed but was on the way home. He responded less than a minute later: *No problem.*

I drove home and pulled into the garage. I opened the trunk and hauled out the two large bags of books. I had to set one down to unlock the door. But when I tried to open the door, it wouldn't budge. That was odd. This door did sometimes stick when we had a lot of rain, but we hadn't had rain for more than a week. I tried to open it several more times, then knocked on the door to attract someone's attention.

That didn't work, either, and by this time I was getting pretty peeved. Something definitely wasn't right. I picked up the bags and carried them out of the garage and around to the front door. I unlocked it and was relieved when it opened easily. I picked up my bags and pushed the door open. The hall was darker than usual, and for a moment I felt a frisson of fear. Had someone broken into the house and was now lying in wait?

Then suddenly the hall came alight with a dazzling effect, and I heard Stewart say, "Surprise!"

My eyes took a few seconds to adjust. I set down the bags beside my feet and gazed around the hall in stupefaction.

The banisters of the stairs had green and gold garlands woven through the balusters and twined around the newel posts. At regular intervals a small wreath had been affixed to a baluster. More garlands, red and gold this time, hung on the walls, strung with twinkling Christmas lights. Ornaments that sparkled in the lights hung from the garlands. All that was needed to complete the picture was the Christmas tree that we would decorate tomorrow night.

I finally saw Stewart standing in the living room doorway, watching me and smiling broadly. "Well, what do you think?" he asked.

"It's beautiful," I said, a bit overcome by it all. "How did you manage to do this? Was I gone that long?"

Stewart laughed. "I didn't do it all by myself. Azalea helped, and so did Laura and Frank."

Laura emerged from the living room holding my grandson. She laughed. "Oh, Dad, your expression is priceless."

Frank and Azalea came out of the kitchen and approached us.

"Thank you all," I said. "This is a wonderful, beautiful surprise." I surveyed their faces, and they all were smiling.

"It was Stewart's idea," Frank said. "His design, too, so he gets most of the credit. We were only the worker bees." He made a buzzing sound, and Laura laughed again.

I looked at Stewart, who I had come to think of more as the younger brother I never had than as a mere boarder.

I walked over to him and pulled him into a hug, and he squeezed me back.

"Thank you," I said softly as I released him.

"Merry Christmas," Stewart replied. "I thought we needed some Christmas spirit around here."

"There's plenty of it here now." I went next to Laura to kiss her cheek and have a look at my grandson. Charles Franklin Salisbury had recently turned six months old, and he was a healthy, happy infant. At the moment he was sound asleep in his mother's arms.

"How long have you been planning this?" I asked.

"For a week," Stewart said. "I wanted to wait until as close to Christmas Eve as possible to put everything up, and I counted on you doing your last-minute shopping this year the way you usually do."

I grinned ruefully. "I guess I'm more predictable than I realized."

"But in a good way," Frank said with an answering grin.

"Where is Diesel?" I asked, suddenly aware of his absence.

"He's in the corral with the babies," Laura said. "Once he made sure baby Charlie is thriving, he wanted in there."

"He sure does love those little ones," Azalea said. "He's going to miss them."

"I know he will," I said, "but they're not going anywhere yet. Until I find out who left them on the doorstep, they're going to stay here."

"No luck with the video?" Frank asked.

"The cameras are working fine," I said. "But the child is one step ahead of me, if not two or three." I heard loud, peremptory meowing, and I knew Diesel wanted out of the cage. "Let's all go into the kitchen. I'll fetch Diesel, and then I'll tell you how clever this child is."

"Sounds good," Stewart said. "I could use some coffee."

"It's ready and waiting." Azalea headed for the kitchen. Laura and Frank followed, with Stewart not far behind.

I walked into the living room to see Diesel standing at the door of the cage, pushing against it with one large paw. "I'm coming," I said. "I'm flattered that you're so anxious to see me."

Diesel trilled in response. I opened the door, taking care that none of the kittens sneaked out with Diesel. "I'll come back and spend some time with you in a little while," I told them. Ramses meowed indignantly at being left behind.

In the kitchen we found Stewart, Laura, and Frank drinking coffee. Azalea held the baby, crooning softly to him. I caught snatches of "Away in a Manger" as she moved around the kitchen with him. Diesel followed Azalea's progress. He wanted to make sure, I supposed, that she was taking good care of his little buddy.

I found a mug full of coffee waiting for me at my usual place, and I slipped into my chair.

"Tell us about this clever child," Laura said. "I'm really curious."

I stirred cream and sugar into my coffee. "The cameras have caught her on video twice. The first time she had the hood of her sweatshirt or coat pulled so closely around her face that I couldn't see anything else. I thought I'd be clever myself and set a trap for her." I paused for a couple of sips of coffee, then explained the so-called trap I had set. "About half an hour ago, maybe a little more, while I was at the sheriff's department talking to Kanesha, I got another video." I paused for effect.

"Well?" Laura said. "Don't be a tease, Dad."

"The child did pretty much as I hoped she would," I replied. "I did get a clear look at her face. The only problem is, she was wearing a gremlin mask."

"The kid must have seen me setting up the cameras," Frank said.

"Possibly," I said. "Or she's simply a very smart child who is very determined to keep her identity a secret until she is ready to reveal it."

"What did you say in the note she took?" Laura asked.

"That I would like to talk to her, basically," I said. "Do you know, she left a note for me before that with five dollars and some change in it, to help pay for the kittens' food?"

"How sweet," Laura said. "She really loves those babies."

"Yes," I replied. "I imagine it's hard for her, not being able to get any closer to them."

"What are you going to do to find her, now that the cameras probably aren't going to help you?" Frank asked. "Would you like me to take them down?"

"No, let's leave them where they are for now," I said. "They might yet provide a clue of some sort. I'm hoping that she will take to heart what I said in the note and come talk to me of her own accord."

"At some point, if you can't find out who she is," Stewart said, "you'll have to make a decision about the kittens. You can't keep all five of them."

"As much as I'd love to keep them, you're right," I said. "This house is more than big enough to handle six cats, but I'm sure I can find good homes for them all." I cocked my head in the direction of Azalea, still walking around with baby Charlie.

Laura and Frank grinned, but Stewart looked doubtful.

"It might not be as easy as you think," Stewart said in a low voice. "With certain parties, at least." He glanced at Azalea.

"I think you might be surprised," I said.

"You don't think you might be tempted to keep at least one of them?" Laura asked.

"I'd be lying to you if I said no," I replied. "Ramses has so much personality, I've become a little partial to him, I'll admit."

"You wouldn't take him everywhere with you, like you do Diesel, would you?" Stewart asked, looking worried. "That might be a bit much, having two cats on a leash. People around here already think you're eccentric, but that might make them think you're loony."

It took me a moment to realize that Stewart was ribbing me, something he always enjoyed doing. Laura and Frank were laughing, and I noticed that Azalea appeared to find it funny as well.

"Amusing," I said. "But you do make a good point. I don't think I could take two cats with me. It wouldn't be fair to leave one of them home alone all the time, either." I had to admit my heart sank a little as I spoke, because part of me really wanted to keep Ramses. *You could keep two of them, then Ramses wouldn't be lonely when you took Diesel with you,* I told myself.

"Now you're thinking about keeping two of them," Laura said. "Aren't you?"

"Yes." I sighed. "If I work at it long enough, I can find

arguments to keep *all* of them, but y'all will simply have to talk me out of it if I start saying I'll keep them."

"We can try," Stewart said, "but you know what you're like when you make up your mind to do something." He grinned to remove any sting from the words.

"You're saying I'm stubborn." I grinned back at him. "I admit it. It runs in the family." I looked pointedly at my daughter.

Laura smiled sweetly. "At least I come by it honestly."

Frank rolled his eyes heavenward. "If y'all only knew what I have to put up with on a daily basis, you wouldn't joke about it." He emitted a sigh, theatrical in its intensity. Laura giggled at him, and he winked at her.

Frank rose from the table. "As much as I would love to stay and tell you all about how stubborn my beautiful wife is, we need to get going."

"Yes, I suppose so," Laura said. "If you'll take the baby, I'll grab his diaper bag."

Azalea surrendered baby Charlie to his father. I insisted on another look at him, but then, all too soon, they departed. Stewart finished his coffee and said he had things he needed to do as well. I thanked him again for the beautiful Christmas decorations before he headed upstairs.

A few minutes later, the front doorbell rang. Diesel hurried to the door, and I followed. I was hopeful that the child had decided to come talk with me, but it was Melba who had rung the bell.

"This is a pleasant surprise," I said. "What's up?" I stood aside to let her in and shut the door.

Melba didn't answer right away. She was too busy with

Diesel. When she did reply, I was shocked by her expression.

"I'm so upset with Jared Carter, I don't know what to do," she said.

She did look miserable, I thought. "What has he done?" I took her arm and led her to the kitchen. Diesel followed anxiously, chirping at his friend.

Melba collapsed into a chair, and Diesel planted himself next to her. Melba stroked his head.

I repeated my question.

"I'll tell you what he's done," Melba said. "I think he killed Gerry Albritton."

TWENTY-EIGHT

▬▬▬▬▬▬▬▬▬▬▬▬▬▬▬▬▬▬▬▬▬▬▬▬▬▬▬▬▬

Startled, I sank into my chair. "Killed her? What possible motive could he have?"

"Money." Melba practically spit out the word.

I was right about Jared's connection with Gerry Albritton, I decided.

"He was her sleeping partner," I said, not considering my choice of words.

"He was sleeping with her, all right," Melba said grimly.

"That isn't what I meant," I said. "I meant he was financing her real estate deals."

"Oh." Melba looked taken aback. "Yes, he was. I think he was having an affair with her, too."

"How do you know about the financial relationship?" I asked.

"I went to see Dr. Carter this morning," Melba said. "It's been bugging the heck out of me, ever since I heard what he said to her at the party the other night. So, I decided to have it out with him."

"Did you go to his office?" The thought appalled me. Surely Melba hadn't made a scene at his office.

"No, of course not," she responded impatiently. "I have more class than that. I was at his house just now. I called him and told him I had to talk to him, and he asked me to come to his house. I think he knew I was out for blood."

Braver men than Jared Carter had quailed before the wrath of Melba Gilley, I reflected. I was surprised he hadn't tried to put her off, though.

"Oh, he tried to put me off," Melba said, correctly discerning my thoughts. "But I told him if he didn't talk to me, I'd show up at his office and throw such a fit that he'd never live it down."

That made me suspicious. This wasn't like the Melba I knew. "Why are you so riled up about him and the fact that he might have been seeing another woman?"

"Because he told me that I was the first woman he'd been interested in since his wife died," Melba said. "I believed him, and all that time he was probably carrying on with Gerry Albritton."

"I think you're letting your emotions get the better of you," I said gently. "It *is* possible for a man and a woman to have a business arrangement without any personal, intimate relationship to go along with it. Do you have any real proof that he was having an affair with her?" I wondered what she'd think if I could tell her what I knew about Gerry.

"No," Melba said in a grudging tone. "I don't."

I suspected that she cared a lot more for Jared Carter than she herself realized or was willing to admit. Otherwise, why would she act this way?

"When I asked you why he would murder her, you said *money*. That doesn't really explain it."

"He told me that money was missing from the account he set up, and he couldn't figure out where it went. He thought maybe Gerry had siphoned it off and put it in a personal account."

"Did he give you any hints as to how much money he was talking about?" I asked.

Melba nodded. "Over four hundred grand. I had no idea he had that kind of money."

I shared with her the figures that I had shared with Kanesha earlier that morning. "He has to have a pretty large amount of disposable income," I concluded, "if he could finance deals like this and still have four hundred grand on top of it."

"He must be rich," Melba said, sounding bemused.

"I think he must be," I said. "I don't know how much dentists make, but I suspect he's been making money from investments on top of the income from his dental practice."

Melba didn't respond to that.

"Do you think he would kill Gerry if he suspected her of embezzling?" I said. "Wouldn't that make it hard for him to get the money back? She could have put the money in a secret Swiss bank account for all he knew. Then he'd never be able to get it back."

She thought about that for a moment. "I guess you're right. I've really made a mess of things this time."

An appalling thought struck me. "You didn't accuse him of murder, did you?"

"Yes," she said. "Then I stormed out of his house and came right over here. By now he must be thinking he never wants to set eyes on me again."

I couldn't argue that point with her. If I were Jared, I'd be pretty upset with Melba right then. I wasn't going to tell her that, however.

Diesel was doing his best to console her, and I left her to his ministrations for the moment. There was enough coffee in the pot for one last mug, and I prepared it for Melba. When I set it in front of her, she looked up at me through her tears and whispered her thanks. She fumbled for her purse and found some tissues. She started blotting the tears from her face and ended by blowing her nose. She held the crumpled tissues in one hand while she lifted the mug to sip at her coffee.

I gave her time, waiting until she indicated she was ready to talk again. After a few more sips of the coffee, Melba stood and excused herself. She grabbed her purse and headed for the half bathroom under the stairs.

When she came back several minutes later, she seemed composed and in control again.

"I stopped for a minute or two to have a look at your hallway," she said. "It's gorgeous. When did you do it? I guess I was too upset earlier to pay attention."

"I didn't do it," I said. "Stewart came up with the idea and the design, so I've been told. Frank, Laura, and Azalea helped put it together while I was out running errands this morning."

"Goodness, how long were you gone?" Melba asked. "Surely that took several hours." She checked her watch. "It's only a quarter to twelve now."

"I was gone a little over two hours, I'd say. I'm amazed they could put it up so quickly myself. Stewart is a whiz at organizing, though, so I'm sure they were prepared to work fast. I am thrilled with what they did. I needed some Christmas spirit, and they provided it, bless them."

"How is little Charlie doing?" Melba asked. "I haven't seen him in three weeks."

"He's doing fine," I said. "Thriving, in fact. Six months have flown by."

"What about Alex? Any more word on her?"

I shook my head. "No, I've been waiting for Sean to call me. Between keeping tabs on Alex's condition and trying to get work done, he's stretched pretty thin. If I don't hear from him in another hour, I'll call."

"Let me know what you find out," Melba said. "I've been so worried about Alex. Breaks my heart to see her go through this."

"Thank the Lord she's finally getting help. I really want to go see her, but I'm waiting until Sean tells me she's up to a visit," I said.

"I hope that's soon," Melba said. "Guess I'd better get going. I've cried on your shoulder enough for one day." She smiled, and the sadness of it made me want to hug her and tell her everything would be okay.

"You don't have to rush out on my account," I said. "If you're not in that big a hurry, why don't you go and visit the kittens? They'll help cheer you up. Won't they, Diesel?"

Diesel warbled a loud and firm agreement, or so I interpreted it. Melba smiled again, a little more brightly this time.

"I think I'll do that," Melba said. "I don't have anything that can't wait awhile longer. Come on, Diesel, let's go play with the babies."

I did not accompany them. I wanted to give Melba the chance to calm down even further, and without me present she could focus on the kittens and hopefully forget about Jared for a little while.

I decided to hang out in the den until Melba was ready to leave. I could check my e-mail while I waited. I was still reading through messages when Melba and Diesel came to the den in search of me.

I set the laptop aside. "How were the kittens?" Diesel jumped onto the sofa next to me.

"Full of energy, and shedding hair," Melba said with a rueful glance at her dark skirt. I started to apologize, but Melba said firmly, "Don't worry. I have one of those lint brushes in the car. Won't take me a minute to get rid of the hair."

"If you're sure," I said.

"I am," Melba said. "I'd still be in there playing with them, but I got a text message. I've been waiting for it for a couple of days now."

I knew Melba and that arch tone of hers. She expected me to ask about the text.

"What's up with the text message?" I asked obligingly. "Is it important?"

"It could be," Melba said. "It took me a while, but I finally tracked down someone I've been looking for."

"Who would that be?"

"Mrs. Ima Jean Norwood," Melba said with an air of triumph.

"Congratulations," I said. "Who is Ima Jean Norwood? Last living relative of the Russian royal family?"

Melba shot me a look of disdain. "You used to be so funny. No, Mrs. Norwood was good friends with Billy

Albritton's mother, and she knew his grandparents, the Albrittons, too. She's in a nursing home here in Athena, and I'm going to talk to her."

"Still on the trail of Gerry Albritton," I remarked.

"Yes, I am," Melba said. "I'm determined to find out exactly who she was."

I really wanted to share the news about Gerry's birth gender, but if Kanesha found out I had told Melba, she might not trust me again with sensitive information. So I kept it to myself.

Melba's eyes narrowed while she gazed at me. "You know something, don't you? What is it?"

"I can't tell you," I said. "Something Kanesha told me, and I can't tell anyone else, not even you."

"Since it's Kanesha, I'm not going to press you. I know how she is," Melba said.

"You think Mrs. Norwood may actually know something?" I asked.

"If she's not gaga, I think she might," Melba said. "I figure she's in her late eighties, at least. I'm praying that she's still mentally all there."

"Good luck," I said. "I hope she can help us."

"I'll let you know," Melba said.

"We'll see you out," I told her.

"No need, I know the way." Melba gave a little wave. "Talk to you later."

"Bye," I said. Diesel added a couple of meows to my farewell.

"Okay, buddy," I said to Diesel. "It's time to wrap some presents. I know you'll help me, but don't help too much, okay?" Diesel was like a kitten around ribbon and boxes. He couldn't resist them. Other than locking him in another room while I wrapped gifts, however, I didn't know how to stop him. The trick was to distract him with a box and some ribbon, and I could wrap while he played.

I needed a large flat surface. I could use my bed, because I knew by now Azalea would have stripped it, remade it with clean linens, and put the bedspread on. The kitchen table would be better, however, and unless Azalea needed it for the next half an hour or so, that would be the best place to work.

Azalea was working at the stove when I entered the kitchen toting my two bags of books. I had left them in the hall, thanks to the wonderful surprise I'd had earlier. I needed to find the wrapping paper, bows, and tape, and then retrieve the other items from the car.

"Azalea, are you going to need the table for the next thirty minutes or so?" I asked.

"No, you go right ahead with whatever you want to do," she said.

"Thanks. I need to wrap some presents. Shouldn't take too long." I set the bags on the table. The wrapping paper and other gift paraphernalia resided year-round in the hall closet. Once I'd retrieved what I needed, I went to the car and brought in the toys I'd bought for the kittens and Diesel, as well as Helen Louise's bottles of perfume.

I didn't need to wrap the toys for the kittens, and they certainly didn't need ribbons to chew on and potentially eat, so I set those aside. I found a suitable box in the utility room and put it down near the table. Diesel immediately crawled into it for an inspection. I tossed him a couple of old bows that had seen better days, and he batted them aside. While he had fun getting in and out of the box and batting the bows around—out of Azalea's way, because he was smart enough to realize he had to stay clear—I started wrapping.

The perfume bottles in their lovely packaging provided little challenge. I knew the books would be a little hard to wrap neatly, at least for me. First I had to sort the books by recipient, but that didn't take long. I wrapped and labeled as I went and soon had a tidy pile of gifts. There was one stack of seven books left over, but those didn't need wrapping, as they were for me. Somehow I always managed to buy books for myself when I went Christmas shopping.

I began to clear the table, but my cell phone sounded. I had a new text message.

From Kanesha. It read: *New information. Call me when available.*

TWENTY-NINE

▐▖▌▖▌▖▌▖▌▖▌▖▌▖▌▖▌▖▌▖▌▖▌▖▌▖▌▖▌▖▌▖▌▖▌▖▌▖

I finished the task at hand and found room for the gifts I'd wrapped in the hall closet. Then I went to the den and called Kanesha's cell phone. I perched on the corner of my desk. Diesel chose the sofa and stretched out to relax.

Kanesha answered right away. "Had an interesting talk with Jared Carter a few minutes ago."

"In your office?" I asked. How long had it been since Melba stormed out of his house? I glanced at my watch. Close to ninety minutes.

"Yes, why do you ask?" Kanesha said.

"Oh, no reason," I replied lamely. "Just wondered. I thought he'd be busy pulling teeth, I guess."

"He made the time to show up here and asked to see me," Kanesha said. "I asked him if he was Gerry Albritton's silent partner, and he admitted it right away. Surprised him, I believe, that I had figured it out. I didn't mention you."

"Good." I didn't want Jared Carter to know I played any role in this. "Was he coming to you to tell you this himself?"

"Yes," Kanesha replied. "He also told me he thought Gerry had been embezzling from the account he set up to fund her real estate purchases."

"That's serious," I said, hoping I sounded surprised enough to fool her.

"The amount he mentioned is serious," Kanesha said. "I asked him how certain he was that Gerry was the culprit. Was there anyone else who could have done it? Also asked that."

"Was there?" I asked.

"He hemmed and hawed a bit, but he finally said that Gerry's assistant, Jincy Bruce, could have done it. He seems to think she's smart enough to have figured out how, but she can't be all that smart if she thought she could get away with it."

I had a sudden thought about that. "Unless you can prove that she murdered Gerry, she could get away with it. That might have been her motive, if she's the killer."

"I'm trying to locate Ms. Bruce so I can talk to her," Kanesha said.

I remembered then that I had seen Jincy earlier, coming out of the office building where Jared Carter had his practice. I related this to Kanesha. While she pondered that, I tried to work out Jared's potential movements this morning. If Jincy had seen him in his office, and Melba had talked to him at his home, and then he had went to Kanesha's office, he had had a busy morning.

"Carter didn't say that he had talked to Ms. Bruce this morning. If she did go to see him, he might have asked her about the missing money," Kanesha said. "I'm going to talk to him again. If he did confront Ms. Bruce, she may have bolted. Talk to you later." She ended the call.

I remained where I was, cell phone in hand, and considered the idea of Jincy Bruce as the murderer. I didn't have any idea how long she had worked for Gerry, but maybe long enough to become aware of her personal habits. For example, her predilection for brandy in a particular snifter. Jincy would know that putting poison in that snifter on a night when everyone else was drinking champagne out of flutes would ensure she'd avoid poisoning anyone else by mistake.

The times I had seen her during the party, she had been at the door. That didn't mean, however, she couldn't have slipped away long enough to add the poison to Gerry's brandy. There were so many people milling around, not many would have noticed her absence from the front door or her presence as she moved through the rooms in search of Gerry and her snifter.

One potential sticking point, when I considered any suspect, was the poison itself. Did Jincy have any kind of access to poisonous substances? It would be a whopping coincidence if she, like Tammy, had the knowledge and skill to distill it for herself. Maybe she and Tammy were working together, I thought for just a moment. But that was a little too far out to take seriously. Identification of the poison that killed Gerry should help narrow down the suspects to only those who had access to it.

For now, I thought, Tammy—despite the alibi she claimed to have—and Jincy were strong candidates for the role of murderer. But I was forgetting someone, I realized. Deirdre Thompson. The conversation Helen Louise and I had heard had been ugly. The women obviously despised each other. What I gathered from Gerry's part of the conversation was that she had something she could hold over Deirdre's head in order to force Deirdre to do whatever it was she wanted from the doyenne of Athena society.

I couldn't recall ever hearing a breath of scandal about Deirdre Thompson. She had the reputation of pinching pennies, despite her rumored wealth, but that wasn't anything to encourage blackmail. I hadn't discussed Deirdre with Kanesha, although Helen Louise and I had certainly related what we overheard to the deputy. Had Kanesha ruled Deirdre out somehow? I would have thought she had as much opportunity as anyone to poison Gerry's brandy. The murder had to be premeditated, because who carries poison on them as a regular thing? Deirdre could have brought it and seized the chance when she saw that snifter.

Even if I didn't recall ever having heard about any scandals involving Deirdre Thompson, I knew two people who might have. One of them was working in the kitchen; the other might be upstairs on the third floor. I headed for the kitchen, texting Stewart on the way. I asked him to join us in the kitchen if he was still at home.

Diesel scrambled off the sofa when he saw me head for the door. He meowed loudly a couple of times, as if to ask me where I was going in such a hurry. "Going to talk to Azalea," I told him.

Azalea wasn't in the kitchen when Diesel and I first walked in, and I started to call out for her. She appeared behind me carrying an empty laundry basket. Startled, I turned when I heard her footsteps.

"Were you looking for me?" she inquired.

"Yes, I wanted to talk to you," I said. My cell phone buzzed, and I checked it. Stewart had responded to my text. *Down in a few.*

"What about?" Azalea set the empty basket on the table and regarded me calmly.

I knew I had to approach this in the right way, because Azalea, as a rule, did not hold with gossiping about anyone. In the past, however, she had occasionally given me useful information about people.

"Why don't we sit down for a minute?" I suggested.

Azalea pulled out a chair and sat. I did, too, and Diesel stretched out on the floor by me.

"It's about the murder that took place at the party the other night," I said. "Kanesha is investigating it, of course, and I'm helping her in my own way."

Azalea nodded.

"One problem is that no one seems to know who Gerry Albritton really was. The other is the motives anyone might have had for wanting her dead."

"I can't help you with that first part," Azalea replied. "I don't know who she was, either. Don't recall ever knowing anybody with that name. Same with the second part, since I didn't know her."

"Fair enough," I said. "I think you probably can help with the second part, though. In the past you have shared information about people you used to work for, or that friends or relatives might have known or worked for. I'm hoping you might have information in this case about one person in particular."

Azalea's tone was not encouraging. "Who might that be?"

"Deirdre Thompson," I said.

"Why do you want to talk about that dreary old biddy?" Stewart asked as he entered the kitchen. "Sorry, couldn't help overhearing. Is that why you wanted to talk to me?"

"Yes, I thought that you and Azalea might be able to answer my questions about her."

Stewart pulled out a chair and sat. "What questions?"

I glanced at Azalea, and she nodded.

"Are there any scandals or rumors of scandals in her past that would embarrass her badly if they became known now? Especially if someone could prove the rumors true?"

Azalea and Stewart looked at each other. Slowly, they nodded, almost in unison.

"Rumors, certainly," Stewart said. Azalea nodded in agreement.

"Rumors about *what*?" I asked. Surely they weren't going to turn coy now.

"There have been several over the years," Stewart said.

"Murder," Azalea said at the same time.

THIRTY

||||||||||||||||||||||||||||||||||||||||

"Murder?" I said.

My two informants nodded their heads. Stewart indicated that Azalea should go first.

"You know she's been married several times," Azalea said.

"Three times. Is that right?"

"Yes," Stewart replied.

"Always older men," Azalea said. "People say she married them for money. Her family's been around ever since Athena started up. Used to be, they had a lot of money, but her daddy wasn't too good with holding on to it. By the time she was grown, they were just barely hanging on to that old house she lives in."

"So, she married money," I said.

"Yes," Azalea replied. "Every time. She was kind of pretty when she was young. Some people said she really loved Mr. Thompson, her first husband, but he had to be nearly forty years older than her. She keeps going back to his name, so I reckon there must be something in that."

"Maybe," Stewart said. "From what I've always heard, he left her about half a million, and she parlayed that into three or four million. She's pretty shrewd when it comes to investments, supposedly."

"If she had that kind of money, why did she keep marrying for more?" I asked. "Wasn't she satisfied with several million?"

"Not our Deirdre," Stewart said. "You know how notoriously cheap she is, right?"

"Yes, I've heard stories," I replied.

"People like her, seems like they always want more money even if they've got a lot," Azalea said, shaking her head. "She grew up poor, but real proud of who her family was, and I reckon she doesn't want to be poor again."

"So, she married twice more, both times to older, rich men," Stewart said.

"I guess murder comes into it because people think she killed her husbands to make sure she got the money before they could spend it all," I said.

"That's pretty much it," Stewart said.

"Is there any basis to these rumors? Did anything particular happen to set people off talking about her?" I asked.

"Mr. Thompson came down with pneumonia real bad," Azalea said. "He wasn't strong to start with—had a few strokes—and that pneumonia, he just couldn't shake it off. Nobody talked about murder when *he* died."

"No, that started when number two died of pneumonia," Stewart said in a wry tone.

"Don't tell me number three died of pneumonia, too," I said.

"Okay, I won't tell you." Stewart grinned, but Azalea simply looked pained.

"Mrs. Thompson has always been real cheap about hiring people to clean and do things like that. Hardly anyone ever stayed with her more than a few months," Azalea said. "She finally found her a strong girl that could do the cleaning and some of the cooking. The girl didn't know enough to realize she wasn't getting fair pay, but I don't think she had any family or friends to tell her different."

"She was slow, as they used to say," Stewart said. "A euphemism for mental impairment. She was the only other person in the house when husbands two and three came down with pneumonia."

"And if she was mentally impaired, Deirdre Thompson could get away with murder, and the servant wouldn't understand what had happened."

"Yes," Stewart said. "Pneumonia can be induced, and the old codgers she roped into marrying her weren't hearty physical specimens to begin with. She picked her pigeons carefully."

"Did anyone—anyone official, that is—ever look into their deaths to find out whether they'd been helped along?" I asked.

"Not seriously, at any rate," Stewart said.

"I don't think so," Azalea said. "People just started talking, not too long after Mr. Reardon died. He was number two. Mrs. Thompson doesn't have many friends. Most people don't like her because she's so stingy. She goes around like some grand duchess and acts like she's always giving money to charity."

Stewart grinned. "I know for a fact she does give

money to charities, because I was briefly on the board of one. I saw how much she gave."

"How much?" I asked, because I knew he wanted me to.

"Twenty dollars," Stewart said. "Other people in her income bracket were giving twenty *thousand* or more."

"That *is* pretty darn cheap," I said.

"Word gets around," Azalea said. "Not much is ever secret, and when you don't treat people right, well, that just makes people talk more because they don't like you and want to drag you down."

I couldn't argue with that analysis. Since I had moved back to Athena several years ago, I had seen and heard such things.

"What happened to the mentally impaired woman? Is she still working for Deirdre?" I asked.

"No, she died six or seven years ago," Stewart said. "She was probably close to forty by then. Don't you think?" he said to Azalea.

She nodded. "She worked for Mrs. Thompson for over twenty years, and she got buried in the cheapest coffin you could imagine." She sighed. "People say by the time she died, she was thin as a rail. Used to be kind of heavyset."

I was considerably appalled. Not only had Deirdre gone for the cheapest possible funeral, she had evidently also kept the poor housekeeper on starvation rations. I wondered if that had any connection to her cause of death.

Stewart caught my eye and nodded. He read my expression of mingled disgust and horror all too easily.

"That woman is truly a piece of work," I said, "if all of this is true."

"Nobody knows for certain," Azalea said. "Lots of

talk, but nobody's ever proved any of it. The funeral par-
lor knows the truth about the cheap coffin and what that
poor housekeeper looked like, but they've never said a
word. I don't know where all that talk got started."

"Is there anything else?" I asked. "I mean, what you've
told me is horrifying enough, but there could be more."

"Not that I'm aware of," Stewart said.

I looked to Azalea. She shook her head. "Nothing else
I know."

"It's my turn to ask a question," Stewart said. "What is
all this in aid of? It must have something to do with Gerry
Albritton's murder."

"It does," I said.

"Was Gerry trying to blackmail Deirdre?" Stewart
asked.

"Possibly," I said. "Look, this shouldn't go any further,
and I know you will both keep it to yourselves." I waited
until they both nodded before I continued. "Helen Louise
and I overheard most of a private conversation between
Deirdre and Gerry at the party. It sounded like Gerry was
threatening Deirdre with something she knew."

"Something she could use to get Deirdre to ease the
way for her with the high-society folk?" Stewart asked,
one eyebrow arched.

"Basically," I said. Stewart startled me by laughing. I
noticed Azalea was smiling, too.

"Okay, what is it? What am I missing here?" I asked.

Stewart was still laughing, so Azalea explained.

"People like Miss An'gel and Miss Dickce don't have
much to do with Mrs. Thompson," Azalea said. "They're
about as high in high society here as you can get, and
those other society folks follow their lead."

Miss An'gel and Miss Dickce Ducote, dear friends of mine, were indeed the true doyennes of Athena society. Given their constant generosity to many charitable causes, I could see why they wouldn't find Deirdre Thompson at all congenial.

"If somebody told Gerry Albritton that Deirdre was her ticket to high society, they were either leading her on or didn't have a clue," Stewart said.

Had Jared Carter encouraged Gerry to cultivate Deirdre? As her silent partner, he was probably the likeliest candidate. He was not in that rarified atmosphere himself, so perhaps he really didn't know the truth about Deirdre's standing with the real aristocracy in Athena.

The question that occurred to me was what kind of proof Gerry could have had to make good on her threat to expose Deirdre. Maybe she was connected to the housekeeper somehow?

"Do you know what the housekeeper's name was?" I asked.

Stewart shook his head. "I might have known it at one time, but at the moment I can't dredge it up."

"Azalea?" I asked.

"I think her name was Glory Smalls," Azalea said.

"Any connection to the Albrittons?" I asked.

Azalea frowned. "I'll have to think about that. I don't believe the girl came from around here. I can ask a couple of friends who might know something."

"Thanks." I knew Azalea would do it discreetly. "If you come up with anything, it could help. Before I forget, is Kanesha familiar with these rumors?"

"Yes," Azalea said.

"All right, I'm done." I smiled at them. "I have no idea

if what we've talked about has a bearing on the investigation, but you never know."

Azalea stood. "Are you ready for lunch now?"

I had been so involved with my quest for information, I had forgotten about lunch.

"My goodness, yes," I said. "I'm sorry, I hope it's not ruined because of my questions."

"No, it's not." Azalea went to the fridge and pulled out a salad bowl, one of the larger ones. She brought it to the table. "Grilled chicken salad. I know you prefer the chicken chilled."

"It looks delicious," I said. "Yes, definitely chilled."

Azalea looked at Stewart. "There's another one, if you want it."

"Yes, please," Stewart said. "I'm in the mood for a good salad."

Azalea took another bowl from the fridge and set it in front of Stewart. Next, she pulled out three bottles of dressing. I almost always chose my favorite, Thousand Island. Stewart varied his choices between balsamic vinaigrette and ranch. Today he chose the former.

After Azalea gave us utensils and napkins, Stewart and I dug in. A glass of sweet tea appeared by my place, and Stewart received a large glass of filtered water before Azalea left the kitchen. Azalea never ate with us even though I would have been happy to have her join. I knew she did eat lunch, but usually when she was on her own in the kitchen.

I put my fork down. Sean. I hadn't heard from him. I wasn't going to wait any longer for him to call. I dug out my phone and hit Speed Dial. The call went to his voice mail after six rings. I ended the call. I decided to text instead. He might have been with a client when I called. *That was me calling. Update on Alex and Rosie?* I set the phone aside and resumed eating my salad.

Stewart had watched me closely. "Are you trying to reach Sean?"

I nodded. "Yes, I want an update on Alex and Rosie."

"I'd like that, too," Stewart said.

We didn't have long to wait. My phone buzzed to announce a new text message. In fact, it buzzed three times, so I knew the message was a long one.

I read through it slowly, making sure I took in the details. Then I heaved a sigh of relief. The gist of it was that Alex was continuing to improve physically, gaining some strength, and beginning to have an appetite again. Her psychological gains were slower but steady, thanks to her therapy sessions. I knew she would need counseling for a while, perhaps months, before she returned to her usual self. Rosie was doing fine with Cherelle, and Sean was extremely pleased with her.

I passed the phone over to Stewart so he could read the update for himself. He scanned the messages quickly. With a smile, he passed the phone back to me. "Excellent news."

"Yes, I'm very pleased," I said. "I was hoping Alex might be able to come here for Christmas, but that might be too much to ask."

"It is the season for miracles," Stewart said.

"I'll be praying for one," I said. "I forgot to ask Sean if she was up to having visitors." I picked up the phone and tapped out another text.

Sean responded quickly, saying that Alex would love to see me. I decided to run over to their house then, before

I got caught up in something else. I was anxious to see Alex.

I announced my intentions to Stewart and hurried through the rest of my salad. I decided not to take Diesel with me. Better not to overwhelm Alex, and I wouldn't stay long anyway. I didn't want to tire her unnecessarily. I was about to run upstairs to brush my teeth when I heard the doorbell. I hoped whoever was at the door wasn't going to take up a lot of my time, because I wanted to get to Sean's place. Diesel came loping out of the kitchen the moment he heard the bell.

When I opened the door, I saw a small figure wearing a jacket with a black hood. The gremlin face was gone, replaced by the solemn mien of a child.

THIRTY-ONE

I recognized the boy immediately. He sang in the choir at Helen Louise's church. In fact, he was the boy soprano soloist, and he had a hauntingly angelic singing voice.

"Hi, Tommy." His name was Tommy Russum, and he lived several blocks away with his mother and stepfather. His mother was a friend of Helen Louise. "Would you like to come in?"

The boy nodded and stepped inside the house. I shut the door, and he pushed back the hood to expose his dark auburn mop of hair. Small for his age—around eleven, I thought—he stood looking up at me, a mute appeal in his expression.

"Let's go see the kittens, shall we?" I said.

"Yes, please," he said softly.

I led the way. Diesel walked beside Tommy, and the boy stroked his head. Diesel purred his thanks.

The minute Tommy saw the kittens, he hurried to the

cage and dropped to his knees, his hands against the wire mesh. The kittens squeaked and chirped as they tried to reach his hands. He looked up at me again. "Thank you for taking care of them."

"I'm happy to do it. Why don't we let them out so you can play with them?"

"Yes, please." He scooted back, and I opened the door. Diesel watched anxiously as the kittens scrambled to get to Tommy, now sitting with his legs stretched out. They crawled over his legs, and Ramses tried to crawl up his arm, claws grabbing at the thick fabric of the jacket.

Tommy laughed as he picked them up in turn and let them lick his face. As I watched, I wondered how an adult could be so cruel to a child, to deprive him of such love and joy. The family wasn't poor as far as I knew. Tommy's stepfather, if I recalled correctly, was a cardiologist and reputedly an excellent one. He could surely afford kitten food for this bunch. He must be the *he* Tommy had referred to in the original note to me.

I pulled a chair close to where Tommy continued to play with the kittens. Diesel stood watch, ready to pounce if one of them tried to make a break for it. At the moment, however, they seemed happy to play with Tommy.

"They haven't forgotten you," I said. "I hope you weren't worried about that."

Tommy regarded me solemnly, his smile gone. "I was kinda worried about that."

"Did you have names for them?" I asked.

He nodded but didn't speak.

"I didn't know what to call them, so I gave them names, too."

"What do you call them?" he asked.

I told him the names and explained the origin of them. He smiled when I mentioned Fred and George Weasley. "I love Harry Potter," he said. "I like your names better. Mine were kinda lame."

"They're your kittens, so you call them whatever you want. I won't mind if you'd rather call them something else."

He shook his head. "No, your names are better." He pulled Ramses off his shoulder to stop the kitten from trying to groom his head. "Tell me about Ramses again and where his name comes from, please."

I told him about the ancient Egyptian pharaoh and his namesake from the Amelia Peabody series. He smiled when I told him about the fictional Ramses's penchant for getting into trouble.

"That's a perfect name for him." Tommy stroked the kitten's head while the others squirmed around his legs, batting at tails and squeaking at one another.

"We need to talk about why you brought the kittens here," I said gently. "Is it because of your stepfather?"

Tommy nodded. "He's mean. He doesn't want me to have a cat."

"You must have a cat if you have these kittens," I said.

"I found their mom in our yard. She looked hungry, and I started feeding her. *He* didn't know about it. Then one morning I went looking for her when she didn't show up."

"But you found her," I prompted when he stopped.

He nodded. "He has this old shed in the backyard. She was in there. I found her with her babies. They were so tiny."

"You looked after her and made sure she had enough to eat so she could take care of the babies, didn't you?"

"Yes, sir," he said. "He hardly ever goes in the shed, and I thought they could stay there. But he went out there a couple weeks ago and found them."

"Did he talk to you about them?" I asked.

Tommy shook his head. "No, he didn't. He talked to my mom about it. I heard them. *She* thinks it's okay to have the kittens, but he doesn't. He told my mom I wouldn't take care of them, and he wasn't going to spend a lot of money on a bunch of damn nasty cats." His lips trembled. "But I *was* taking care of them. I was buying their food out of my 'lowance. My mom gives me that, he doesn't. She has a job, so it's her money, and she doesn't care how I spend my 'lowance."

"I appreciate the money you left for me," I said. "It's very responsible of you, but you can have it back if you need it."

Tommy shook his head vigorously. "No, you keep it. I get more next week, and I'll give that to you, too." He looked at Diesel. "You must have to spend a lot of money already to feed your kitty. Do you think one of mine will get that big?"

"No, they're not the same kind of kitty that Diesel is. He's a Maine Coon, and they're a breed that is pretty large."

He seemed disappointed, and I tried not to smile.

I would love to have a talk with his stepfather and his mother. I knew it wasn't my business, and they would have to handle this situation themselves. The stepfather ought to know how much these kittens obviously meant to Tommy, and the fact that the child was doing his best to see after their welfare ought to count for something. I didn't know the man, but I already disliked him.

"Do you think if I talked to your stepfather, he might let you bring the kittens home?" I asked.

Hope flared in Tommy's eyes but faded quickly. He shook his head. "No, he's too mean. He doesn't want cats in the house. But they couldn't stay in the shed forever. It's too cold. That's why I brought them here, so they could come inside."

Such a loving, kindhearted child, I thought. This made me even angrier at his stepfather.

"They're safe and warm here," I said, "and they're getting plenty to eat. There is a problem, though."

Tommy frowned. "Are they pooping on the floor?"

"No, it's not that," I said. "They're using the litter boxes just fine. They're growing, and they're going to get a lot bigger. I can't keep them in the cage once they get too big. As much as I would love to keep all of them, I can't. That would mean six cats in the house, and that's too many."

"What are you going to do with them?" Tommy sounded fearful.

"That's what I want you to help me decide," I said. "We need to do what's best for them, right?"

He nodded. "Yes, sir."

"I believe I can find good homes for them. Not all five together, though."

"Won't they miss one another if they're separated?"

"Yes, for a while," I said. "I hate to separate them, but in order for them to have a good home, we have to do it. Someone might take two or three of them, I think, but not all five."

"I understand," he said. I could tell he was trying not to cry. "I want them to be safe."

I felt like an ogre who had stolen his beloved kittens. I knew that was ridiculous, but I felt so bad for him.

"I won't let them go to anyone you don't approve of," I said. "If it's possible, I want you to meet the people who will adopt them."

"Really?" After I nodded, he said, "I guess that's okay then." He removed the kittens from his lap and off his legs to stand. "I think I'd better go home now. My mom isn't at work today, and she doesn't like me to be gone long."

"We don't want your mother to worry." I rose from the chair to start gathering kittens. He helped me put them back into the cage. He stood there a moment, watching them, then turned and ran toward the front door.

I hurried to catch up with him before he was out the door and gone. I called out to him, and he slowed down to wait for me.

"Tommy, you can come and see the kittens whenever you like," I said.

"Anytime?" he asked.

"Well, not at three o'clock in the morning," I said in a solemn tone. He giggled at that.

"I'll wait until four," he said. I had to smile. Smart boy.

I opened the door for him. I expected him to run out, but he stood looking up at me.

"What is it?" I asked.

Suddenly he threw himself against me and hugged me hard. I patted his head, trying to swallow the sudden lump in my throat. Tommy turned me loose and ran out the door.

I shut the door and realized that Diesel was watching

me. He meowed as if asking me a question. I stroked his head. "I don't know yet what I'm going to say to his step-father," I told the cat, "but one way or another I'm going to talk to that man and tell him what I think of him for the way he's treating that poor little boy."

THIRTY-TWO

I returned home from my visit with Alex feeling encouraged about her progress and the eventual outcome. Her face had lost that sunken look, and her skin had taken on a healthier-looking tone. She was still depressed and prone to self-recrimination, but there were signs of improvement. Before I left, Sean brought Rosie in to her mother, and Alex immediately reached for her baby. After a few minutes, I left the three of them together, saying a silent prayer of thanks.

When I neared my driveway, I spotted Melba's car parked in front of the house. I remembered she had gone to visit an elderly lady in the nursing home, Ida Norwood. No, that didn't sound right. *Was it Ima?* I asked myself as I pulled into the garage. *Yes, that was it. Ima Jean Norwood.*

Diesel met me at the door, chirping happily, no doubt informing me that his buddy Melba was here. I glanced toward the table to see Melba sipping from a mug. She was frowning when she looked across the room at me. Her face cleared, and she smiled. "I'm glad you're back. Tell me, how is Alex?"

"Doing much better, I'm happy to say."

Azalea came into the kitchen. "She's doing better?" she inquired.

"Yes, thankfully." I shared some of the details with them.

"Surely the worst is over now," Melba said.

"I think so," I said, "but we have to pray that she doesn't have a relapse. This is not something a woman recovers from in a day or two. It will take time."

Azalea said, "I'll be praying for her, and if she needs me for anything, I'll be glad to do it."

"Thank you," I said. "I know how much she will appreciate that. If you have time to visit her, I think she would love to see you."

"I'll be sure to go," Azalea said. "Would you like coffee? I made plenty."

"Yes, thank you." I could have served myself, but Azalea bustled toward the coffeemaker. I pulled out my chair from the table and took up my usual position.

While I stirred my coffee, I looked at Melba. Moments before, she had seemed happy about Alex, but now her frown had returned. "What's the problem?" I said. "Didn't you get any useful information from your visit with Mrs. Norwood?"

"I'm not sure," Melba said. "It's a strange story, and I'm not sure it makes much sense or has anything to do with what happened a few days ago." She lapsed into silence again.

"I won't know that until you tell me," I said to prompt her.

Melba sighed. "Okay, but let me tell it my way, and don't interrupt me."

"All right," I said. "Please proceed."

"Now, like I told you before, Mrs. Norwood was friends with Billy Albritton's mother. She lived on a small farm near theirs. This was around seventy years ago. They were all hardscrabble kind of folks, not a whole lot of money. Billy's daddy and his daddy had to do a lot of hunting to keep food on the table, because there were so many of them. Billy's dad, Jack, had twelve brothers and sisters, and he was one of the oldest. Jack had brothers and sisters the same age as his oldest kids, Billy and his sister." She paused for coffee and stared unseeingly in my direction.

I waited patiently for her to continue, not wanting to break her concentration.

"Where they lived was pretty far out in the county. No such thing as indoor plumbing, even at that time, when everybody in town had it. Mrs. Norwood said the day her family moved into a house with an indoor toilet she sat in the bathroom for two hours just marveling at it. The point I'm getting at is, they were poor. A lot of mouths to feed, and not always enough to go around. Billy's mom kept having kids, and a couple of them died not long after they were born.

"When Billy was about eight—did I tell you Billy was the oldest? I meant to. Well, Jack Albritton went out hunting one day with one of the little ones, a boy going on four years old. When Jack got back that evening, he didn't have the boy with him. Claimed he lost sight of the boy in the woods, and even though he searched and called for him for hours, he never found him." She shivered suddenly. "In those days there were still bears and panthers in the woods. I remember my mama telling me how they would hear the panthers scream at night, and she and her sister would get under the bed and hide." Her hands were shaking a little as she grasped her mug and brought it to her mouth.

"Sounds pretty terrifying," I said.

Melba nodded. "Jack's daddy said a bear or a panther must have gotten the boy, but they never found any trace of him. Wasn't long, though, before Jack came home with a new rifle and some new clothes for himself and his wife. The kids got new things, too. Jack claimed he'd done something to help a man with money, and the man was so grateful that he gave Jack a big reward. I guess they had no choice but to believe him, because he swore up and down it was true.

"The family didn't move to Athena until some years later, around when Billy was ready to start high school. Billy's mama wanted him to have an education so he could do better than she and his daddy had done. His daddy got a job as a mechanic, plus a timber company bought their land. The Norwoods' land, too.

"This would have been about six years after the little boy disappeared. Mrs. Norwood said one day when she was shopping, she came across a woman and a boy about nine or ten—he was a little on the small side, she said. Anyway, the boy looked kind of familiar, Mrs. Norwood thought, but she couldn't place him right off. She didn't know the woman's name, although she found out later on. Turned out it was Mrs. Halbert."

Melba must have noticed my perplexed expression. I had no idea who Mrs. Halbert was.

"She was Deirdre Thompson's mama," Melba said. "Deirdre was a Halbert."

"Okay." I had an idea where this rambling tale was leading, but I had a piece of the puzzle Melba didn't. I waited for her to continue and finish the story.

"Everybody knows that Mr. and Mrs. Halbert had only one biological child, and that was Deirdre. But about six years before Mrs. Norwood saw Mrs. Halbert with this boy, they came back from a trip—or so they said—and had a boy with them. Claimed he was the son of friends of theirs who'd died suddenly. The Halberts had adopted him. Named him Ronnie."

I didn't remember Ronnie Halbert at all, but I knew Melba would enlighten me.

"Mrs. Norwood saw Mrs. Halbert and Ronnie a couple times more, and it finally hit her why he looked familiar. She thought he looked a little like Mrs. Albritton, Billy's mama. Billy and his sister took after Jack in looks."

I finally couldn't resist a question. "Did Mrs. Norwood talk to Mrs. Albritton about this?"

"She couldn't," Melba said. "Mrs. Albritton had died about a year before that, not long after Jack had moved him and his kids to Athena, along with his parents and some of his youngest brothers and sisters.

"Mrs. Norwood didn't care much for Jack, she told me. Thought he was a pretty rough character. She wasn't about to go up to him and ask him if Ronnie Halbert was really his little boy. He would have denied it, of course, but Mrs. Norwood has always believed that Ronnie Halbert was Jack Albritton's little boy, Jerry."

The name clinched it for me. She really had been Gerry Albritton all along, although somewhere along the way Jerry had become Geraldine—after being Ronnie Halbert for a number of years. Was this the key to her murder? I thought it had to be. Deirdre Thompson, in my mind, suddenly moved to the number one spot on the list of suspects.

"Tell me about Ronnie Halbert," I said. "I don't remember anybody by that name. He had to be around eight to ten years older than you and me."

"Close to ten, I think," Melba replied. "I remember seeing him around town. He always dressed nice and had his own car. Mr. Halbert spoiled him rotten. He and Mrs. Halbert couldn't have any more kids, and he wanted a son more than anything. So Ronnie got anything he wanted. Ronnie was good-looking, and he had girls running after him all the time."

"Sounds like he was on the wild side," I said.

Melba nodded. "Yes, but he never got arrested for anything. Mr. Halbert paid people off, I always heard. One day, though, as the story goes, he had a big fight with Mr. Halbert. He ran off and never came back. People said he went into the army or the navy, but nobody knew for sure. Killed his daddy. Mr. Halbert grieved himself to death."

"That's a really sad story," I said, and I meant it. So much unhappiness, and Gerry had been at the center of it, but not by choice.

"What I don't get is what this has to do with the murder," Melba said. "Unless Ronnie Halbert was dressing as a woman and going around and calling himself Geraldine, since he maybe used to be Jerry Albritton. He might

have been ashamed to show his face around here as Ronnie Halbert again."

Melba had hit close enough to the mark, and I thought
it was all right to let her see it that way. Until the truth was
made known, Melba could think Gerry was simply mas-
querading.

"I'll bet Deirdre was fit to be tied when she figured out
who Gerry really was, if that's what happened," Melba
said. "They say Mr. Halbert left Ronnie a lot of money in
his will, but since they never could find him, Deirdre finally got everything."

Another strike against Deirdre. Given her miserly reputation, I had little doubt that she would not want to share
what she had with anyone else. She might very well be
willing to murder her adopted sibling, not only for the
money but also to keep quiet about that sibling's gender
reassignment.

"We need to tell Kanesha this story right away," I said.
"I think this could be the link she needs to bring this case
to a close."

"So you believe Gerry Albritton was really Jerry Albritton and Ronnie Halbert?" Melba asked.

"I do." I pulled out my phone to text Kanesha that I had
vital new information for her.

Melba shook her head. "I wonder why he was pretending to be a woman. I might have recognized him as Ronnie Halbert, although it's been at least forty years since he
left Athena. I'd swear he had plastic surgery, though."

"You had no idea that Billy Albritton actually did have
a little brother named Jerry?" I asked as I tapped out a
message.

"No, I'd never heard about him before today. I don't

think anyone in town knew," Melba said, "though I could be wrong."

"Billy Albritton must have known who he was," I said as I hit the icon to send the message.

"I guess he did," Melba said. "Do you think Billy killed him?"

I shrugged. "He could have. Would he have welcomed the return of a long-lost brother who was basically sold to another family?"

"No, I don't think he would," Melba said. "Especially since his daddy's still alive. He's close on a hundred years old. Lives in the nursing home where Mrs. Norwood is."

My cell phone rang, and I saw from the caller ID that it was Kanesha.

She spoke immediately. "I'm across the street right now. I'll be over in two minutes." She ended the call.

Frowning, I put down the phone. "Kanesha says she's across the street and will be here in two minutes." I got up from the table. "I'm going to look out the front door and see what's going on."

"I'm coming with you," Melba said. She and Diesel were right on my heels as I hurried to the front of the house.

I opened the door, and we looked out to see a couple of police cars, plus a county patrol car, pulled up in front of Gerry Albritton's house. As we watched, one of the policemen came out of the house, accompanied by Billy Albritton. The officer led him to a patrol car and put him inside.

Kanesha came out of the house carrying a bag. She stopped to speak to the police officer before she came across the street toward us.

When she reached us, I asked her, "What's going on?"

At the same time, Melba asked, "Are you arresting Billy?"

Kanesha said, "Let's go inside, why don't we?"

We obeyed her request, and when I had shut the door behind the deputy, she faced our inquisitive expressions and explained. "Yes, Mr. Albritton is being arrested for basically breaking into the house. The police officer caught him trying to sneak out with this." She brandished the bag, and I recognized it as an evidence bag.

"What's in it?" I asked.

Kanesha pulled a tissue from her pocket and then carefully extracted the object with the tissue—to protect any fingerprints, I supposed.

She held an old notebook that appeared to be falling apart.

THIRTY-THREE

▮▮▮

"That doesn't look much like it could be worth risking arrest for," I said as I led the way to the kitchen.

"It must be," Kanesha said, "because he did risk it, and got caught."

"What's in it?" Melba asked.

"Let's find out." Kanesha turned to me. "Would you mind laying down a couple of clean paper towels for me to put this on?"

"Of course," I said. As I was placing the paper towels on the table, Azalea returned to the kitchen.

Mother and daughter eyed each other. Kanesha spoke first.

"Hello, Mama, how are you?"

"Fine," Azalea replied. "How are you?"

"Fine," Kanesha said.

Melba and I exchanged glances. Watching these two women reminded me of two lionesses circling each other, one waiting for the other to make a false move. Kanesha had not softened her stance on her mother's chosen employment, and Azalea had not given in on her right to work however she saw fit.

This standoff could go on for a while. I coughed, and Kanesha's gaze shifted to me. "Can we see what's in the notebook?" I asked.

I looked down at the ragged old thing, frayed around the edges. It was really more of a tablet, now that I got a better view of it.

"That looks like those tablets we used to take to school in first grade," Melba said. "Remember them? And those big pencils we learned to write with?"

"That's exactly what it is." The red cover had faded badly, but if you peered at it closely enough, you could see the words *Big Chief* and the design of a Native American in a feather headdress on it.

Using the tissue, Kanesha drew back the cover, and we all bent to see the words written there. The first page was covered with one sentence, line after line: *I am Jerry Albritton.*

Kanesha flipped a page. The same thing: that one sentence written over and over in childish printing. She kept turning the pages. The writing began to change, the printed letters becoming more precise, more to scale. Eventually the print gave way to cursive writing. Every single page, however, contained nothing but that one sentence, line after line.

I glanced at Melba, and I could see the tears ready to flow. I knew how she felt. That poor little boy, doing what he could to hold on to his identity. I could only imagine how he felt, being ripped from his family and given to strangers. He was old enough to remember his own name, though he immediately was given a new one. From the evidence of the tablet, with the handwriting changing over time, Jerry had been determined never to forget who he really was. It was heartbreaking.

Melba sank into a chair and delved into her purse for tissues. While she dabbed at her eyes, I pulled out my handkerchief to wipe my own.

"This means something to you both," Kanesha said. "Is it related to what you wanted to tell me?"

"Yes," I said. "You'd better sit down." I pulled out my chair and settled back, handkerchief curled up in my right hand. Diesel, from the first moment he sensed Melba's emotional state, had moved to her side, rubbing against her legs and meowing occasionally. She smiled gratefully down at him and rubbed his head.

She looked up for a moment. "Charlie, will you tell Kanesha the story? I don't think I could get through it right now."

"Sure." I first explained the source of Melba's information, then launched into the story. I pruned as many unnecessary details as I could, but it still took several moments to relate. Kanesha had her notebook and pen ready from the moment I started, and she jotted things down throughout my retelling of the tale. When I finished, she put down her pen and stared broodingly at the tablet.

Azalea, who had hovered in the background the whole time, suddenly blew her nose, startling all of us.

When I glanced her way, I could see she was upset. Kanesha got up, apparently concerned, and approached her mother. "Mama, what's wrong? Are you all right?"

Azalea nodded. "That's such a sad story," she said. "I

remember that boy Ronnie. Every time I saw him, I knew he had a sad heart. I never saw real joy in him."

Melba began to cry again, and I struggled not to get emotional myself. Even Kanesha seemed to be affected. She stared at her mother, and Azalea reached out and touched her daughter's cheek. Kanesha sighed, Azalea's hand fell away, and Kanesha resumed her seat.

No one spoke for a moment. Kanesha closed the tablet and put it back into the evidence bag. To break the mood, I decided to ask a question.

"Did Billy Albritton say anything about this?" I gestured toward the notebook. "I'm wondering how he even knew about it."

"Didn't say a word," Kanesha said, "even though the officer caught him with it in his hands. It will have his fingerprints on it, so he can't deny having it in his possession."

"Do you think Gerry showed it to him?" Melba asked. "Maybe that was why they were arguing that day when you heard them."

"Sounds reasonable," I said. "She must have shown him. Where did she keep it?"

"In a dressing case with a false bottom," Kanesha said. "He had to have known ahead of time where it was. The officers who searched the house had overlooked it. I checked it, and it would have been hard to spot unless someone knew what to look for."

"Dressing case?" Melba said. "Not many people use those anymore. I don't."

"It's an antique one," Kanesha said. "Heavy and not too practical, if you ask me, but it's well-used."

"One thing I still don't understand," Melba said. "Charlie wouldn't talk about it much, but maybe you can answer it. Why was Ronnie Halbert going around pretending to be a woman?"

I wondered if Kanesha would come clean with Melba. I watched the deputy as she regarded Melba with her usual cool detachment.

"She wasn't pretending," Kanesha said in a matter-of-fact tone. "Ronnie Halbert went through a gender reassignment operation twenty years ago or more."

The revelation obviously shocked Melba. She now appeared incapable of speech. Not a state she often found herself in, I knew. She stared at Kanesha and continued to stroke Diesel's head.

Ronnie Halbert. I didn't know why it had taken me so long to make the connection, but I suddenly figured out the use of the name *Ronni Halliburton.* Close to Ronnie Halbert, but different enough so that people probably wouldn't connect the two. Unless they happened to know who Ronnie Halbert really was, I decided.

"Is this story going to help your case?" I asked.

"It's filled in the major gaps in Gerry Albritton's history," Kanesha said. "Now that I have the name *Ronnie Halbert*, I should be able to dig up more information and find out where he was for all those years."

"I wonder if Ronnie joined one of the armed forces," I said. "That was apparently the speculation at the time he disappeared."

"We'll search military records, too," Kanesha said. "The most important point about this backstory, however, is the connections it gives me to the suspects."

Melba finally seemed to have recovered from the shock of learning about Gerry's sex change. "Are you any closer to making an arrest?"

"Maybe," Kanesha said. "I'll be questioning Mr. Albritton about breaking into his sister's house. He has a lot of explaining to do. I found two more witnesses from the party who say they also saw him briefly."

"His other sister was there, too," Melba said.

Kanesha nodded. "Yes, I've been tracking her movements as well, based on witness statements."

"His other sister?" I asked, puzzled. I remembered Melba had mentioned this sister several times, but I couldn't recall if she had mentioned a name.

"You know her, Charlie," Melba said in a chiding tone. "She lives down the street from you."

When I still looked blank, Kanesha said, "Mrs. Betty Camden. Married to the lawyer."

Light dawned. *Betty Camden*. Now I remembered Melba mentioning a sister named Betty when she said she wanted to talk to Billy Albritton. She hadn't told me that she was Betty Camden, of all people.

"Honestly, Charlie, you don't know anything about the people who live around here," Melba said.

"For the most part I know what I need to know," I replied with some asperity. "I'm not a walking genealogy of everybody in Athena like you are, for Pete's sake. I was gone from here for thirty years, remember?"

Melba grimaced at me, but evidently she decided to let the remark about being a walking genealogy pass without comment.

I turned to Kanesha. "I had never even considered

Betty Camden as a suspect," I said. "You must have, since you knew the connection."

Kanesha nodded. "Yes, I was aware of that, and frankly, I thought you knew, even though you never mentioned it. Otherwise I would have said something about it."

I shrugged. "That's okay. I guess I'm going to have to start paying more attention to who's related to who in this town. You can get tripped up pretty easily if you don't know."

"You certainly can," Melba said. "I never dreamed you didn't know about her."

"I remember you said you don't like her, and she doesn't like you," I said. "You never said why, though." I thought for a moment. "She's got to be several years older than us, so surely it wasn't something to do with high school."

"No, it wasn't," Melba said. "Chip Camden was a widower, about twenty years ago, and I went out with him for six months. Then Betty Jones—she was a widow—started chasing him. He dropped me for her, and she went around bad-mouthing me, saying she had *saved* Chip from a terrible mistake."

That all this still rankled, even after two decades, was obvious. Melba wasn't usually one to hold a grudge, but I could understand why she held on to this one. What a nasty thing to do.

Kanesha had listened to this without reaction. Once Melba stopped talking, the deputy looked at me for a moment.

"Since you weren't aware that Mrs. Camden and Mr. Albritton are siblings, you might also not be aware of Mrs. Camden's background in education."

"I know she is a retired teacher," I said. "But I have no idea what she taught."

"Yes, she retired three years ago," Kanesha said. "She taught high school chemistry and biology for twenty-five years before that."

THIRTY-FOUR

Chemistry. The word resounded in my brain. If she was adept at chemistry at all, then Betty Camden would be as capable of making her own cyanide as Tammy Harville.

The suspect list now included Deirdre Thompson—still my favorite—along with Billy Albritton, Betty Camden, Jincy Bruce, and Tammy Harville. The final two on my list I considered less likely, although if Jincy had embezzled all that money, that was a strong motive. I thought the family connections that Gerry had had with the other three were far more likely to be the source for the motive to kill.

"Any hard evidence that points to one of the suspects?" I asked.

"Not yet," Kanesha replied. "I really need to track down that brandy snifter. I don't know how the killer managed to get it out of the house."

"In a purse," Melba said. "A man couldn't have smuggled

it out without a bulge under his jacket, I'd imagine. So probably a woman."

"I've considered purses. The poison certainly could have been brought into the house that way, or in a pocket," Kanesha said. "But the purses I saw when I arrived were all those small bags that women carry at parties. I didn't notice one that would have been big enough to conceal that snifter."

An image popped into my head. I had no idea of its source, but it sparked an idea. "When the house was searched, did you turn up any fragments of glass or crystal?"

Kanesha regarded me thoughtfully. "No, we didn't. I thought of that, because that would have been a way to destroy the evidence and make it difficult to analyze. What are you getting at?"

"Here's a possible scenario," I said slowly, visualizing it as I put it into words. "The murderer, in this case a woman, picks up the snifter while everyone is staring at Gerry, collapsed on the floor. The woman, pretending to be overcome by the shock, stumbles away and takes refuge in the bathroom. She locks herself in, puts her purse and the snifter aside. Then she takes one of the hand towels set out for guests, unfolds it, and wraps the snifter in it. Then she puts it on the floor, wrapped, and stomps on it."

"And now that it's broken into a lot of pieces," Melba said, excited by my idea, "she can stick it into her purse, still in the hand towel, and slip out of the house. In all the confusion, probably nobody will notice she's gone until later."

"Exactly," I said. "I don't recall seeing either Deirdre

Thompson or Betty Camden after the cops arrived. Certainly they were not there when we were all shepherded into the dining room. Either one of them could have absconded with the broken snifter the way I described it. With Melba's help." I grinned at her.

"It could work," Kanesha said. "And if I can get a hold of the purses they brought to the party, they can be examined for traces of the snifter and the poison." She shook her head. "It's a long shot, but if the evidence is there, the lab should be able to find it."

"Do you think you'll be able to get search warrants?" I asked.

"I believe so," Kanesha said. "With the story Ms. Gilley heard from Mrs. Norwood, which I am going to verify with her as soon as possible, and the fact that Mr. Albritton broke in to the deceased's house, I think I can make a pretty good case. It will depend on the mood the judge is in today."

"Are you going to be examining anyone else's purses?" I said.

"Yes," Kanesha said, "along with pockets in jackets and pants, even in dresses, depending on what the suspects wore to the party. I've got good descriptions from several people of what the women wore, though not so much the men."

"Good luck," I said. "I hope you can solve this thing soon."

"She will," Azalea said unexpectedly, startling the rest of us. Kanesha regarded her mother with her frustratingly unreadable expression, but mother and daughter appeared to understand each other.

Kanesha rose. "Thank you both for all the information, and the idea about how the snifter could have been taken out of the house. If that is how it was done, I hope I won't be too late in finding any remaining evidence."

I started to rise, but Kanesha waved me back. "I can find my way out," she said. "I'll be in touch later."

She headed out of the room with our further wishes for good luck following her. Azalea stared after her daughter for a good thirty seconds, her expression every bit as unreadable as Kanesha's. The two women were so much alike, it was uncanny. I wasn't sure they saw that, however, perhaps each thinking the other was the truly difficult, frustrating one. Azalea departed the room, and moments later I heard her heading upstairs.

I chuckled as another thought popped into my mind.

"What's funny?" Melba asked.

"All of a sudden I thought about how things have changed since that first murder several years ago," I said.

"You mean Godfrey Priest?" Melba said.

I nodded.

"What's changed?" Melba asked.

"Kanesha," I said. "In the beginning I always thought I was about to be arrested as the chief suspect. Now, even though we're not bosom buddies, she actually seems to respect my opinion on certain things. Although," I continued slowly, "I don't think she'll ever truly like me as long as Azalea works here."

"That's her little quirk," Melba said. "And her mother's. You can't help that."

"No, and at least now she doesn't glower at me the whole time I'm in her presence." I chuckled again.

"What's that word they use?" Melba asked. "Détente?"

278

"Yes, that's it. Kanesha and I have achieved détente."

Melba suddenly changed the subject back to the murder. "Who do you think did it? I know who I think is guilty."

I thought about it briefly before I answered. "In some ways, frankly, I don't really care which of them did it. I don't know any of them, really, except for Betty Camden. I don't know her well at all. But if I had to pick one of them, I'd say Deirdre Thompson. From everything I've heard, she's the most unpleasant of them all. There's the financial motive as well, if Gerry could have been successful in getting what Mr. Halbert left her in his will."

"I think Betty Camden did it," Melba said. "And not because I don't like her to begin with. She likes to pretend she's *so* classy because she married Chip Camden. He's from an old Athena family, one with class *and* money, unlike her. She barely managed to get through college. She had to work and get scholarships, and then she married a bum named Wally Jones."

"What's the point in this?" I asked, tired of waiting for her to get to the crux.

"The point is," Melba said, glaring at me, "she's so status-conscious it's ridiculous. Do you think she'd want people in this town to know about the brother that her father *sold* to Mr. Halbert? The brother who turned himself into a sister? No siree Bob, she wouldn't. She's not exactly the enlightened type. I think she'd do *any*thing to keep that news from getting out."

"I'll take your word for it," I said. "I'm hoping Kanesha finds the evidence soon."

"If it's there, she will." Melba rose, giving Diesel a last rub on the head. "I'd better get going. You're probably ready for a little peace and quiet."

"I'm fine," I said. "Before you go, would you like to look in on the kittens?"

She hesitated. "Oh, why not?"

Diesel trotted ahead of us to the living room. He sat by the cage and watched the kittens, all asleep at the moment.

"They're so precious," Melba said.

"One or more of them could be yours soon," I said.

"Have you found out where they came from?" she asked.

"Yes, earlier today." I told her about the note I had left. "Turned out to be Tommy Russum, the solo boy soprano in the choir at Helen Louise's church."

"Did he give you the full story behind his bringing them to you?"

"Yes, the case of the mean old stepfather, according to Tommy," I said. "His stepfather is a cardiologist, Henry McGillivray. I often see him and Tommy's mother, Ellen, when I go to church with Helen Louise."

"I've heard the name," Melba said. "He's supposed to be top-notch, but that's all I know about him."

"He can be a little gruff, in my experience," I said. "Never downright rude, but he always gives the impression that he doesn't have much time."

"Those people are always irritating," Melba said. "Usually think they're way more important than you."

"That might be the case with Dr. McGillivray, though Ellen McGillivray is a genuinely warm and friendly person," I said. "I know nothing about Tommy's father, though I think he passed away when Tommy was small."

"So the good doctor doesn't want cats around the house?" Melba asked.

"According to Tommy," I said. "I'm trying to make up my mind whether I should try to talk to the man and Mrs. McGillivray about the situation. I don't want to cause trouble for Tommy, but it really burns me up that Mr. McGillivray seems to be ignoring how important those kittens are to the boy."

"I hope you do talk to him," Melba said. "The man needs to learn a little compassion, seems to me."

"We'll see," I told her. "I expect we'll see them at the church on Christmas morning. I'm not in the mood to tackle him right now."

"Good luck," Melba said. "See you Sunday."

Diesel stared after her forlornly as she headed out the door. I felt curiously flat myself, now that the murder investigation was so close to an end—provided, as always, that there was reliable evidence for Kanesha to make an arrest.

"How about we go play with the kittens?" I said to Diesel, and he warbled and darted toward the living room. I followed slowly, continuing to think about the investigation.

Odd how it seemed to happen like this pretty much every time. Insert one previously unknown piece to the puzzle, and things shifted around and gave you a much more complete picture. Putting together Gerry Albritton's background and finding the connections with the two siblings and her adoptive sister had been the key.

Jincy Bruce was an outlier. There was still the matter of the embezzlement. She and Gerry appeared to me to be the only suspects. Surely Jared Carter wouldn't embezzle from himself. Jared was even more of an outlier than Jincy. Unless his relationship with Gerry was more than simply a business arrangement? Things could have turned ugly if Jared hadn't known Gerry's full story. He might not have understood the true significance of her use of the name *Ronni Halliburton*. Did he know anything about Ronnie Halbert? That would be for Kanesha to figure out.

As much as I detested Deirdre Thompson, now that I knew so much more about her, I wasn't sure she really was the murderer. I simply thought she was the nastiest of the bunch and the most likely to kill to protect her family name and her money. People had murdered in the past for each of those reasons on its own. Combined, they became even more powerful. Billy and Betty were probably motivated by the desire to protect the family name. Billy was a politician, and he might have ambitions for a higher office than that of city councilman. Betty might want to protect her brother as well as herself. Chip Camden was high-powered, and they moved in pretty important circles in town and in the state. He also nursed political ambitions, and a scandal like the truth behind Gerry Albritton's identity might harm his chances irreparably.

I realized I had been standing in front of the cage, blind to the kittens who were now awake and wanting to be let out. Diesel had been meowing at me, too.

"Sorry, kids," I said. "Time to play." And time to push all thoughts of murder out of my brain for a while. I settled down to enjoy the kittens and think about them instead.

THIRTY-FIVE

|||||||||||||||||||||||||||||||||||||||||||||||||||||||||||||||||||||||||

To my great joy and relief, Sean informed me before lunchtime the next day, Christmas Eve, that Alex felt strong enough to spend time with the family that evening. I happily scrapped my rather chaotic plans to try to take Christmas Eve to her and instead concentrated on everything I needed to get done around the house.

Despite my inability to carry a tune in a bucket, as the old saying went, I scurried around the house that day singing snatches of my favorite Christmas songs, chief among them "Silent Night" and "Joy to the World." Not for the first time did I wish that the joyful noise I was making could be in tune as well. Both my children had pleasant singing voices, especially Laura, who had done musicals in high school and college. It had to have come from their mother's side of the family, because I didn't remember that either of my parents could sing any better than I could.

Stewart helped bring the decorations down from the attic, and he had arranged for a friend with a pickup to deliver the tree he had picked out at a local Christmas tree farm. The tree was scheduled to arrive no later than three this afternoon. That would give us time to get it set up before family started arriving around four thirty. We would start decorating the tree together then.

The doorbell rang a little after two, and I went to answer it, expecting to see Sean's friend with the tree. It took me a moment to recognize the man on the doorstep. Dr. Henry McGillivray, noted cardiologist, and stepfather to Tommy Russum, appeared to be in an irritable state of mind.

"Good afternoon, Mr. Harris," he said. "If you have a few minutes, I'd like to talk to you about my son."

"Certainly, I'll be happy to talk to you about Tommy." I stood aside and motioned him in. I noted with interest, and approval, that he referred to Tommy as his son, not as a stepson.

A tall, powerfully built man who exuded an air of authority, Henry McGillivray was around forty. He seemed uneasy, however, and that surprised me. All the times I had seen him in church, he never appeared in the least unsure of himself. He had impressed me as a man who was always in control and was a stickler for detail.

After taking his overcoat and putting it on the rack in the hall, I led him to the kitchen. I didn't want to confront him with Tommy's kittens right away.

"Please have a seat," I said. "Can I offer you something to drink? Sweet tea, a soft drink? The mulled cider isn't quite ready yet."

"No, thank you," McGillivray said. "I don't want to take up too much of your time."

"Don't worry about that. I'm glad you came by," I told him as I took my place at the table. "I've been wanting to talk to you about Tommy and his kittens."

In a brusque tone he said, "I'm happy to reimburse you for any expense you've incurred because of them." He reached inside his jacket.

"There's no need," I said. "Tommy actually gave me money to help pay the expenses." I watched him closely. He was obviously surprised at this information. His hand faltered, and then he pulled it back.

"Really?" he asked. "Where did he get the money?"

"He said it was from his allowance. It seemed important to him that he helps pay for them."

McGillivray frowned. "That's good, and it shows he does have a responsible side after all. But his allowance isn't large. It can't be enough."

"It's enough for me," I said, trying to keep my tone level. "I'd say Tommy is quite a responsible boy. I have no reason to doubt what he told me. He found a starving cat, took care of her and fed her, and then he found himself with five kittens. He was doing what he could to look after them, despite apparent parental opposition. When he felt he could no longer keep them safe and warm, desperation drove him to me. I guess everyone in the neighborhood knows about me and my cat."

Mentioning Diesel made me realize that he wasn't with me. He must have gone upstairs with Stewart to fetch another box or two from the attic. I wondered how he would react to the doctor.

"Yes, everyone has seen that big cat of yours," McGillivray said, his irritation growing, it seemed. "What do you mean, *parental opposition*? What did Tommy tell you?"

"I'll show you." I got up and went to the drawer where I had placed Tommy's notes to me. I found the first one and brought it to McGillivray. He took it and stared at it. As I watched him, I could see what looked like remorse in his expression.

He put the note on the table and ran a hand across his face. "I *never* said I wanted to drown those kittens," he said, sounding for the first time unsure of himself. "As far as I can remember, what I *did* say was that farmers used to drown kittens they didn't want to bother with. I'm not even sure why I said it, but I didn't say it to Tommy. He must have heard me talking to my wife. I'd had a rough day at the hospital. I'd lost a patient on the operating table earlier that day. When I came home and found those kittens in the shed, I just didn't think about what I said. I honestly didn't realize those kittens meant so much to him."

He looked at me, obviously shaken. "Mr. Harris, I love that little boy like he is my own flesh and blood. I wouldn't want to hurt him." He paused. "When I'm upset, I say things that come out of frustration and exhaustion. I put in twenty-hour days sometimes. I was angry with myself because I couldn't save my patient. I took it out on my son and those helpless kittens. I can't forgive myself for doing that to him." By the time he finished his short speech, tears streamed down his face.

I didn't quite know what to do or say. Unless he was a consummate actor or a sociopath, I had to believe that he loved Tommy and was heart-stricken that he had hurt the child so badly. After a short time, he managed to regain control of his emotions. He pulled a handkerchief from a pocket and wiped his reddened eyes.

"I'm so sorry," he said. "My wife and I, Tommy's mother, lost a baby two years ago, and the thought of losing Tommy terrifies me. I can't believe I made him afraid of me. Made him hate me."

"Children listen to us," I said gently, "and our words can do harm even when we don't truly intend to hurt them. I have a son myself, an adult now, and we went through a period a couple of years ago when we hardly ever talked to each other. It was my fault, and it started with things I said. I never meant to hurt him, but like you, I was so wrapped up in my own emotions, I was careless."

"Thank you for telling me that," McGillivray said. "I feel like scum right this minute, but you obviously repaired your relationship with your son. I only hope to God I can do the same."

"Tommy is a very loving boy with a big heart," I said. "I bet he will forgive you." I smiled. "Especially if you tell him he can bring those kittens home."

McGillivray nodded. "He is such a sweet kid. He never asks for much, not toys, not video games. Books sometimes, but he seems content with what he has most of the time. Of course he can have those kittens, and we'll keep them all if that's what he wants. I just want my son back."

I was struggling to hold on to my emotions. Talking to McGillivray brought back my own feelings over my estrangement with Sean, and all the guilt had resurfaced. If sharing my experience with this man helped him heal his relationship with his son, I would count it as a blessing.

"Just go home now and talk to him," I said. "I'm sure

he will understand. I have a box that you can put the kittens in if you want to take them now."

He shook his head. "If you don't mind keeping them another hour, I'd like to talk to him first. Then we'll come and get them and take them home together."

"I think that's a wonderful idea," I said. "I'll have a box ready with their toys and food that you can take with you."

McGillivray stood and extended his hand. I grasped it, and we shook. "Thank you," he said. "Merry Christmas, and God bless you."

I showed him out, and Stewart and Diesel came down the stairs as I shut the door behind McGillivray.

"That wasn't Joss with the tree, was it?" Stewart glanced toward the spot in the hall where the tree would stand. "No, I guess not."

"That was Dr. McGillivray, Tommy's father. We had a talk about Tommy and the kittens. It was basically a misunderstanding. He's going home to talk to Tommy, and they'll be back in a little while to take the kittens home. He said Tommy could keep all of them, if he wanted to."

"That's wonderful," Stewart said. "We'll miss those kittens, won't we, Diesel?"

The cat meowed loudly. I had no clue whether he understood what Stewart meant. I knew he *would* miss the kittens, but we would all adapt. I wouldn't miss that cage in the living room, however. I wondered if Dr. McGillivray would like to take it home, too. Haskell had engineered it so that it was mobile.

Joss appeared about twenty minutes later, and he and Stewart wrestled the tree, a beautiful six-foot Leyland cypress, into place. Stewart had located a Christmas tree farm not too far from Athena that grew these beautiful trees. I thought his choice was excellent. Joss, a lanky, taciturn man around fifty, refused payment for his services, averring that he owed Stewart a favor or two and was glad he could help.

I felt full of goodwill and Christmas cheer when I climbed the stairs a little later. All I needed now was a shower, clean clothes, and my family around me, ready to decorate the tree.

THIRTY-SIX

▖▖▖

I woke on Christmas morning even more full of goodwill.
Watching my family interact with one another last evening while we decorated the tree together, seeing the real
love and affection among them all, gave me the joy I had
always associated with the season. I had gone through a
period of a few years after my wife died when I feared the
holidays, because all I could think about during that time
was my loss. Trapped in grief, I couldn't find the joy in
anything, not even in my children.

Time helped heal those wounds, and gradually I came
to enjoy the holidays again. Having my family and friends
around me made that possible. Whereas before there were
only my children and me, I now had my children's spouses,
their own children, my beautiful Helen Louise, and dear
friends Melba, Stewart, and Haskell. My cup did indeed
run over.

Another blessing this Christmas morning was the

memory of a smiling, happy Tommy Russum, hand in hand with his father when they came to collect the kittens. Dr. McGillivray once again thanked me as he watched Tommy interact with the kittens. He carried the box with the toys and the food, and Tommy carried the kittens carefully in their box out to the doctor's car. McGillivray declined the cage. Tommy wanted to keep the kittens in his room, and his parents were not going to contest that.

I thought Diesel might try to follow the kittens and Tommy out of the house, but he remained by my side in the doorway while we watched father and son load the boxes in the car. Tommy ran back up the walk to hug me and thank me again. Then he hugged Diesel and thanked him, too. Diesel meowed as if to tell the boy he was welcome.

After I closed the door, Diesel and I wandered back into the living room. The empty cage would have to be taken down soon. I didn't want to have a reminder that the kittens were no longer with us. I would miss them and their playfulness, and I would certainly miss the headstrong, mischievous Ramses. I had held him for a moment before he joined the others in the box. He squirmed the whole time, always wanting to be loose and free to roam.

We woke early that morning, Diesel and I—earlier than usual, because today's service at Helen Louise's church started at nine. I had a few more things I wanted to do before I needed to shower and dress for church. I wished I could take Diesel with me, but the church would be full to overflowing. He would be better here at home. This would be one of the few times he was left all by himself in the house. It would be for only a couple of hours; then everyone would gather here to open presents and have our Christmas luncheon. I had hoped for a text or a call from Kanesha yesterday or even this morning, but so far, I hadn't heard from her. I wondered whether she had found the evidence she needed to make an arrest. Perhaps my hunch about the brandy snifter had been a dud. Though I still thought Deirdre Thompson wasn't as strong a candidate for murderer as Betty Camden, I knew that my wanting her to be guilty was colored to some degree by my intense dislike for the woman.

When I picked Helen Louise up at eight forty for the drive to church, she surprised me by telling me that Kanesha had come to see her yesterday evening after she got home from the Christmas Eve festivities.

"That was pretty late for her to be going around talking to witnesses," I said.

"It was barely nine o'clock," Helen Louise said. "I hadn't been home long, and I wasn't quite ready for bed then."

"What did she want?" I asked.

"She wanted me to tell her anything I could remember about the movements of Betty Camden and Deirdre Thompson."

"Were you able to give her any helpful information?"

"I think so," Helen Louise said slowly. "I told her that Betty and Deirdre were involved in what looked like a fairly intense conversation before I joined them. I don't know what they were talking about, but neither of them appeared happy."

I hadn't yet had time to share with Helen Louise all that we had learned yesterday. The Christmas Eve gathering was not the time to talk about murder. By the time we pulled into the church parking lot, I had managed to share the salient points. Helen Louise looked bemused by my rapid summation.

"It will be interesting to see who's in church this morning," she said as we got out of the car. The Camdens and Deirdre Thompson were members of the congregation.

"Yes, it will be," I said as I took her arm to escort her into the church. We found Sean inside with Laura, Frank, and baby Charlie. Sean explained that Cherelle had agreed to take care of Rosie until the church service ended. He would then run home to pick up Rosie and Alex and take Cherelle to her home so she could go with her family to church.

We found a pew near the middle of the nave where we could all sit together. Church members continued to arrive, and I watched with considerable curiosity as they began to settle in their accustomed spots. I saw Dr. and Mrs. McGillivray and nodded to them. Tommy was in the choir, and I hoped to hear him sing a solo this morning.

The church continued to fill at five minutes to nine. Thus far I hadn't caught a glimpse of Deirdre Thompson or Chip and Betty Camden. Absence on their part didn't automatically indicate an arrest on murder charges, but they wouldn't lightly skip this service. They considered themselves pillars of the community.

I suddenly felt my phone vibrate in my pocket. Thankful that I had remembered to silence it before leaving for church, I pulled it out to see that there was a text message from Kanesha. My heart suddenly beat faster. Had she arrested someone?

I read the message, then read it again, unsure that I had grasped its full import.

Arrest attempted. Subject found dead. Suspected suicide by cyanide from vial found near body. Betty Camden.

Mutely I passed the phone to Helen Louise as the choir filed in. She shook her head as if she couldn't believe what she was reading. I supposed that the humiliation Betty thought she would face once the truth was known about Gerry Albritton was too much for her. Not to mention the disgrace of being on trial for murder, with her husband a prominent attorney from an old family.

I found out later from Kanesha that after the search warrants had been obtained, and the evening bags and clothing had been collected, they found the residue of broken glass in Betty Camden's bag. My hunch had paid off after all. Billy Albritton confessed to destroying the Christmas decorations at Gerry's house. He wanted to frighten her, but evidently Gerry hadn't been intimidated in the least.

Off and on during the church service that morning, I found myself, as I often did, thinking of families. My own family, now strong and united, stood in contrast to the Albrittons, with their legacy of a sibling taken from them and the eventual devastating consequences. I wondered what had motivated Gerry to return to Athena. Had she sought revenge against her adoptive sister? Against her blood relatives, Billy and Betty? I wondered if Billy would tell his father what had become of his youngest son. Somehow, I expected not.

Kanesha also told me that, as suspected, Jincy Bruce was the embezzler. Terrified that she might be charged with Gerry Albritton's murder, she had gone to Kanesha and confessed. Though she promised to return the money,

Jared Carter was still considering whether to press charges. I hoped he would be merciful. It was Christmas, after all.

Jared had also settled the question of why he had been willing to finance Gerry Albritton's real estate wheeling and dealing. He and Ronnie Halbert had been best friends in junior high and high school. They had stayed in touch, at least intermittently, after Ronnie disappeared from Athena. Jared had been the only friend that Gerry had trusted with the true story of her journey from Jerry to Ronnie to Geraldine.

I settled in to listen to the choir. As the familiar notes of "Silent Night" issued from the organ, I smiled. Tommy Russum stepped forward to sing. His voice rose sweetly, seemingly effortlessly, over the organ and the choir as he sang the familiar words. I listened, deeply moved, as the notes poured forth from him, pure and true. By the time the hymn ended, I knew that mine were not the only eyes wet with tears. The sheer beauty of the young boy's voice surely had reached even the most hardened heart that morning. Nothing could have projected the spirit of Christmas more perfectly.

Later that day, after the exchange of gifts, when my family and I were in the dining room enjoying our Christmas feast, I occasionally fancied that I heard Tommy singing over the hubbub of conversation. As usual, I felt a welter of emotions, but what I primarily felt was joy. I saw it in every face I observed from my place at the head of the table, and I hoped that, in the coming months, we could all remember this day and these feelings when we needed lifting up.

I also thought with sympathy about Chip Camden and

Billy Albritton and the sorrows they faced, as well as the sad, painful legacy of Gerry Albritton. Now that I knew the truth about her, I wished I could tell her how much I admired her strength and courage in overcoming such a horrible childhood. I felt pity for Jack Albritton, now an old man in a nursing home, who many years ago had traded his child for money. It was not my place to judge him. He might have no memory whatsoever of what he had done. He had been desperately poor at the time and trying to take care of his family. I was profoundly thankful that I had never been faced with such a dilemma.

I turned my gaze toward Diesel, who sat by the bassinets on the side of the table. The bassinets that held my priceless, precious grandchildren. He stayed by them and watched them anxiously lest either one woke and turned fretful. He would remain their devoted servant as they grew, and I hoped they would love him in return.

I felt the prick of claws on my thigh. Sighing, I looked down to see Ramses starting to climb my leg. I thought I had left him safely in the utility room with his own version of Christmas lunch and plenty of water. But the little escape artist had somehow managed to get out. I must not have closed the door tightly. I plucked the kitten from my leg and put him in my lap. When Tommy Russum had showed up at the front door two hours ago with Ramses in a basket with a large bow on it, I didn't have the heart to turn down his gift. I wasn't sure I could handle a rambunctious handful like Ramses, but as he climbed up my torso to rub his head against my chin, I decided he would probably be worth the effort. He was one of the most memorable Christmas presents I ever received.

Turn the page for a special sneak peek of

CARELESS WHISKERS

the next Cat in the Stacks
mystery by Miranda James.

I stared at my daughter in considerable alarm. I couldn't remember ever seeing her like this, grabbing at her hair and stomping around my office. Suddenly she stopped in front of my desk and glared at me.

"I swear, if I could get my hands on Trevor Percy right this minute," Laura said through gritted teeth, "I'd pull every tooth right out of his head."

"Laura, sweetheart, surely it can't be that bad," I said in what I hoped was a soothing tone. Beside me, Diesel, my Maine Coon cat, chirped in distress. Always sensitive to heightened emotion, he seemed to be growing more agitated along with Laura. "What on earth has this Trevor Percy done to make you so upset?"

The glare did not abate. Nostrils flared as she expelled a harsh breath. "What has he *done*? What has he *done*?" She threw her hands up and started roaming around the room again. "He's gone and ruptured his appendix, that's what he's done, the bloody idiot, and now he's out of commission, stuck in California where he's bloody useless."

"I think you ought to have a little sympathy for him," I said. "A ruptured appendix is no fun." I tried not to shudder as I recalled my own experience some twenty years ago. "I'm sure your agent can find someone else to take his place."

"You have no idea, Dad." Laura's stormy expression, as she continued with her restless pacing back and forth, worried me. I wasn't sure she had heard me. "This could be an unmitigated disaster. 'When sorrows come, they come not single spies. But in battalions!'"

I recognized the quotation from *Hamlet*. In reply, I offered another line from the same play, 'There is nothing either good or bad, but thinking makes it so.'"

Startled, Laura stopped pacing and glared at me. "Do you honestly think I'm imagining all this? Come on, Dad, you know me better than that."

"I understand you're upset," I said, a little tartly. "You've also got Diesel on the verge of a nervous breakdown. You have to stop this ranting and calm down."

Laura looked stricken. Her gaze shifted down toward the cat, as if she were only now aware of his presence in the room. She dropped to her knees and held out her arms. "Come here, sweet boy," she said, her voice low and steady.

Diesel hesitated a moment. She called him again. This time he trotted right into her embrace, and she stroked his head, speaking in a reassuring tone. "I'm sorry, sweet boy, I didn't mean to upset you." He responded with a loud meow.

"I think he forgives you," I said, relieved that the storm seemed to have broken.

Laura remained on her knees for perhaps a minute more, rubbing the cat's head and stroking down his back. Mollifying the cat evidently soothed her as well. When she stood, she appeared calm.

"That's better," I said. "Now come sit down and discuss this. Hasn't your agent found another guest star for you?"

Laura sank into the chair in front of my desk, and Diesel took up position beside her. He rubbed his head against her jean-clad thigh. "Yes, she has. *That's* the problem."

"Why?" I asked. "Who is it?"

"His name is Luke Lombardi."

I detected an undertone of distaste in the way she said the name.

"What's so bad about him? Is he a terrible actor?" I asked.

"No." She drew out the syllable. "He's a terrible person, but he's actually quite a good actor." Then she added, almost grudgingly, it seemed, "He was nominated for a Tony a few years ago."

That sounded promising, but I still had no idea what lay behind my daughter's obvious dislike for the actor. "Have you worked with him before?"

Laura nodded. "In a community playhouse production in Connecticut one summer, a couple of years before I moved here. *After* he'd been nominated for the Tony." She snorted. "He worked it into conversations every day."

I could understand her irritation, but I had other concerns about the man. I put it to her bluntly. "Did he harass you?"

"Good Lord, no." She laughed. "I am *so* not his type."

"Is he gay then?" I asked.

She shook her head. "Oh, no, he's definitely straight. He likes his women dumb and stacked." She glanced down at her chest and giggled. "I have two strikes against me."

"I see," I said wryly. Laura, like her brother Sean, had graduated near the top of her class in high school, and had done extremely well in college. "What are your objections to having him as guest artist then?"

The theater department at Athena College put on a spring production every year, and they always tried to find an actor of some reputation to play a leading role, not only as a draw to sell tickets, but also for their students to have the chance to work with a seasoned professional. Laura had the leading female role in the play, and her husband, Frank Salisbury, was directing. Laura had professional experience, having spent several years in Hollywood, with bit parts in television shows, as well as theater productions there and back east. She was not a big name, however.

"He's a gigantic drama queen," Laura said. "He throws fits at the drop of a hat if something isn't to his liking. He tries to cow the director into doing what he wants and doesn't take direction well. He can be a bully. And he drinks."

What a charmer, I thought. I began to understand Laura's concerns over having to work with this man.

"Isn't your agent aware of this man's reputation?" I asked.

"She is," Laura said. "He's one of her clients, too, however, and she said he needs the work." She made a guttural noise. "I could kill her. She swore up and down that she had a perfect replacement for us, and then she sticks us with Luke."

"I suppose it's too late for her to find someone else," I said.

"The contract is signed, and it would cost a lot to get out of it. On top of all that, there's absolutely no time," Laura said. "Plus, rehearsals with him start next week. You're welcome to come by any time." She hesitated. "I'd love it if you did, in fact. I know Frank won't mind, and if Luke knows my father is watching, he might behave better."

"If he's as obnoxious as you say, I can't see that my presence will inhibit him," I said.

Diesel uttered a couple of chirps, as if in agreement. Laura patted his head and laughed. "It probably won't," she replied frankly, "but it would make *me* feel better, and it might keep Frank from taking Luke's head off."

"I'll do what I can, then, but I don't know that I'll be able to make every rehearsal."

Laura flashed me a smile full of gratitude.

"When does Lombardi arrive?" I asked.

"He's supposed to be here Saturday morning sometime. He's flying into Memphis on Friday and spending the night there, and Frank is going to pick them up in one of the college vans," Laura said. "There's a big reception for him at the Farrington House Saturday night, where he'll be staying for the duration. The department has reserved their best suite for him and his entourage."

"Entourage?" I said. "That sounds pretty grand."

Laura shrugged. "All it probably means is a couple of people, his personal dresser and whatever unfortunate woman he's got dangling at the moment."

I had to admit to a considerable amount of curiosity about Luke Lombardi. He sounded like he could be a nightmare, but I also had considerable faith in my son-in-law to handle the situation. Frank was young, but he had a strong character and was not easily cowed or pushed around. He had to be strong, working as he did with the often histrionic personalities in the theater department.

I expressed these thoughts aloud.

"Yes, you're right, Dad," Laura said. "I know Frank can handle him, but Frank does have a temper, and Luke has a knack for finding your buttons and stomping on them."

"I still put my money on Frank," I said, though privately her words caused me a few misgivings. I trusted Laura's judgment about her fellow actor, and I could foresee trouble ahead.

A knock at my office door caught both Laura and me off guard, and we turned to see Melba Gilley, my longtime friend and the administrative assistant to the library director, standing there.

"Is everything all right?" Melba asked, frowning. "I could hear a loud voice when I walked out into the hall a few minutes ago on my way to the lounge for some coffee."

The first floor of the antebellum mansion that housed the archive and rare book collection, along with my office, also contained the library administrative office on the first floor, along with a staff lounge and small kitchen. There were two reception rooms as well. If I left my office door open, as I usually did while working, I could hear sounds from downstairs, and vice versa. I hadn't realized Laura's voice had reached a loud enough volume to attract anyone's attention.

"Sorry." Laura grimaced. "I was ranting to Dad about the guest performer who's coming in for the play, and I didn't know I was so loud."

Melba laughed. "Honey, that's okay. Wouldn't be the first time I heard somebody up here yelling at your dad." She bent to rub Diesel's head. She spoiled him rotten, and he adored her. "What's wrong with the guest performer that you're getting so riled up for?"

"He's a toad," Laura said. "A total drama queen with an ego the size of Memphis."

"Goodness gracious," Melba said, visibly taken aback by the heat of Laura's tone. "Who the heck is this guy?"

"Luke Lombardi," I said. "I'd never heard of him until today, but Laura worked with him doing summer stock in the northeast." I glanced at my daughter. "Is that the correct term?"

She nodded.

"Luke Lombardi," Melba said, her expression thoughtful. "I saw him in a play a few years ago on Broadway, when a couple of friends and I spent a week in New York during spring break. As I recall, he was terrific."

"He's got talent," Laura said. "I'm not disputing that."

"As a human being, though," Melba said, "he must leave a lot to be desired if you have that kind of opinion of him."

Laura shrugged. "I'm not president of his fan club, that's for sure. Maybe he's mellowed a little by now. He's been having trouble getting work, I think, so I'm hoping he's learned to rein himself in." She picked up her backpack and purse. "I've blown off enough steam now. Time to go home and see my offspring."

"How is baby Charlie doing?" Melba asked.

"Thriving and crawling all over the place," Laura said. "He's trying to pull himself up to stand now."

"He's nine months old," Melba said. "That's on target.

Just wait till he starts walking. You'll be running all over the place after him."

Laura grinned. "We're doing that already. He crawls fast."

"Give him a hug and a big kiss from me," Melba said, as Laura headed for the door.

"Will do," Laura said. "Bye, Dad, and thanks as always for listening. Bye, Melba and Diesel." Diesel chirped unhappily as he watched Laura leave.

"You'll see her again soon, sweet boy," Melba crooned to the cat.

Diesel responded with more chirps.

"I didn't want to mention it after Laura said what she did about him, but I actually met Luke Lombardi in New York," Melba said.

"Did you tell me that before?" I asked, surprised.

Melba shook her head. "I don't think I ever did."

"How did you come to meet him?"

"One of the friends I went with, Katrinka Krause, has a nephew in New York. He's an actor, but so far he's only had minor roles," Melba said.

"So he was in this play with Lombardi," I said.

"Yes, he was. That's the main reason Katrinka wanted to go to New York. It was her nephew's first big play on Broadway," Melba said. "He was good, though he wasn't on stage all that much."

"Was Lombardi good?"

Melba nodded. "He was terrific. Anyway, we got to go backstage after the play to visit with Joel, the nephew, and we also met the rest of the cast." She paused. "Lombardi slobbered all over Katrinka. It was embarrassing, and it made Katrinka really uncomfortable. Joel saw it and got mad and threatened to punch Lombardi if he didn't leave Katrinka alone."

"Sounds like a thoroughly unpleasant scene." It didn't take much imagination to envision it.

"It was, and it got worse. Katrinka was trying to calm Joel down, and Lombardi kept blustering, trying to provoke Joel, and finally the stage manager had to intervene. Joel got fired the next day, actually. Lombardi insisted, and the manager caved."

"I'm sorry for Joel's sake," I said, "but good for him for standing up for his aunt."

"His mama raised him right," Melba said. "Katrinka was fit to be tied when she found out Joel lost his job. I swear if she could have got her hands on Luke Lombardi at that moment, she would have slapped him so hard his neck would have snapped."

Miranda James is the *New York Times* bestselling author of the Cat in the Stacks Mysteries, including *Claws for Concern*, *Twelve Angry Librarians*, and *No Cats Allowed*, as well as the Southern Ladies Mysteries, including *Fixing to Die*, *Digging Up the Dirt*, and *Dead with the Wind*. James lives in Mississippi.

Ready to find
your next great read?

Let us help.

Visit prh.com/nextread

Penguin
Random
House